All That's Left to Tell

Daniel Lowe teaches writing in Pittsburgh,
Pennsylvania, and received his MFA in fiction writing
from the University of Pittsburgh. His fiction and poetry
have appeared in a wide variety of literary magazines.
All That's Left to Tell is his first novel.

All That's Left to Tell

Daniel Lowe

PICADOR

First published 2017 by Flatiron Books

First published in the UK in 2017 by Picador
an imprint of Pan Macmillan
20 New Wharf Road, London N1 9RR
Associated companies throughout the world
www.panmacmillan.com

ISBN 978-1-5098-1056-7

1 3 5 7 9 8 6 4 2

A CIP catalogue record for this book is available from the British Library.

Printed and bound by CPI Group (UK) Ltd, Croydon, CR0 4YY

For my children, for Erin

When I was alive

I was dust which was,

But now I am dust in dust

I am dust which never was.

—The Arabian Nights

1

Now the sunrise.

Now this plate of boiled grain, the spoon in my hand.

Now the walk around the perimeter of the building and the sunset call of the muezzin.

In the long hours between her visits, he used the other events of the day as a refuge.

Each time, before she came into the room, they bound his hands and blindfolded him. Often Azhar, whose few words of English he'd likely learned from the woman, smiled apologetically before he knotted the scarf, drawing it slowly tighter so as not to pull the hair on the back of his head, while Saabir, whose English was only slightly better, yanked the scarf so hard with his calloused fingers that he thought it would leave its bright pattern imprinted on his skull. The room was small, perhaps ten by fifteen feet, partially underground with a half-finished floor, the other half hard-packed dirt; there was a single high window through which, when she wasn't there, he could occasionally see the feet of men walking by, and when she spoke to him, her voice—he thought she must be fairly young, despite its melodic depth—resonated slightly off the blank walls from where she sat on the other side of the room. Most times Azhar or Saabir seemed to remain in the room with her, but he couldn't be certain. He had been here six days, and this was the fourth time she'd come.

"Good morning, Mr. Laurent," she said. Her English was perfect, and if there was the slightest inflection of a Pakistani or Afghan dialect, it likely came from the time she'd spent in those countries. She could easily have been American, was likely American, because while he was no expert in local or regional culture, and had traveled here after absently reading a couple of books, it was unfathomable that a faction in this country that would kidnap him would use or train one of their own women for this purpose. He was stunned they were using a woman at all.

"Can you say *good morning* to me, Mr. Laurent?" she said, addressing him not as a child, but as someone from whom she expected a courteous response.

"Good morning," he said, clearing his throat. "I'm sorry. I still don't know your name."

The blindfold was wide and thick, and even if the sun had

been angling through the high window, which it never did, and he'd held his eyes fully opened, he would likely have been able to make out only her silhouette.

"You can call me Josephine these mornings I visit," she said. "If I told you my real name, you would start to worry."

The few times she'd spoken to him to this point, never for more than ten or fifteen minutes, she'd been similarly ambiguous in her choice of words, and he'd lacked the courage to ask what she'd meant. But this time, he said, "Worry about what?"

She let out a brief sigh, perhaps a quiet laugh.

"Maybe that you couldn't pronounce it," she said. "Or maybe, if I told you my real name, you would start to think that you would never be leaving here."

He had come to the country for the wrong reasons and stayed for worse ones. He'd volunteered to open new opportunities for Pepsi while operating out of Karachi, a city he would have had trouble placing in Pakistan before he'd volunteered, or rather insisted that he go, using the relatively light weight of his executive position to make the move for no more than six months. Gregory, his boss, and younger than he was by ten years, but with more international experience, had said, "Six months will seem like an eternity. Pakistan's a young country. But you'll feel something ancient there, and every now and then it doesn't feel good. Not saying you won't meet some wonderful people, even walking around in the markets. Hell, you can buy a Big Mac if you're homesick. I don't mean to be unnecessarily grim, Marc, but you watch the news. Educate yourself and be careful." He'd done neither adequately.

The first times she'd come in, she had mostly asked for names of people in the States who would ransom him. Though she loosely accused him of being a spy, he had been kidnapped in order to exact a sum of money that would either finance her cause or that of the people she represented. He had been wandering where he shouldn't have, out toward the slums of what he was told was Lyari Town, hoping to soothe his heart with images of greater poverty, when a cabdriver who spoke some English warned him of the danger and offered a ride back to his hotel. Because it was toward evening, he'd accepted the ride, and two blocks later the driver had slammed to a stop, and a man toting a machine gun emerged from a small shack and aimed the gun at his head while the driver climbed into the backseat and blindfolded him. They'd driven for hours; whether it was in circles or all the way out to Waziristan he had no way of knowing, though they weren't in the mountains. When Azhar or Saabir, each afternoon, walked him for exercise around the perimeter of a house near the one where he was held, the air still seemed damp with the occasional salt-scent of the sea.

"You look no worse for the wear," she said to him. "I see you have a change of clothes. Eating well?" He'd been given simple but generous meals of grains and peas and bread. "It would be an affront for a Pakistani not to act hospitably," she added without irony. She said something to Azhar in what he believed he recognized as Urdu, and he heard the door open and close. She pulled the chair across the floor to the point she was only a couple of feet away. When she sat down, some damp fragrance briefly invaded his nostrils.

"Mr. Laurent," she said. "May I call you Marc, now that we know each other a little better?"

"May I call you Jo?" he said to her, the first undercurrent of sarcasm he'd managed since his capture, because even in his state he'd bristled at her use of the word *hospitably.*

He expected she would leave the room, or call a man back in to slam his chair to the ground, or to slap him—something for this first expression of impertinence—but instead she said, "When I'm in the room alone with you, you're certainly welcome.

"Mr. Laurent," she continued. "Marc. We called some of the numbers you gave to us. Business associates. More business associates. Mr. Gregory McGuire expressed grave concern for you. But not one family member. None among that list of numbers."

"No one in my family has the kind of money you're looking for."

She laughed lightly at this, a few high, musical notes that gradually deepened.

"You're not talking to Saabir, who thinks all Americans are wealthy. I know what kind of money your family doesn't have. And I don't think for a minute the Pepsi corporation is going to hand over ten million dollars for a mid-level executive. Easier to promote someone else than sell that many cans of soda."

"Thank you."

"No offense intended. But a corporation being what it is, they'll work harder to keep your capture a secret than to ransom you. Which is why we need the numbers of family members. We can find them ourselves in good time, but that's only likely to extend your stay."

"Are you American?"

"That you will never know for sure. Regardless of what happens, you'll never see my face."

"They must pay you well."

She shifted in her chair at this and resettled herself.

"We won't be talking about my motives. Or how I became *radicalized,* as they say."

"I can't believe you're a woman," he said.

"Can't believe it or don't believe it?"

"Either. A fundamentalist Muslim group would not hire a woman as its interrogator."

"Is that what this is? An interrogation? Does it feel that way to you? And as I said, you have no idea who I am, who we are, and what our motives may be."

He strained to loosen the rope around his wrists, not because he hoped to escape, but because sitting in the chair with his arms behind his back made his shoulders ache. He'd held no thought of escaping from the moment of his capture; the despair and fear that most would feel were numbed by the presence of all the days of these past two months, and even the weeks before them that had followed him onto his flight. He used to be terrified of flying, but midway over the Atlantic, when out the window he watched the unvariegated water meet in a distant haze the indifferent blue of the sky, he thought if the plane nose-dived at that point, he would feel no terror because of despair. And then he'd felt his face warm with a different kind of panic: that this move at age forty-seven, after his wife had left him, was an anguished effort to reignite a life that had never burned with a particular fervor in the first place.

"I'm sorry about the bound hands, but it's the only way."

"You think if you untied them that the first thing I'd do is snatch the blindfold from my eyes? I don't care all that much what you look like."

"After a while, maybe we'll see."

He felt the familiar tightening of his grief in his larynx but forced it down.

"So, Marc, you had a wife."

"Yes, I had a wife. Did you find out her name on the Internet?"

"We did. Lynne. Lynne Laurent. Why do so many people seem to choose to marry for the musicality of their new name?"

"It's as good a reason as any."

"That may be true. Did she take you for everything you had?"

"No. She didn't take me for anything." Which had ultimately proven true in other ways. But in the isolation and confinement of these last six days, the gilded edges of his early memories of her—that morning when, from the porch of their first home together, she turned back to smile at him as he left and her robe slipped from her shoulder, or the time she'd cut her forearm so badly that it had to be stitched, and she'd winced when he gripped his homemade tourniquet with his hand, and later he'd contemplated her dried blood on his fingers in ways that had unsettled him—had begun to glow with increasing heat.

"No affection for you at all?"

"I'm not saying that. But she's not going to fund-raise for the cause, if that's what you're thinking. I haven't spoken to her since I arrived here." Which was true but for the two voice messages she'd left. "What you'll get for your phone call is maybe a measure of concern. Maybe."

"No brothers? No sisters?"

"Two sisters. One lives on a farm in Indiana in a little ranch home on sixty acres they rent to local corn growers in order to make ends meet. The other lives in a tiny apartment in Chicago where she's trying to patch her life back together after bouts of alcoholism. She borrows money from me."

"No children?" she asked.

At this he felt his eyes tighten under the blindfold and sting at the corners.

"No children," he said.

He heard her stand up then; her garments rustled, as if she were resettling them, and then she took a quiet step or two, and he felt her shadow as she stood over him; he heard her exhale in his ear.

"Marc," she said. "Your only daughter was murdered a month ago. She was nineteen. You know this. And you didn't even go home for the funeral."

She breathed again in his ear and then pulled away, dragged her chair back over to the far wall, opened the door, and closed it behind her.

2

When Azhar came in with the plate that evening, his gun slung over his shoulder, for the first time there was a serving of meat cut into small pieces. After Azhar handed him the plate, Marc lifted a bite with his spoon and looked up to where Azhar stood by the door.

"Lamb," Azhar said. "For muscle."

He flexed his arm and showed his lean biceps.

"Strength for the long haul?" Marc asked, though he knew Azhar wouldn't understand. Azhar smiled at him. His eyes were large and wet, almost pretty. He had a beard that he occasionally stroked thoughtfully, and when he was sitting watching over Marc for long stretches of time, he tended to stare up and out the window, as if something other than dust or a few feet of the nearest building might become visible. It occurred to Marc that sitting and guarding someone who posed no threat and with whom you shared no language must lead to almost depthless boredom.

Azhar stood and watched him eat. Marc had developed the habit through the days of his capture of separating out each spoonful of grain in order to extend the meal.

"You should bring a plate of your own next time. I don't much like eating alone." He lifted his fork toward him.

"Lamb," Azhar said, and then a sentence in Urdu.

The room where Marc was kept had a crude toilet that sometimes managed to flush. A bucket in which to wash that either Azhar or Saabir emptied each morning. The room was part of a small house or building, and he occasionally heard muffled thumps or a muted voice at night when he was sleeping on his thin mat. Whichever man had the night shift slept in front of the threshold of the door.

When Marc finished eating, Azhar took his plate and set it on the empty chair. "Walk," he said. He readied his gun in an almost desultory way that had deepened with each passing day, and he opened the door for Marc and followed him out into the late-evening sun. Even its waning brightness was for a moment too much, and Marc shielded his eyes, the sky seemingly saturated with pigment. There was the same smell of dampness in the air mingled with the nearly constant odor of something burning, and more distantly something foul, perhaps sewage. Azhar never led him around the perimeter of the building where he was being kept, but rather the neighboring one that had two or three windows that were often covered, but today Marc could peer through a pane where there were chairs and a table with three cups. He stopped to look in, surprised that he found himself missing even the anonymous faces of others, but Azhar said no and pushed him along with the hand that wasn't holding the gun.

Two times around the perimeter, after Marc felt the muscles in his legs start to stretch and warm with the movement, Azhar stopped him, put his hand on his shoulder, and turned him around. The gun was at his side, and he was reaching into his pocket. Azhar pulled from it a photograph and handed it to him. The picture was of a girl, maybe ten years old, in a plain dress and a bright blue scarf. She was smiling slightly, her mouth closed. Azhar said something in Urdu and then tapped his chest. "Daughter," he said with difficulty. Marc handed the photograph back to him, but Azhar didn't take it immediately, and when Marc looked at his face, Azhar's eyes were narrowed slightly, the lines near them deepened with sadness. "I"—he struggled to find the word—"sorry." Then something in Urdu again, and then he gestured with his gun and took Marc one more time around the perimeter.

The sun between the low buildings was nearly at the horizon, a red orb hung over collections of one-story buildings and the gently rolling hills. Marc could have been outside the Midwestern town where he grew up, as far as the sun and hills were concerned, but they were pretty nonetheless, the dusty deep and pale greens tinted orange before the coming twilight, and he felt his eyes fill. Remarkable that these glimpses of beauty under a darkening sky opened the gates of emotion more than the photograph of Azhar's daughter.

When they walked back into the room, Azhar picked up the plate, lifted it toward him, and smiled.

"Thank you for the lamb," Marc said, and Azhar nodded and then backed out of the door and was gone for half a minute before Saabir came in with the blindfold and, without speaking, wrapped it around Marc's eyes and tied his hands. For the first time, he was to get an evening visit from the woman.

When she came in, he heard Saabir walk out and close the door, and the woman once again pulled her chair across the floor of the room so she could sit close to him.

"It's a beautiful evening," she said first. "Soon they'll be calling for the sunset prayer."

"I wouldn't know what kind of evening it is," he said.

"That's not true, Marc. I saw Azhar walking you outside. I saw the way you looked at the sky."

"You can't be Muslim," he said.

"The call to prayer is moving even if I'm not. The way its rhythms bring your attention in equal parts to your devotion and your mortality."

"I would think it would get tedious after a while."

"Maybe," she said. "Maybe it's like washing your face.

Most days you do it without thinking, but now and then, as you're patting your skin dry, you catch a glimpse of yourself in the mirror that's such a surprise that it affirms your faith in the familiar."

Perhaps she was both a jihadist and a poet, he thought.

"That would depend on the face, I think."

"Yes, I suppose. I saw Azhar show you the picture of his daughter."

He tightened his eyes again beneath the blindfold. "Did you ask him to do that?"

"No. I did tell him that your daughter had been killed." She left the words suspended in the air for several seconds. "He's softhearted. He's a butcher by trade, but, like any butcher I've known, gentle and funny away from his work."

"Less gentle seeming when he's carrying a gun."

She shifted in her chair, and he heard her resettle her garments. Even with the blindfold, the room seemed to have darkened with nightfall.

"We reached your wife. You underestimated her, I think. She seemed very concerned about you. But perhaps that was just a manifestation of her grief."

"Don't," he said, shaking his head. Like everything else, he'd held at bay what could have been easily imaginable images of Lynne getting the phone call about the murder, or answering the knock at the door, or receiving mourners alongside the coffin, near which photographs of their daughter at various ages—

finger-painting in blues and yellows at age five, and water-skiing on a lake where one summer they rented when she was twelve, and laughing, arms linked, with girlfriends at age fifteen at a birthday party—told the half truths of a half-happy life.

"She wasn't angry with you for not flying home, or for not answering her calls."

"You must have had quite a chat."

"Woman to woman. She used the words *lost soul,* and seemed to suggest that ransoming you wouldn't change that."

This he knew was false. "You didn't talk to her at all, really, did you?"

"Does it make any difference?"

The peculiarity of the conversation struck him then, where the threat of her asking about his wife and daughter seemed more present than the blindfold, the rope around his wrists, or the man outside with the machine gun.

"What is this, exactly?" he asked.

"What do you mean?"

"I have no value to you. I'm not a journalist. I'm not rich. Yesterday you used the words *mid-level executive.* We're sitting here talking about my ex-wife. My daughter. I don't understand why anyone would kidnap me."

"You're an American," she said. "You were wandering where you shouldn't have been. We didn't choose you, especially. You happened by, more or less. You could have been anyone. What you were doing in Lyari I can't imagine."

"I was— I wanted to see how other Pakistanis live."

"Don't do that," she said. Her tone was suddenly cold.

"Do what?"

"Don't look for the suffering of others as a salve to your own wounds. It's arrogant. You see where that gets you."

"It wasn't a salve. I was trying to—I don't know. Put things in perspective."

"Well, did you?"

He didn't answer her, and she was silent for a while. Then she said, "Marc, you might be here for a long time for the simple reason that we hope to get something of value for you. I can't promise that I—" She stopped herself for a moment and then cleared her throat before continuing. "When I heard that your daughter had been killed. And that you didn't go home when you heard. I admit that interested me in ways that have nothing to do with your ransom."

"You're interested in a murder of someone you don't know? In this country where innocents are killed almost daily?"

"Unlike your country? No one is ever shot dead in your own country? Where your own daughter died?"

He flinched at these questions. He would be unable or unwilling to muster a political argument even if it weren't for his circumstances.

"Perhaps she wasn't an *innocent,* but I'm sorry your daughter was killed," she said eventually. "And you're right to think, for me, she's as faceless as any other daughter who lost her life senselessly. But I'm more interested in the story of a man who didn't even return home when he heard she'd been murdered."

"Why?"

"Why? Because I've seen many men grieve. Say what you want, but men here are not afraid to show their grief. Or rage. Or how one feeds the other."

"You think I'm not sad or angry?"

"What I think," she said, and he heard her bring her hands down with a light slap on the top of her thighs. "What I think," she said again, "is that you will have many long days here. At least you should be hoping for that. Here, with me. Or with Saabir or Azhar. You've noticed that their company doesn't involve much conversation. And so you will mostly only have me to talk to. And I am—compensated for talking to you, for getting information from you that might lead to more money. But I am not in charge of your fate, and I'm not at liberty to jump into an SUV and travel across the border or take a plane to London. I'm trapped here, in many ways, just as you are. More or less alone with my first language. So almost every day, we'll talk. If you want to talk about the weather, we can do that. Or stock prices at PepsiCo, and whether a bullish year for your company might loosen the purse strings of your ransom. Or we can talk about something else."

"Like my daughter."

"I assume you loved her?"

He felt the question like a low-voltage shock.

"What color were her eyes? I've never seen your eyes. Were they the same as yours?"

It was a strangely intimate question. He had not thought of his daughter's eyes, specifically, in years, but they had been a kind of green-gray, like neither his nor her mother's.

"Her name was Claire," she said. "A French name, of course. Claire Laurent. France, home of your ancestors."

"Another imperialist nation," he said, still resisting memory.

"I've been to Paris. Parts of it are beautiful. The way the sun lights those buildings on the first warm days of April. But to the extent that all that architecture arrives on the backs of the poor—well, many parts of Karachi are beautiful, too. You must have made it down to the ocean to watch the sunrise."

"So I'm still in Karachi. On the outskirts."

She shifted in her seat again and coughed once. She'd lowered her guard.

"You may be," she said. "You may not be. But it's no real comfort either way. Would you feel any closer to home?"

But he felt he'd gained some slight advantage, whatever that may have meant.

"Who were you traveling with in Paris?"

"Well, it wasn't your daughter," she said. "My guess is Claire Laurent never made it back to her ancestors' homeland."

He was stricken again at the mention of her full name.

"She wasn't the kind of girl to go to the senior prom, was she? But an attractive young woman. Her hair cut close to her head. That tattoo on her left shoulder. A tree with no leaves and one bird. Pretty in a lonely sort of way."

"So you must have seen—" But his voice caught. "You must have seen her eyes."

"She drank too much," the woman continued. "There's a picture of her drinking straight from a bottle of whiskey. And she liked to read. One photo has her lying on a bed with Jack Kerouac. His book, I mean."

"Stop it."

"Your wife—Lynne. Lynne said that she'd enrolled in a community college for the start of the next semester. Had finished her GED. She was turning her life around, though I admit I've never known what people mean when they say that."

"Please stop."

"How do you turn your life around once it's been turned inside out?"

If his hands had been free, he would have stopped up his ears.

"I do not—" He was trying not to choke on the words. "I do not want to talk about this. How do you know these things?"

"I'm not a mind reader, Marc. But I know where to look. There aren't very many secrets out there anymore, except among the poor. And no one cares much to hear any of those."

He heard himself breathing heavily, and recognized the same separation between his state of mind and body that he'd had since he arrived, even before he'd heard Lynne's message on the machine. In the first weeks, walking the most urbane streets of Karachi, with men in suits, women without scarves, their hair shining in the sun alongside others whose eyes peered out of their hijabs, and the odd juxtaposition of an exotic written and spoken language among images of American companies he recognized (hell, represented), he was a stranger to himself, his life up to this point a kind of caricature that sat on his left shoulder and occasionally whispered its mundane preoccupations in his ear: What was the score of last night's game? Sweetheart, this is a fine cup of coffee. It's springtime. Time to throw some grass seed on the bare patches of lawn.

He heard her stand up then, and he thought she would leave without saying anything else, but instead she walked over in the direction of the window.

"Saabir won't leave me alone with you for much longer." Her clothes rustled, and the joint at her knee quietly popped. "You know, if you stand right up against this wall, and stretch, you can see the stars."

Despite himself, he laughed.

"You have no idea how odd that sounds from where I sit."

"No," she said. She was quiet for a while, apparently contemplating the sky. "When I was in Paris, I was with someone I loved. It was years ago now. We traveled quite a bit because he had money. Money from his father, but money nevertheless. I loved seeing different places in the world. I may have been more in love with them than I was with him. But like many young men who come from money, he was taken with the people who lived on what he called *the fringes*. He gave those people his money, and some of those organizations did things to others that you would deplore. I deplored them, too. But I was young, like your daughter. I loved what I thought was the adventure. I loved him. He was killed, ultimately. Here. His throat cut. It's not that it's commonplace, but it's common enough. For men like he was."

"Why are you telling me this?" he asked. But she seemed to ignore him.

"I hate the word *radicalized*," she said. "As if people can be programmed to do awful things against their will. Do you know what I think *radicalizes* most people? Other than poverty. Do you know what *radicalized* me?"

She waited several long moments for him to answer, but he didn't.

"Grief," she said.

And then she took three steps to the door, knocked on it once to alert Saabir, and quietly closed it behind her.

3

When he woke in the morning, for the first time since his capture, no one was in the room with him. He sat up on his mat.
Saabir's had been rolled up and set against the wall in what he'd
learned were Saabir's meticulous habits of neatness. Saabir
swept the floor every few hours with a broom he kept outside,
even when no one had passed through the door. He brought in
a short ladder to keep the window free of dust, but removed it
immediately afterward. The emptiness of the room struck Marc
as oppressive more than either Saabir or Azhar, as if, unknow-
ing, he'd been delivered from a dream of friends and woken
into destitution, with the last word the woman had said before
leaving still resonating in his ears.

Outside, in the distance, he heard two men talking. About
what, he had no idea, but he thought he understood the tone of

their shortening sentences—they were exchanging lines of a familiar story—and then a burst of laughter from both. They walked on. To most everyone back home, but especially to those who questioned his move to Karachi (among them his mother, seventy-five now, who had begun forwarding e-mails with the names of Muslims serving in the president's cabinet—as a safeguard or a warning, he wasn't certain—and the post-separation friends who narrowed their eyes and said, "Marc, Pakistan? How about China or Brazil? You trying to punish Lynne?"), he'd fluorescently blathered on about the commonality of the human experience, how we were more alike than different despite fences, despite more profound religious and cultural barriers. But listening through the wall to conversations he couldn't understand, at those moments a recognizable language would have seemed like a clothesline on which you could hang a worn, comfortable shirt and let the breeze sweeten its scent. At what point, at what age, he wondered, had he passed from longing for the exotic to longing for what had once been familiar?

Saabir came through the door with his rifle strapped to his back, and without looking at him handed him a bowl of rough-cut fruit mixed with grain. Saabir sat in the chair across from him and watched him eat, almost unblinking. Marc swallowed the cereal with difficulty, his throat dry from sleeping on the floor.

"Can I have a cup of water, please?"

But Saabir only continued to stare at him blankly.

"Some water," Marc said again, and motioned as if lifting a

cup to his lips. Saabir stared for another moment, and then slowly shook his head, averting his eyes in disgust. He stood up and put his hand on Marc's chest and looked at him.

"Stupid," he said, and shook his head slightly. "No stupid."

Nevertheless he left and came back with the water, and stood only two feet away while Marc drank. When Marc finished he set the cup in his lap.

"You," Saabir said. He was gazing down at him with his deep eyes narrowed, as if he were trying to make a calculation. He was handsome enough to star in films. Saabir reached out and laid the tip of his index finger on Marc's forehead, lightly, letting it rest there, and then drew the finger gently down the length of his nose and chin until it came to rest again on his Adam's apple, where he pushed slightly harder. The pressure made Marc swallow involuntarily. "You," he said again, then with effort, "tell me. Tell me." And then he removed his finger.

"I don't know what you want me to say," Marc said. Oddly, he was not feeling terribly threatened. Saabir stepped away.

"No time," he said. "You do not. No time," and then a sentence in Urdu that he spoke very quickly, as if in relief over a language that he knew well.

After this, Saabir pulled a scarf and a rope from the pocket of his salwar kameez—Saabir's was more formal than many Marc had seen, a long, flowing black shirt over loose white trousers—and first tied Marc's hands, then wrapped and knotted the scarf around his eyes. Saabir didn't leave immediately to get the woman, and Marc sensed him standing in front of him.

"Blind man," Saabir said, and then Marc heard him turn away and go out the door.

When she came in, she didn't speak. She seemed to be moving about the room, taking an inventory of things. When she lifted the cup from his lap, he flinched because he hadn't recognized she was that close. He again caught the fragrance of her clothes. She handed the dishes to Saabir outside the door, who spoke to her in soft, almost pleading tones. She closed it then and pulled the chair across the floor and sat down, remaining silent.

"Saabir," he said, "might be in love with you."

She offered something close to a snort. "Why would you say that?"

"You can hear it in the way he speaks to you."

"How do you know he wasn't saying, *When do we get to kill the son of a bitch?*"

This silenced him for a moment, and he turned his head. "Well, if he did, he said it with affection."

"You know," she said, "there are over twenty million people in Karachi."

This seemed an odd non sequitur, so he said nothing, despite the fact that she had affirmed where he was being held.

"And you can still—" But she didn't finish her sentence.

"He touched me in a strange way."

"He touched you?" She sounded surprised.

"Yes. He put his fingertip on my forehead, then ran it down my face and pressed it on my throat. He said there was no time."

"I see," she said, and then it sounded as if she were impatiently brushing crumbs from whatever she was wearing. "Saabir is a complex man. We are only in control of so much, you know. When there's a bombing, or something like a drone strike, even in a different part of the country, some people get upset. Almost everyone sees themselves as innocents, at that point. And some want revenge. You're nearby, and you're not an innocent, but in some ways, for them, it would be even better if you were."

"So others know I'm here."

"Twenty million people, Marc. It's hard to keep a secret. We may have to move you at some point."

"It's not like I was getting comfortable here."

"No." She sat quietly for a full minute, and then said, "We spoke to your mother. She has a charming Midwestern accent."

"My mother." He doubted it.

"We heard a dog barking in the background."

"Penny," he said involuntarily.

"Pardon?"

"The dog's name."

"Of course. She kept saying, your mother, if you'd only come back for the funeral. If you'd only come back for the funeral, you would be safe. Now she's worried about losing both of you. Both you and Claire."

"I don't believe you even spoke to her."

"Both you and Claire," she said again.

"Look," he said. "If I had some information you could extort from me, why not call in Saabir and have him beat it out of me?"

"Yes. As if that's all he's good for," she said. "As if that would do nothing to him."

"There's not a thing I can tell you, Josephine."

His use of the name she'd told him took the edge from her voice.

"We don't want information. You know that. We want money."

"Yeah, money. Right."

"Your mother said she still lives on the little lake in southern Michigan where you grew up. She lived there even after your father left. You have to truly love a place to stay there after you've been brokenhearted."

"You must have a great Internet connection."

"She said that you were a fearless little boy, at least with regard to the lake. There was a raft that floated on empty oil barrels at the place where the water got deep. When you saw your older sisters sunning themselves on it, past the point you could reach, you taught yourself to swim at age five so you could cannonball off the tip of that raft in order to splash them and get them to scream. She told me that you and Penny Senior used to wander around in the shallows of the reeds, and when you weren't tossing a tennis ball to the dog, you were trying to attract leeches that you'd joyfully pluck from your skin then drop in salt water just to watch them squirm. She said that you used to have underwater races with your friends, and that you were so good at holding your breath that once one of your friends started crying when you didn't come up because he thought you'd drowned."

His face flushed warm, and the images spun through him like water down a drain. He could see his dog, a springer spaniel, poised above the shallows of the lake, her tail vibrating in anticipation, her brown eyes the color of her coat open wide as she searched for minnows before plunging her head beneath the surface. The blindfold left him increasingly vulnerable to memory because he couldn't use his vision to distract himself with objects in the room.

"It's strange, isn't it?" she said. "The mundane things that rack your heart when you're away from everything you've known."

"I—" he said. "Some of those things were right. Some weren't. You have a very good imagination."

"Which weren't right?"

This he wouldn't answer.

"And yes, I do have a very good imagination."

"Can I ask you a question? How old are you?"

"I can't tell you that. It's not that I would mind you knowing in other circumstances. But when and if you leave here, that's not information I want you to have."

"But you told me yesterday about the love who brought you here."

She didn't respond to this, and sat quietly, and it dawned on him that the more he learned about her the less likely it was that he would leave alive.

"It's funny in a way," he said.

"What is?"

"That you would use childhood memories of your hostages as a means to get a ransom."

"Missing home can be more powerful than *a good beating,* as you put it."

"I didn't say that."

"No, you didn't. You're very careful with the words you choose, I think. That would be much harder if we were to sit here for hours with you blindfolded. But for now we don't have that much time."

"What do you do when you're not here? Do you have other guests assigned to you?"

"Guests." She laughed. "Why do you ask? Are you jealous?"

"Did you actually talk to my mother?"

"Someone did. She's older now, and a little lonely. So for her, it works the same way as it does with you. You tug at a loose string of something she remembers, and other details come pouring out. You can't be surprised that the first things she spoke of were about you as a small boy."

"Why?"

"It's the first thing any mother would say about her grown child, whether he's a hostage or on death row. If she can make him be seen as a boy, as someone who was once innocent and sweet, then there's a chance he'll be set free."

"You sound like you know something about it."

She stood up then and walked over to the window. He imagined her arching her neck to look outside.

"You were wrong about the leeches," he said. "I was terrified of them when I was a kid."

"No mother would tell a story of torture on her captured son. Even if the subject was leeches."

"It was an interesting choice of details. You must know something about Midwestern lakes."

"As if that were the only place there are lakes and leeches."

He heard her step quietly back to the chair and sit down.

"You asked me about what I do when I'm not here. What do you do when I'm not here?"

It had been, he believed, over a week since his capture, but already the days had begun to run into each other, like a bleak version of a Florida vacation he'd once taken with Lynne where the sun and the ocean gave the illusion there were days and nights, but neither accumulating. Had he been more afraid, he supposed, the hours would have passed even more slowly, but with nothing to read, no conversation, no television or phone, and nowhere to move other than along the walls of the small room where either Saabir's or Azhar's eyes followed him as if they were watching a distant boat move along the horizon, he was consumed by tedium. At times, it was a blunt weapon that helped him fend off what he knew would be a disorienting sorrow, but other times it had become so unendurable that it would part unexpectedly, and an image of Claire riding on his shoulders (a photograph his sister had taken), or something commonplace, like Lynne setting a plate in front of him, would come slicing through.

"Nothing," he said. "I look forward to eating. To counting each bite of food. I think I'm even starting to look forward to your blindfold."

"So when you sit here for all those hours with nothing to do but think. No dreams? No erotic fantasies?"

He laughed at this. "You've got to be kidding."

"Those things don't disappear just because you're a captive."

"Well, they have for me." He couldn't help but wonder what she looked like, but he hadn't for a moment thought about her sexually, much less anyone else in the past weeks with the possible exception of Lynne, with whom sex, infrequent as it was, had become a comfort.

"I'd like to propose something for you to think about," she said. "For both of us to think about, given we have little else to take up our time together. I can only spend so many minutes plying you for a ransom, and you can only hope for so long for freedom or escape."

"I'm not looking to escape."

"I can tell that about you, which is why I'd like to propose this to you."

"Do I have a choice?"

"Your daughter. Claire. It's a pretty name. I mean that with all sincerity. A hopeful name, in its meaning."

The sound of it was like a hand closing over his heart.

"How well did you know her?"

"How well did I know her? She was my daughter, for Christ's sake."

"Don't insult my intelligence. Or yours. We both know that doesn't necessarily mean anything. My own father showed almost no curiosity about me once I'd left home. Or once I was caught between childhood and puberty, to be honest, and my arms and legs no longer fit his pet name for me."

He thought she'd want him to ask what it was, but he didn't.

"So if you think you knew Claire well, I have a proposal for you. I would like you to tell me the story of her life."

Something came hurtling at him from the inside, and he turned his head.

"I know about her death," she continued. "A murder. By someone looking for someone else, though she shouldn't have been in the room with that someone else. I'm sorry about that, Marc. About this. But here, in the slums of Pakistan, that's an undramatic way to die. I'm sorry, but it is. It's what everyone has come to dread, but half expect. And you probably don't want to know the story of her death, or you would have gone back home for the funeral. Except for one detail, and that's what she was thinking at the moment she was killed. And you can never know that."

"I do not want to know that," he said defiantly.

"Why not? I would want to know. Though I think it would usually disappoint us. I read once about Einstein's death, and how his nurse couldn't understand his final words because they were in German. As if, you know, he'd revealed a new scientific insight or was somehow translating for God in those last minutes. It was just as likely he could have been remembering a picnic he'd had with his mother when he was a boy. More likely."

"What good would it do for you to know Claire's story?"

"Good? It would do no good for anyone. Maybe for you. It might open some kind of window for you. I don't know what might fly through it with you trapped in this unhappy place. But as for me. As for me and you, together, waiting here, I wonder about her past so that we can learn to tell the story of her life if she had lived."

The thought of this under the blindfold made him feel more helpless.

"Don't—there's nothing—that's the whole point. I don't want to—I can't believe you'd want to do this. I'd rather you torture me, if I had a choice."

"No, you wouldn't. Believe me."

"You just said murder is commonplace in Pakistan. Suicide bombs. Drone attacks. Yesterday you spoke about how openly people grieve here. Well, would you ever ask those people to tell you about what they're grieving? Are they grieving over the ones they've lost, or for the stories their loved ones won't get the chance to live and no one will ever tell? You can't know those stories. Claire was nineteen. If she were ninety, maybe you could know them then."

He was grinding his teeth between sentences, wanting to tear away the blindfold and run out the door.

"When you were nineteen," he said, "would you have imagined a time when you'd be sitting in this fucking building across from a bound and blindfolded man while trying to drum up a ransom for some kind of failed cause? I can't fucking believe this. Just leave me alone."

He heard how much he'd raised his voice, and he waited while the sound of it echoed off the bare walls, but Saabir didn't come through the door.

"When I was nineteen," she said calmly, "I was a theater major at a small college in upstate New York. One summer, we did a performance of Harold Pinter's *The Homecoming*. Do you know that play?"

"No, I don't know that play," he said, shaken and exasperated.

"There's only one character that's a woman. The other five are men. I was too young for that part, all of us were, but the director wanted to do Pinter. So I was Ruth. I was in love with the boy who played Teddy. That was my husband in the play. We would rehearse for hours, you know, in this theater with no air-conditioning. It was one of those summers where the world outside the theater seemed flattened by the heat. The grass dried to the point that it looked like someone had set it on fire, and in the afternoon, when the wind blew, which it always did, the trees under that sun seemed gray rather than green. You couldn't be outside for long through this string of ninety-degree days, so after a while, it seemed like our rehearsals, and then our performances, were the lives we were living. And afterward, that boy—because he was a boy then—that boy and I would go up to his apartment, and we would make love almost till dawn on that bed, with the window fan blowing the barely cool air over our bodies. I don't mean constantly make love. I mean the kind of lovemaking where you would finish, you know, both of you calling out in the way that it seems rare when it's still new to you, and you'd both be almost slippery with the sweat on your skin, and the sounds of passing cars and insects out your window would lull you to sleep so that you didn't know you were asleep, or you were simultaneously sleeping and listening to the world outside, then one of you would lay a finger on the still-damp place on the other's neck, or in the small of his back if he'd turned away from you, and then you would be probing other places, and his breath and the sound of your own blood would rise and recede into the streets again. It was like that then. It was like waves. And after you woke up in the morning, you felt shy, a bit, at what your body revealed about who you were, so maybe the first thing you'd say were lines from the play. *The last thing I want is a breath of air. Why do you want a breath of air? I just do. But it's late. I won't go far. I'll come back."*

Her words hung in the air, and forgetting how he was bound, he tried to lift his hand to reach for them. As she was speaking, he had forgotten his anger, and for the first time, really, he'd almost forgotten where he was, and the heat of the late-spring Karachi morning had become the heat of Midwestern July. Only she'd said upstate New York, hadn't she? He sat still, waiting for her to continue.

"So that's where I was when I was nineteen, and I don't know that I aspired to be anywhere else. Well, no, of course I did. But when you remember, I mean when I think back—I can't recall any particular performance, any particular rehearsal. It's as if they all happened at the same time. I remember the nights afterward. If Claire had lived, I wonder how she would remember age nineteen, years from now."

"She was not like you."

"You don't know how I was."

"She wasn't the way you described yourself that summer. If she'd been that. If she'd had that." The room was returning to him, slowly. Someone's feet shuffled outside the door. "If you had died at age nineteen, and your father knew that story, I wonder if that would have been a comfort to him. To know that you had those months."

"Like I've told you, my father was not like you, Marc."

"The kind of father who would travel to Pakistan for half a year not knowing where his daughter was sleeping at night?" Marc asked. "Not even knowing for certain the city she was sleeping in?" But he knew better than to berate himself. It was what had led him to Lyari.

He said, "I couldn't help you with the story of who she was when she died. So I can't help you with the story of who she might have become."

"So there's nothing you remember from her childhood? A time where you knew things were changing? I don't believe for a minute you don't know some of her story."

He was aware that beneath the blindfold his eyes were open, as if he were looking at her. But then he closed them.

"She was—" He pulled at the ropes on his wrists, and the memory tumbled forward as his resistance eased away. "Maybe twelve. Fifth grade, I think. Maybe sixth. I was in her room gathering laundry. No, I wasn't the house domestic, but I tried to pitch in, and Lynne had trained me to go through pants pockets."

Claire's room appeared to him then. There were no posters of boy bands, or photos of friends, or Disney princesses. Instead, a poster of Jimi Hendrix after Claire had started playing guitar, a large, blue drawing of his head with a joint in the corner of his mouth. Harmless, Lynne had said, when he'd questioned it. Bob Dylan as a young man in the streets of New York. Janis Joplin in her wire rims, and a rapper who'd been murdered whose name he couldn't remember. "I like your wall of dead friends," he'd said to Claire.

"Bob Dylan's not dead," she'd told him.

"Depends on your perspective."

She'd smiled.

"What did you find in her pockets?" the woman said, and he realized he'd fallen silent. "A note, I assume?"

"A letter. A letter from an older school friend when, you know, even then kids were texting. So I was surprised. The girl's name was Sally. It was a pretty long letter, with names of kids, only some of which I'd heard of, and the girl, Sally, was going on about how she was so sorry that she'd taken away Claire's innocence. I had no idea what that meant. Claire was twelve years old. But at the end of the letter, the girl wrote that she wasn't being serious when she asked Claire to cut herself to prove that she loved her, and that she couldn't believe she'd done it and she should never do it again. I didn't tell Lynne right away. But that night, when Claire was asleep, I walked into her room. She was a sound sleeper, and it was a hot night, and her blankets were off. She still had these thin legs and arms. She was a child. Still a small girl. But high on top of her thigh was a long slice, still scabbed over. I woke her up on the spot. She was disoriented. She told me she'd dropped a pair of scissors when she was wearing shorts, but I didn't believe her. I stood over her, asking again and again, 'Did you make the cut? Did you make the cut?' As if I were asking whether she'd made the girls' softball team."

"Did she tell you the truth?" the woman asked quietly.

"Not then. Lynne bought her story. She told Lynne that she'd lied to Sally about cutting herself. Then years later, about the time she turned eighteen, when she was applying for colleges, I was sure she wouldn't get in because of her grades. She was a smart kid, good test scores, and all. A good writer, but didn't give a damn about her high school classes. Then she was accepted by the University of Chicago, which no one expected. She called me the day the letter came, and after reading the first paragraph, she said, 'So, Dad. Looks like I made the cut.' And when I said something innocuous like, 'That's for sure,' she said, 'No, Dad, get it? I made the cut. I made the cut.' "

The woman laughed loudly at this. "That's a good line," she said. "She had a sense of humor."

He nodded. "I suppose I don't find it particularly funny right now. She dropped out of high school soon after that."

He heard the door open, and Saabir came in and asked something in Urdu in a tone of insistence. She turned her head and explained it to him in firm, but patient, detail. He offered a curt sentence in return, and closed the door.

"He heard me laugh," she said. "I have to go soon."

"You're not allowed to laugh?"

"We're not supposed to be enjoying ourselves in here."

"Little risk of that."

She let out a long breath. Beneath her garments, she seemed to cross and uncross her legs.

"So Claire is thirty-two," she said.

"What?"

"So Claire is thirty-two. Her birthday is in—?"

"June."

"June. And she's thirty-two now, and she's living far away from you. Far away from Lynne. In a small town out west, in Montana, maybe, or eastern California. It's a town on a highway, not an interstate, but a state road. It's traveled more heavily in the summertime because tourists pass through going from one place to another, but they do not come to this town to sightsee. There's a range of mountains, and on clear days you can see one that's snowcapped, but it's too far away once you've lived in that town for a few years to think about driving there to cool off in the summer heat. Claire and her husband own a small motel where mostly truckers stay, and the people passing through who don't want to spend the money on the Best Western a few miles farther up the road. There are twelve rooms all on one level, with paneling inside, and the musty smell of bedspreads Claire smilingly describes as 'vintage'; they bought the motel over a year ago, and they talked about making improvements, but others in that town that too slowly warmed to them told them they loved the place as it was, and anyway, shortly after they'd bought it Claire had become pregnant, wasn't particularly happy about it, and now the baby is three months old. She uses cloth diapers to save money, washing them in the big machine along with the soiled sheets of the guests of the motel. But the diapers she hangs on a clothesline behind the building because she thinks the sun and the wind coming down off the hills scent them in ways that a drier sheet never could. The clothesline is worn, and breaks on occasion, and money's tight enough that she's stubborn about buying a new one, and one day, while repairing it again, she's pulling it so taut, anchoring it under her foot so she can draw it level with the sky, that it snaps on the other end, flies at her, and whips across her thigh just under the hem of her shorts, and leaves a long welt. She curses once, and rubs it, and sees it running almost parallel to an old threadlike scar. And she remembers then this girl she loved when she was a child who asked her to put it there, the first person she'd ever loved, a girl she had kissed so as to know what kissing was like. And then she smiles, looks down at the baby sleeping in her bassinet, and goes back to fixing the clothesline."

After she stopped speaking, he was aware that he was clenching his eyes, not in pain, but out of the effort of trying to imagine Claire in this place. He was holding his mouth open, as if he could breathe in the possibility.

"I'll be back later tonight," the woman said. "Azhar will be here this afternoon."

After she left, Saabir untied his hands and removed the blindfold, and for the remaining hours of the morning the walls felt so familiar that they were like a second skin.

4

Throughout the afternoon and into the evening, Marc sat with Azhar in the rising heat; at times, Azhar dozed in his chair, his gun slipping down his shoulder to the floor, and it occurred to Marc that, in the right circumstance, it would have been relatively easy to slip out the door if he had any chance of knowing where he was once he got outside. He wasn't sure what that circumstance would look like, but he imagined himself running down one of the narrow roads, taking hold of someone's sleeve, and pleading into an impassive, uncomprehending face.

Azhar left the room frequently to bring in cups of water for both of them, along with plates of food in the early evening. Azhar ate quickly and then watched Marc carefully portion out on the plate each spoonful of grain. Toward nightfall, Azhar lit a lantern, and the light fell across his hands as he held his cup, and Marc saw a heavy scar between two of his knuckles and other places where there had been nicks or cuts that had healed. When Azhar saw him staring at them, he put his cup down and held his hands up for Marc to see, turning them at the wrist. The lines on his palms were long and dark.

"So you work as a butcher, Josephine says, and then you spend hours on end watching over me so you can catch up on your sleep."

He wasn't sure how much Azhar had understood, but Azhar nodded and smiled at him, and then pointed at the deepest scar. Then with his other hand he made chopping motions in the air, as if he were handling a meat cleaver, and brought the invisible cleaver down between his knuckles so that Marc would understand how the scar got there.

"Boy," Azhar said. He pointed toward himself, and then laid his hand flat in the air several feet above the ground. "Boy," he said again. Marc gathered that Azhar must have cut himself when he was a child and learning the trade.

"Not a mistake you'd make more than once," Marc said to him.

Azhar smiled. He took the gun off his shoulder and placed the tip of it in the area of the dirt floor in front of his chair. He moved it slowly across the floor with careful deliberation, and after a couple of minutes, Marc could see that he was drawing a remarkably accurate outline of a cow. Azhar even added a tail and legs with hooves, and lastly a pair of wide eyes and a mouth turned up into a grin. He tapped the tip of the gun on the cow's smile and then gestured with his free hand as if to say, "Why not?" He then drew lines through various parts of the cow, cordoning it off into sections. He tapped a section of the cow about two-thirds toward the tail, and then looked up into Marc's eyes and with a smile on his face began chewing slowly, savoring something imaginary, and then with his fingertips starting at the corners of his mouth, ran them down into his beard as if the juices of the meat were overflowing. "Good," Azhar said, and Marc realized he was teaching him which parts of the cow were most tender and flavorful.

Marc stood up from his chair, and Azhar didn't raise the gun as he had during the first days. Marc knelt next to the drawing and pointed to the section at the rear end of the cow.

"What about here?"

Azhar nodded, and then cupped his hands in the shape of a bowl and hollowed it out with his fingertips. He then used his finger as a knife as if he were cutting pieces, and then stirred it with an imaginary spoon.

"Ah, soup," he said. "Good in a soup or stew."

Azhar grinned. He said the word in Urdu.

"You're a good man, Azhar, even if you are a terrorist."

But this was a word Azhar recognized, and he frowned and touched the shoulder strap that held the gun.

"I'm sorry," Marc said, and then knelt back on the ground

and drew a crude image that was supposed to look like Azhar, and then images of small children—stick figures, really—behind him.

"How many children do you have?" he asked.

Azhar smiled again, and held up three fingers, and with his free hand held up two, and said, "Boy."

"Two boys and a girl," Marc said, nodding.

Someone knocked on the door then, and Azhar stood up and pulled the blindfold and rope from his salwar kameez. He tied Marc's hands first, lacing them carefully, and then wrapped the blindfold around his head, passing his fingers on the surface over Marc's eyes in order to smooth out a wrinkle. Marc heard him open the door, exchange a word with the woman, and then close it behind him.

She stood for a while in front of him as if she were surveying the situation, and then Marc realized she must have been looking at Azhar's sketch of the cow.

"He was teaching me about his trade," he said. "Showing me the best cuts of beef."

"So I see," she said.

"You can't blame him. My god, he sits here for hours on end with nothing to do. He must be bored out of his mind."

"It looks like a petroglyph."

"A what?"

"A petroglyph. Like a cave drawing. I've seen them in different places here. This reminds me of an elephant I saw in the north that was etched onto this blue stone. There were the same kinds of lines dividing it into parts."

He had taken a trip to Arizona once where he saw similar drawings, though they weren't in caves. Images of animals, some quite beautiful, and human handprints.

"It's funny," he said. "You don't think of the ancient history of a place like Pakistan when you're thinking about coming here."

"No," she said. "Most people don't. It's a beautiful landscape conquered by many. The Aryans, the Greeks, the Mughals. The British. Now Americans think of it as foaming at the mouth."

"Which it is, sometimes."

"Like everywhere else, and never only that. Because the truth is, here we have this butcher who drew a perfect image of a smiling cow. And someone taught him this. You can think of the country that way, too."

She sat down in the chair where Azhar had been sitting without moving it closer because she didn't want to destroy the drawing.

"We'll have to sweep this away before Saabir comes in."

"Not an art lover?"

"Ha. No, it's not that." She was silent for a few seconds. "Do you know, if you were to be killed, it would probably be Azhar, and not Saabir, who would do it?"

The thought had occurred to him, especially given Azhar's profession.

"Does that mean you have some news for me?" he asked.

"No. As I told you before, things can change quickly here."

For the first time, he recognized her vulnerability in her work. If he were to be discovered, she was unlikely to live much longer herself.

"And if someone decided you should be killed?" he asked.

"There would be many who would volunteer." She sat quietly for a while. "So have you been thinking about Claire?" she asked.

He shifted his feet, and somewhat absently strained at the rope around his wrist, which loosened slightly.

"I don't want to think about her."

"You seemed transported this morning."

"I wouldn't say transported. It feels good in the way a dose of morphine does, in that it makes the pain go away for a while."

"Was she an affectionate little girl?"

"I—" he started to protest. "All little girls are affectionate."

"That's not true, you know."

"Well, were you?"

"I could be. I liked exploring. Finding things. Presenting them to my mother."

"I assume you loved her?"

But she ignored this question. "She kept many of them. We lived near a school with a playground, and some nights, when the other children had been called in or had gone home, I'd go out and sit in one of the swings, kick myself high, and survey the playground for anything they had left. It was about what you'd expect. A Popsicle stick. The missing limb of a doll. Kite string. If it interested me, I'd jump off the swing and pick it up and bring it back to my mother, who would arrange them into some kind of display that she'd place for the evening on the windowsill. So if I was lucky enough to find the cracked eggshell of a killdeer, and, say, a gum wrapper and a ribbon, she'd wind the ribbon into a kind of crude nest, place the broken shell in it, and cut out of the wrapper a small chick that she'd place in the shell. Next morning, when I got up, it would always be gone."

"This was in upstate New York?" But it was another question she ignored.

"One time I was looking through the attic of her house, and opened a small box that had my name on it. And there they were, a tangle of these things I'd brought to her from that time. An assortment of junk, really. A dirty flip-flop. A mitten. Two or three toy cars. But what was strange was how few there actually were, and it seemed she'd saved them all, without storing them carefully, or anything like that. The eggshell was in bits. But I thought I'd done this a hundred times, and there were maybe two dozen items in that box. Not much larger than a shoebox, to tell you the truth."

"Did you hold on to it?"

"No. Hardly. All those things were so plain or broken or torn. You can't reinfuse them with how you marveled at them as a child. If I marveled at them at all. I picked them up because they seemed to please my mother."

Behind the blindfold, he saw a fleeting image of a girl hanging from her knees on a bar, reaching for a coin she saw on the ground.

"So would you describe that as affectionate?" she asked, but he didn't answer her. "Anyway, so you see how this works, Marc? Do you think that the baby we dreamed up for Claire this morning—"

"You dreamed up."

"No, we dreamed up. Do you think that the baby we dreamed up for Claire today is a girl, and that there's a school in that highway town out west where her mother and father live, and that she'll wander around the dirty playground and pick up bits and pieces of refuse left by other children and bring them home to her mother and present them as a prize?"

"I can't imagine you as a little girl. I'm sorry. I've never even seen your face."

"You don't have to imagine me as a little girl. You have to imagine Claire as having one. And you have to stop trying not to remember her. Why did you refuse to fly back home when you heard she was killed?"

In the blindfold, he felt the question was as confining as the walls of the room, and as ever present.

"It wouldn't have brought her back."

She laughed.

"That's not the answer. That's the answer anyone would give."

He was sweating now, and couldn't wipe it from the back of his neck.

"I couldn't face it. Please. I was a coward. I am a coward. Like all Americans."

"Stop that crap," she said, so sharply there was a faint echo off the walls. "You may be a coward. But you can't keep me away with this one-dimensional sarcasm." He heard her stand up, and he could feel her shadow near him. Was she going to slap him? Then her hand was on his forehead, or rather some edge of her gown wiping away the perspiration, and then her fingers themselves on the back of his neck, and he flinched at their light, calloused touch. She sat back down.

"Why are you sweating so much? It's a cooler night than that," she said quietly. No one had touched him with anything approaching tenderness in months. Then she said, "I think we both know the reason why you didn't go back home, but it's such a sentimental illusion."

"What is it, then? You tell me."

"When the man I loved was killed here—I told you his throat was cut—I was nearby. A few blocks away from where they found and laid out his body. Someone had come and told me, and I was shaking, shaking. Not crying yet. And the impulse I felt—you must have felt this impulse—was to run to the place because I didn't want to believe it. I wouldn't believe it until I saw for myself. I'd seen violence at that point. I'd seen the aftermath of a bombing, the blood, the limbs. But I also knew that if I saw his face after what they'd done, I could never remember it in any other way. So I didn't want to walk those few blocks. I knew he was dead, but I knew if I didn't go, I would be freer to remember him as he was. Or believe that he might still be alive."

"The thing that radicalized you," he said, but she didn't respond.

"So what did you do after that?" he asked.

"You know what I did. I'm sitting here in front of you. And yes, I was unprepared for it. I'd lived something of a protected life to that point, maybe more so than your daughter. I was unprepared for that depth of grief. But, Marc, it's a sweet little illusion that by staying in Karachi, by not answering your wife's calls, that you somehow were keeping Claire alive wherever she may be back home. But it's sentimental, and she deserves better."

He felt his eyes go heavy, but the knot of cold in his chest remained. He thought she was only partly right. "And how is it not sentimental, then? How is it not sentimental to tell the story of a life she'll never live?"

"Because it will not be a father's story for his daughter. It won't be the idle, hazy dreams a father has when his daughter is young."

"How do you know that?"

"Because you will tell the story of her past. Honestly, I hope. You're the only one who holds it now. Forget Lynne, and Claire's friends, her lovers. Their stories are thousands of miles away, and you may never hear them again. And I'll never hear them at all. Her story is yours to tell here with me. But the story of the life she'll never live—that belongs to both of us."

"It turns my stomach to think of doing this here. With you."

"Good. People spare the pretty details when their stomachs are turning."

"I still think you're waiting for me to say something that you can turn into a ransom."

"I'm not saying that isn't true. And I'm not saying that what I've told you about my own life to this point is true, either, and that what I might say in however many days we may spend here will be true. If you ever go home, I don't want to become a target. But whatever happens to you, it's not as if my life here is necessarily secure. Claire's isn't the only story we will tell."

"It seems desperate," he said.

But she didn't respond to this. They sat quietly for what seemed a long time. They were past the hour for the evening prayer, and now he heard only occasional voices in the distance, unable to discern what they were saying even if he had understood the language. Sounds of insects nearby were punctured by a dog that barked three times. Two children passed by, saying, "Shh. Shh." But someone, probably Azhar, chased them away.

"After Lynne asked for the divorce," he said, his voice louder than he'd anticipated, "she called me. Claire called me. From someone else's phone, I'm sure, because she didn't want me to have the number. I'd already moved into an apartment in the city, and it was late at night. I couldn't sleep. Hadn't slept. I was playing music from twenty years ago, Bruce Springsteen, or something like that, trying to pretend that it was sometime other than now. My phone was in my hand, and I was trying not to call Lynne. I was pretty sure she was seeing someone. And it wasn't that I was enraged, but it was strange how sex mattered again after not mattering for years. I had a physical craving for her that seemed apart from the habit of her. Which is what you miss most. The habit, I mean. Friends had warned me about that. So I was sitting there, probably at 2:00 A.M., three weeks after I'd found the apartment, my phone in hand, on the verge of either calling Lynne, or, because this craving wouldn't let me sleep, on the verge of speaking to the habit of her—I mean, as if there were a person lying on the other side of the bed with whom I could have a conversation—when the phone rings, and I nearly jump out of my skin. I had a fleeting sense that it might be Lynne, that we were somehow lying awake on opposite sides of the city conversing with the habit of each other, but it wasn't her number that came up, and no one else would be phoning that late. A wrong number, I was sure. But I answered, anyway, because any voice would have been better than none. And it was Claire."

"How long had it been since she'd called?" the woman asked. It struck him that, in the blindfold, it was easy to imagine he was still sitting in that apartment.

"I don't know. A long time. Weeks. Maybe two months. I had to ask Lynne if Claire even knew we were separated. She wasn't exactly calling Lynne for a daily mother-daughter chat, either. But that night, when I answered the phone, the first thing she said was 'Daddy.' Which she hadn't called me since she was probably nine. I suppose I spoke her name like it was something holy. She didn't say anything in response, so I said, which is what I asked anytime she called, 'Where are you?' She said, 'You always ask that, Dad. I'm sorry I'm calling so late.' As if we'd talked just yesterday. 'So late, Claire?' I said. 'Are you kidding?' She was quiet for a few seconds, and then she said, 'I'm calling to say I'm sorry about you and Mom. It must be hard for you, living away from that house.' Which struck me as an odd thing to say. 'The house? I don't miss the house.' 'Yes you do,' she said. 'You worked hard on that house. Painting and fixing things. And now there's another man sleeping in it.' My heart turned over, and I asked, 'Who?' but she didn't answer. I heard someone on her end, and she turned away from her phone and quietly said, 'No. Shh.' I hadn't overheard the question. She seemed to be walking somewhere, because her voice kept changing modulations. 'Are you coming home sometime?' I asked. 'Sometime, Dad.' And then I felt a wave—I guess I don't know how to describe it other than to say I felt sorry for myself down to the base of my spine. My wife fucking another man. My daughter maybe in some unnamed city instead of coming by to visit and hold my hand and tell me I'd be okay. So I said, 'I don't understand any of this, Claire. Any of it. Your mother. You. Why you've both abandoned me like this. I have nothing now. Nothing.' She continued to hold the phone to her mouth. She was walking. Maybe uphill. I could hear her breathing. And then she said, 'You shouldn't have kissed me.' And then she hung up."

He stopped speaking, and then strained at the rope on his wrists to dispel the physical discomfort the memory had left. The rope was loose enough that he probably could have pulled out his hands with another minute or two of effort. Azhar was too kind with his knots.

" 'You shouldn't have kissed me'?" the woman asked.

"Yes. That's the last thing she said to me." He was unable to add "ever," but it hardly mattered. "That was like Claire ever since she was sixteen. You'd be having a talk with her about anything. It could have been about an accident on the freeway that held up traffic for an hour. And in the middle of the conversation she'd drop in some memory out of the blue that left you stunned."

" 'I made the cut.' "

"Yes. Exactly."

"Why did she want you to stop kissing her?"

"It wasn't like that. It was something else."

He was resisting this image of Claire, but his mind finally focused on the one that flickered when she was fourteen and asleep on the couch. He wondered, briefly and wryly, if psychiatrists ever employed a blindfold and a gun. But he didn't say this to the woman.

"She was thirteen, maybe fourteen. I want to think younger

than that, but she probably wasn't. One of those days in late August when it's been hot and humid, but the day winds down into a cool evening that reminds you September is coming, then fall. I was sitting in an armchair in our living room with the newspaper, and Claire was reading a book on the couch. We didn't have air-conditioning, but the ceiling fan was circling slowly above us. Claire had reached the age where it was pretty rare to have her home on any summer evening, since she was usually out with friends. Her skin shone in the lamplight where she was reading, and she kept pulling her hair behind her ear, since this was the time before she cut it short. I was watching her read. It seemed like she'd make it through a paragraph, and then she'd look at the fan slowly spinning, close her eyes for a few seconds, then go back to the book. I was trying to remember what it was like to be fourteen, for it to be August, and a few weeks, yet, before school started, but close enough that you savored the days because summer was no longer stretched out before you. And it was easier to remember those days while sitting in the living room watching Claire read—a memory that anyone would have—"

"Not anyone."

"Okay, Josephine, maybe not anyone, but most of us who grew up there at that time. Driving to a lake after sunset with a six-pack of beer that you'd talked someone into buying for you, drinking that beer with your friends, girls in their bathing suits who you'd never touched slipping into the velvet water. Those nights that stirred together the familiar with some hoped-for possibility. And I was watching my daughter while remembering this, and she laid her book down on her chest then, and her eyes followed the slow circling of the fan until she closed them, opened them again, following the fan, and then closed them, and when I looked closely they still seemed to be tracing the fan's path under her eyelids and lashes.

"She was so—pretty lying there. I could see her as my daughter, but also see her as someone who was almost a woman, young and beautiful, on the edge of this final wave of summer, stretching out over the shore as if the crest of the wave had hands with this infinite capacity for gentleness, and they would leave her nestled in the shimmering and soft sand without her so much as turning over in her sleep. And in the living room, I found myself standing next to her as she lay on the couch, then kneeling down, her eyes still moving under her lids, maybe following in a dream, now, the circling of a waterbird, and I leaned over and kissed her on the lips, leaving my own lips lingering there for probably several seconds."

He stopped there, and knew the woman probably couldn't see him wincing because he still recognized the source of the kiss while for another moment he held off the memory of its consequence.

"And then what happened?" the woman asked, a thickness in her voice.

"Her eyes snapped open, of course. She said, 'Dad!' My face must have seemed larger than the moon. I pulled away instantly, and she sat bolt upright. The book that had been on her chest fell to the floor. I said something like, 'I'm sorry, Claire. I can't believe I just did that.' And she said, 'It's okay.' And then, as if this would explain it, I said, 'I'm just so proud of how beautiful you've become,' which made it only worse, of course. Her eyes looked glassy, and then I sort of backed into my armchair, and she stood up and walked toward the stairs to go up to her room. I felt a moment of panic and said, 'Your mother shouldn't—' but Claire stopped almost midstride and glared at me, and I didn't finish my sentence, and then she went upstairs without looking back."

He had never been a great storyteller, and now, telling this story, he wondered at how memory worked, his eyes closed, capturing images of Claire on the couch, on the stairs, but never in continuous motion, not like a film, but more like a flipbook where, when possible, someone paused while thumbing through to see how the illusion of motion was created. But it wasn't always possible to linger like that, and the storytelling was fluid even if the memory was not, as if it had collected evidence and assembled its case.

They sat without speaking for a while, long enough that when the dog barked again, and roused him, he was sure minutes had passed.

"It's getting late. I'll have to go soon," she said.

For the first time he had an unexpected impulse to ask her to stay.

"Okay," he said weakly.

She shuffled her feet on the dirt floor, and then stood up and quietly opened the door. He thought she was gone, but then she said a few words to Azhar, and came back in and closed it, and he listened to her sweep away the image of the cow that Azhar had drawn earlier. She set the broom against the wall, and then he heard her walk back to the window, and when she spoke he was sure she was turned away from him.

"Claire," she said, and then stopped to clear her throat. "Claire is driving east. She's left her husband to attend to the motel while she's gone, and their daughter is three years old now, old enough to be without her mother for a few weeks, though Claire worries about this, and she comforts herself by knowing that her husband's mother—the kind of grandmother that children dream of living in a gingerbread house—will be there to help."

"Despite everything," he interrupted, "the thing about the run-down motel and cleaning other people's sheets. And hanging diapers on the clothesline. I would have hoped for more for Claire."

She walked back from the window then, and pulled the chair closer than it had been and sat back down.

"Don't be a fool," she said. "Why would you think this has anything to do with what you had hoped?"

5

A truck roared past her, the first she'd seen in a while, and pushed her closer to a sign along the highway that read, *Fire Danger Today. Extreme.* The dry air that blew in through the open windows felt like someone lightly sanding her lips. She could travel these endless Western roads for a long time and see few other cars, a half hour, an hour on the same stretch, her mind swept elsewhere, away, absent, a dream of a mind. But then a tractor-trailer approached, or she'd see a dead animal in the road, and she'd have to steer around it, and once she was alert again it seemed as if an invisible hand had lowered her from the enormous sky onto this highway while a mouth whispered to her through the hum of the tires, "Your father is dying."

She was entering a national forest, it hadn't rained in weeks, though it was still only late June—an intermittent years-long drought—and they were worried any careless spark might set everything ablaze. She realized she was hungry. Hadn't eaten before she'd left. She and Jack had made the quick decision for her to drive rather than pay for a last-minute airfare that they would be months paying off, since her father, hospitalized with heart problems, though gravely ill, would likely live a few more weeks. A three-day drive like she hadn't taken in years, since she and Jack had come west, in fact, and it had been many more years since she had seen her father.

She pulled off the highway into a town that had been carved out of the forest; it had a couple of streets with run-down homes set back from the main road where there was a small grocery store, and next door, for some reason, what looked to be a onetime antiques shop with a small trailer out front and a sign that read *Ed's Deli*. Three picnic tables were set out in the dirt parking lot, and an older man and woman were sitting at one of them under a canopy that shielded them from the heavy sun. When she pulled into the lot in the tiny used pickup truck she and Jack had purchased to move supplies to and from the motel, she raised a cloud of dust, and was grateful that the slight breeze carried it away from the man and woman.

When she stepped out of the truck, the couple looked her over, smiling. They were sitting at the table with no food, but just outside the front stoop of the trailer was a gas grill where burgers were cooking. Inside she could see the shadow of someone moving back and forth in front of the window. There were signs in marker on whiteboards that listed the sandwiches and beverages, and in quotation marks below the phrase "All ingredients fresh from next door," and then a red-markered arrow pointing to the small grocery store.

The man at the picnic table watched her looking at the menu and then said, "Everything's good!"

She smiled at him and said, "Is that so? Any recommendations?"

"The burgers are great. That's what we're waiting on," he said. "So's the turkey. You're not a vegetarian, are you?"

"No."

"Good thing, because you'd be out of luck."

The man who must have been Ed stepped out of the small screen door in his trailer. He was younger, with a blue T-shirt that read, *I may be unemployed, out of shape, short on cash, and drunk, but I sure am fun!* He nodded at her as he looked her over, lifted the cover of the grill and flipped the burgers, and then turned back to her and said, "Happy to help you now." He took out a pad of paper and a pen, and she ordered a turkey sandwich.

The man at the table said, "Hell, Ed, it's not like you got a line of folks here. Can't you remember a simple turkey sandwich?" Ed didn't smile, but instead gave a half salute without looking, and walked back into the trailer.

She waited at a separate table in the sun. She was unused to having nothing to do with her hands, since at the motel she was either changing sheets, sweeping floors, attending to guests, or playing games with Lucy, her daughter, who stood at the knees of the truckers and campers while they were checking in at the desk, and often asked, "You stayin' at my house?" At the end of the day, when she and Jack lay back in bed, usually with Lucy asleep between them, she would sometimes say, "Mercy," which was a word her grandmother had used to express surprise, but, in Claire's case, she thought of the work at the motel, loving Lucy, attending to Jack, as a form of mercy that framed her life in ways she had, before this, never found imaginable.

"Where you coming from?" the man at the table asked.

"A little town just south of Merced."

"And where you heading to?"

"Michigan."

"No kidding?" He looked from her to the truck and back to her. Ed came out of the trailer with two prepared buns alongside chips, and flipped the burgers off the grill and closed up the sandwiches. When he slid them in front of the man and woman, he saluted again, and said, "Turkey sandwich is coming up."

"It can take a while," the man said after Ed had gone back in. "Sometimes you'd swear he'd wandered off into the woods to hunt the bird."

The man and woman began eating their burgers. It struck

her that the woman had yet to say a word. Claire looked directly at her and asked, "Do you live here in town?"

The man turned, and pointed toward the houses that lay along two stretches of road above the highway. "The blue one there. We walk up most afternoons to have lunch here with Ed."

Finally, the woman spoke. "Michigan? That's a long way to drive all on your own."

"It is," she said. "But I really didn't have much choice."

"Visiting family?" the woman asked.

"You could say that, I guess."

The woman was wearing a hat with a large white brim. Claire began to feel her own scalp prickle with the heat.

"Could you say otherwise?" the man asked.

"My father's ill," she said. "Congestive heart failure. He's in the hospital. So I'm going back to see him."

The man looked down at his sandwich, and his face darkened, as if this revelation was something he didn't want to witness. The woman said, "I'm so sorry."

Inexplicably, Claire felt compelled to add, "The woman who called and told me he was in the hospital—I didn't even recognize her name. I haven't seen him in years. I haven't even spoken to him, and I don't even know if he knows he has a granddaughter."

The man looked up at her again, started chewing with some speed, swallowed with difficulty, then said, "Why the hell not?"

"I'm sorry?"

"I said, why the hell not? How can it happen that a man has a granddaughter and doesn't even know it?"

"Charlie, that's not our business," the woman said.

"The man has a granddaughter, Maeve. Child of his only child. And she never even told him."

Claire watched him go back to his burger and take an over-sized bite.

"How do you know that?" she asked. "How do you know I'm his only child?"

He waved his hand at her; through his teeth as he chewed, he said, "It's written all over your face. All over your face. I've seen a thing or two in my time. What a shame."

At that point Ed banged through the screen door with her sandwich in a paper bag, and walked it over to her and took her money. "Threw in a pickle and chips no charge," he said with an apologetic smile. "Never mind him," and he jerked his head toward the man at the table. He'd clearly overheard the conversation. "Figures he's the local savant. Retired from the railroad, and he sits here every afternoon and guesses about the people come through. Last week he guessed someone was a circus clown. Turned out he'd done a stint as a rodeo clown, and the guy was amazed. Charlie here said he could tell by the way he walked."

She thanked him and then climbed back into her truck, and when she came around the woman raised her hand and said,

"Have a safe trip to Michigan," but the man wouldn't look up and just shook his head.

Back out on the highway, the wind streaming through—the air-conditioning barely worked, and in the high sun she was better off with the windows down—she thought about it. She had never planned on not speaking with her father. With her mother, either. After she'd nearly been killed, they had taken good care of her, one or the other of them in the hospital until she was released, and then through the long months that her back and shoulder healed. Sometimes when her mother was at work, or was out with her new boyfriend, her father, who had flown home the day he'd heard of the attack, would come by and spend time with her; they'd play Scrabble, or watch daytime TV, or sometimes she would put on music and they would listen together. But he would never ask where she'd been when she'd been stabbed, why she was there, and what it meant that she'd never heard from the man she said she'd loved after the night she was hurt.

One afternoon, when she was strong enough and angry enough at her confinement, and neither of them was at home, she'd packed a suitcase and left a note thanking them for everything. She'd told them she'd be in touch. And then she never was.

Occasionally, a postcard or letter would catch up with her, an e-mail after which she'd change her address, and once or twice a phone call, but when she heard either of them on voice mail, she'd shut down the message after listening to a few words. *Claire, please, if you get this . . . If you only knew how much . . . I wonder what I've done . . .* They'd done nothing, really, to deserve it, and eventually the messages stopped coming.

Now, two birds were circling high in the heat, taking updrafts that pushed them above what had once been a huge lake, but now was mostly dried lake bed with edges where grass grew and cows grazed. She did not like to think about those years, did not want to remember them, that purposeless rage that drove her from town to town, and she could remember them less and less as Lucy grew and even her own childhood seemed dimmed by her daughter's—her sweetness, her milky breath when she fell asleep in her arms, the coins and gum wrappers and occasional key she'd find in the motel rooms while Claire cleaned that she would later offer to Claire like treasures. All spring, she'd been fascinated by the swallows that were nesting under the eaves of the motel.

She liked to think of her life beginning at the moment she met Jack. She thought everyone would be better off if they could make that choice, to cancel out what had happened before, even if it were a matter of looking back, of negotiating with God, if there was one, and saying, "All right, I was thirty-one. I was working as a waitress outside of Lincoln, Nebraska, and a man walked in. It was like a country-western song. I want my life to begin with that song. I'll give up the final ten years of my life if you cancel out everything before that and it begins with that song."

From his booth seat, that first evening he had come in, Jack said, "Jesus, maybe I should find another diner." He looked like many men who ate there, a brown face and brown arms, hair lightened by the sun, handsome in a wholesome sort of way.

"Good luck with that," she said. "You'll have to drive into Lincoln."

"Well, the food sucks here."

"Is that why you stopped by?"

"First time I've been here in my life."

"So how do you know the food is terrible?"

"Looking at you. You sure aren't eating it. Take a look at this." He grabbed hold of her wrist and his thumb and forefinger met around its circumference. "Pretty eyes, though."

"I take it you like corn-fed Nebraska girls."

"I like most kinds of girls, but you're not from Nebraska."

He'd stayed late, and she'd gone out with him after her shift. What drew her was the ease with which he told the stories of his life, far more easily than most men, especially those from farm country in the Midwest, and it occurred to her then that someone might supplant the stories from her own life with those of another, especially if she could make herself fall in love with that other. She thought she knew even at that moment she probably could never love this man the way she wanted, but she invited him back to her room, anyway. He seemed surprised.

"You move pretty fast, Miss Claire," he said.

"At this point in life, if you don't move fast, you spend more time being lonely."

"You spend a lot of time being lonely?"

"Everyone does. You do, too."

Their first night together was like first nights with other men, not that those were frequent anymore, now that she was thirty-one, and the fevered ache of her appetites had been curbed by years and experience. He had good hands, calloused palms just below the fingers, and fingertips worn hard by work, but smooth like sanded wood, and he moved them along her thighs and belly unhurriedly, knowing the right places to touch, but wanting to be certain.

After the second time, they lay back in her bed and watched the ceiling fan spin, cooling their bodies.

"I like the way you smell," she said to him.

He laughed lightly and said, "Gotta admit I haven't heard that one all that often."

"I'm serious. I do. You smell sweet. Like alfalfa. Or corn silk."

"Got me pegged for a farmer, do you?"

"It's not a hard guess out here. Look at your arms, your face." His forearms to his biceps were deep brown, but his chest and shoulders were pale, his skin almost translucent.

"My dad was a farmer. Corn and soybeans on a hundred acres. A few head of dairy cows," he said.

"My aunt lives on a farm. Or at least she used to. She leased the land for others to plow and plant."

"What do you mean *at least she used to*?" he asked. "Does she now, or doesn't she?"

"I don't know. We're out of touch."

He nodded but didn't pursue this. He rested his arm over his forehead and watched the ceiling fan.

"Dad couldn't make a go of it. The farm had been in the family for two or three generations, but he couldn't compete with the mega-farms, and he eventually sold out. I work on the equipment. A man's tractor or combine breaks down in the field, they don't always have time to haul it in for service. So I'll drive out to his land and fix it if I can right out in the sun. That explains the farmer tan. And maybe the smell of hay."

She turned over on her side and laid her hand lightly on his chest, and he flinched.

"It's been a while, hasn't it?" she said.

"Does it show that much?"

"Not in the way—I mean, believe me, you made me feel good. But it seems like you're not used to being touched."

He smiled slightly, but didn't say anything.

"When was the last time?"

He put two fingers to his lips and patted them twice, as if he were used to smoking.

"Over a year ago." He paused. "We hadn't talked about getting married, or anything."

"But otherwise it was pretty serious?"

He propped up on his elbow and looked at her. "You really want to hear this?"

"Sure."

He fell back and lay flat again, staring at the ceiling.

"She was a veterinarian."

"What was her name?"

"Emily. Of course she loved animals. Adored them, really. And she had a small ranch house with a tiny office where she'd see local dogs, you know, the occasional little girl coming in with a cat that got nicked by a car, or kicked by some bent neighbor kid. But mostly it was farm animals. A cow having some trouble calving, or a goat that got its head tangled in a line of barbed wire. Thing I admired about her was that she didn't get sentimental about it. Didn't try to save an animal that had only a ten percent chance of making it. She'd take care of it quickly with a needle. She couldn't stand pain. Pain of any kind. And she said the hard thing was to measure the chances of taking the pain away and for the animal to get better, against the chance of the pain never going away, and making the animal suffer for no good reason."

He stopped there, reached up to scratch his knee, and let his fingers trail up his thigh.

"It's funny, talking about it. I don't want to make it sound like this."

"What do you mean?"

"Well, I was in love with her, you know? We had a good year together, a little more. We traveled for a couple of weeks in August up to the Porcupine Mountains—easier to get away for a while before harvest. In the upper peninsula of Michigan there, a place called Lake of the Clouds."

"That's where I'm from," she said.

"Lake of the Clouds?"

"No, Michigan. But the lower peninsula."

"Yeah? It's beautiful up there. Cool in August, at least that August. Some of the leaves even starting to turn. We camped up there next to that lake, and then spent a few days in a run-down cottage right off Lake Superior. That lake was cold, I'm telling you. Freezing. I mean when it was almost sundown, people would be lighting fires on the beach just to keep warm. But Emily insisted on swimming. One of those few nights when the big lake was dead calm, and she's out there maybe seventy feet off the shore, doing the backstroke into the setting sun. That woman was strong. Blue when she got out of the water, but strong. I wrapped her up in a blanket, and we sat by the fire while she shivered, and one of the others on the beach walked up in a parka and asked, 'Are you an Olympian?' and

Emily just laughed through chattering teeth. 'No, I'm cold,' she said."

Claire continued to listen through closed eyes, imagining the woman in the lake.

"I remember thinking even at the time if we could just stay there . . . You know, you have those days in your life, and mostly it's when you're looking back. But every now and then, even at the time you're living it, living in that minute, you say to yourself, 'Well, I'll just stay right here. We'll stay right here. No sense in going home. We'll open up our own little cottages or hotel on the lake, and we'll deal with the hard winters, and learn to love them for the beautiful summers.' Of course it never works out that way."

He was quiet for a while, and she listened to the ceiling fan spin.

"You still awake?" he asked.

"Oh, yes. What else?"

"Well, there isn't a lot more. Of course we went home to Nebraska, and we made it through Christmas. But after that, she started pulling away. It wasn't because of anything I'd done, which she told me over and over. Sometimes I think you can't love animals like she did and love people, too. Or it's harder that way. You love something who can't tell you why it hurts, it's harder to love someone who can tell you why it does. And what I meant earlier was, I think she could see the pain it was causing me, that distance of hers. Causing her, too, I guess. And she judged after a while that there was maybe a ten percent chance of saving the thing, and it wasn't worth the suffering, so she put an end to it."

After that he stopped talking for what seemed a long time, and she had a light dream of him as a sleek, brown dog, wagging his tail as he searched in the shallows of a lake for small fish.

Then she felt his lips on her mouth, lingering there, and she sat bolt upright.

"Don't do that," she said. "Don't ever do that."

"I was just kissing you."

"I know. Just—not that way. Not when I'm not expecting it."

"Sorry. Most of the time I tend to forget I'm a stranger."

"It's not that. It's not that you're strange."

"Well, maybe. I guess it's an intimate thing to be kissed when you're sleeping. More intimate than sex, in some ways."

"It's not that, either."

"You want to tell me about it?"

She turned over on her side with her back facing him.

"I'd rather hear your stories. You're better at telling them," she said, though she'd always thought she might have many she would tell if she had found the right listener.

And then she felt his sanded fingertip, cool and light, along the length of the scar where the knife had entered. She let out a slight gasp.

"There's a story here, too, isn't there?"

Her skin tingled along the length of her spine.

"Did you notice it right off? Most men do, but pretend they don't."

"I noticed it. It's not something you ask about right off the bat. But it doesn't bother you, does it?"

"No, not at all."

"You seem more ashamed about the kiss."

"I'm not ashamed of anything," she said.

Her back still facing him, she felt him lean close, and he exhaled deliberately with his mouth inches from her spine, and then with closed lips moved his mouth over the scar, stopping every quarter inch to leave a light kiss. Finally, she moaned, and he reached around her shoulder and pulled her back to the bed, and then kissed in the same way the slightly shorter scar that rose above her left breast. She felt a current run through her, and she arched her feet.

"God, it must have hurt," he said, but she was still feeling her body respond to him.

"Did you fight back?" he asked.

"Of course I did," she said, her breath thick. For a moment, that other dark room loomed, and she swept the image away. "Why would you think I wouldn't?"

"I don't think that," he said. "I can tell by the way kissing it brings you alive."

And at this she pushed him away, pushed his chest hard so he lay flat and so she could mount him, and even with him deep inside her she still could see his eyes moving over her body, fixed briefly on the scar, and then trailing down over her breasts and belly, as if it ran the whole length.

Afterward, she collapsed onto him, her head on his shoulder, and with the same measured, light pressure, he touched each vertebra in her backbone as her breathing eased.

She put her mouth to his ear, flicked her tongue at the peak of it, and whispered, "Do you still dream of opening a little hotel someplace where we can love the beautiful summers?"

He shifted away from her to get a better look at her face.

"We've had just this one night."

"So?"

She had passed into Nevada, remembering. They hadn't moved from Nebraska as quickly as she wanted; she'd had to work double shifts at the diner to raise the money, and he was reluctant to leave home, to shake the hands of friends and farmers whom he'd known most of his life who wouldn't say so, but thought he was crazy. And then they'd driven this very highway west, and they'd stayed in the motel they eventually bought because the proprietor had said to them at the front desk, "You just made it under the wire. We're closing next week," and they'd decided the coincidence was too profound, and why not here, anyway, though there was no beautiful lake or even mountains closer than half a day's drive away. And then she'd become a manager, an accountant, and a maid; she was nothing she had ever been, and was grateful. And Jack had become a handyman who repaired the motel's plumbing and tacked up new paneling and worked odd jobs in the evening to make ends meet. And then she'd become a mother, and Lucy looked like Jack, she had to admit, even those mornings when they sat in the little kitchen closed off from the motel lobby and drank coffee, and she thought sometimes that she loved Jack like a brother, which was good enough, and at other times she'd stare at him and think, *I hardly know you. Why am I running this dilapidated dump with you? After everything, you're still a stranger to me who is not at all strange,* by which she realized she meant uninteresting.

But that was unkind, and Jack was never unkind. She had never told him about her father's kiss. And, like most other elements of her past, it wasn't a memory that lingered. Neither she nor her father had mentioned it again, except for one phone call, in that dark time. She had never probed the meaning, but the kiss had marked the end of her perception of him as her father first, and a man second. At the time, he had said something about her beauty, that that was somehow a reason, and even though she hadn't felt at all beautiful, she knew that her father, who was almost forty, was looking at her as a woman rather than his daughter, that a forty-year-old man kissing a sleeping fourteen-year-old was an amplification of the scope and depth of men in the world that she did not want to meet. And yet, after that was precisely when she had begun to meet them.

Now she was heading east, back home, and it was as if the horizon itself were narrowing its length, the opposite sensation of heading west, and all the promise and possibility that she still felt during their once-a-year trips to the Pacific were being funneled away toward a father who might very well be dying and a mother who had told her when she called that she had never stopped marking the passing of the seasons with Claire's unnatural silence.

Ahead now, out of the shimmer of the highway and against a backdrop of gray mountains, she saw a figure rise out of the shoulder of the road, and turn toward her and extend an arm. She rarely picked up hitchhikers, and never had while driving alone, but she was surprised to see this was a woman, in shorts and a shirt tied in back, carrying a small backpack, and with a scarf pulled over her head to protect it from the sun. She was hitchhiking alone. Claire steered the car over to the shoulder, and in the rearview mirror watched the woman turn and jog up to the passenger door. When she pulled it open, Claire had a moment when she thought the woman was a man, but the woman undid the scarf and revealed a head of black hair that hung to her shoulders, and said in a light voice, "Thanks so much for stopping. It's unbearable out there."

"No problem at all," she said. "How long were you waiting?"

"God, I don't know. Fifty cars must have passed before you stopped."

"Jesus. Everyone's so cautious nowadays. Where you heading?"

"If I can get there, Chicago."

"No kidding?" Claire asked. "I'm heading to Michigan."

"Really? Can you stand the company for a couple of nights? I'll pay for gas."

The woman's cheeks were tanned from the sun, and her eyes were dark gray, almost depthless. She was smiling hopefully.

Claire extended her hand and said, "My name's Claire."

"Genevieve," she said. "I'm so grateful to you. I'll be happy to drive some if you want."

The woman's hand was warm and damp with sweat, and she held her fingers for a moment before letting them go.

6

When Saabir came in after the woman left, and untied Marc's blindfold and undid the ropes around his wrists—with a one-word curse at the looseness of the knots—Marc hardly stood up before going to his knees and rolling out his mat and falling deeply asleep. In the middle of the night, he woke once, and in the dim light that came in through the window, he saw Saabir sleeping across the threshold of the door with his gun strapped over his shoulder. When Marc raised his head, Saabir opened his eyes, but they seemed black with unconsciousness. Toward morning, he dreamed he was driving in Nevada, into Reno, the only Nevada city he'd ever visited, and along the road was a man who was hitchhiking while wearing one shoe; the other he carried in his free hand. When he pulled over, the man became a woman, and the shoe a high heel, and she said, "I wonder if you could drive me into Reno and see what I can get for this at the pawnshop." "For a single shoe?" he asked the woman, and she said, "No, for a single girl," and then the woman became Claire and the shoe a blindfold, and she was tying it around his head, and she said, "How far do you think you can drive without seeing?" and he woke up.

Saabir was sitting in a chair, looking at him with his head cocked sideways, and then he gestured with his fingers along the side of his face, and as Marc sat up, he realized his face was wet. Saabir reached into his pocket and pulled out a small square of cloth and handed it to Marc. "Thank you," he said, and wiped his face dry.

"No cry," Saabir said, and put a finger to one eye and shook his head.

"I wasn't crying," he said. "I was—was I crying out in my sleep?"

Saabir nodded. Marc was remembering the dream, and the story the woman had told the night before, Claire on the highway after marrying a man named Jack. She'd described how Claire remembered the time he'd kissed her, and how she was traveling east because Marc was in the hospital probably dying. While she spoke, Marc had gone completely still. He couldn't recall a single footstep, a single voice outside the room, and the blindfold had become like a drive-in movie screen. He knew even then, though, that in this storytelling the woman would never let her arrive, and the woman who Claire had picked up along the highway—Genevieve—likely had no better intentions than Josephine herself. Inexplicably, he found himself worrying over Claire.

He handed the piece of cloth back to Saabir, who folded it neatly and slipped it back into his pocket. This kindness led him to take a risk.

"Josephine," he said.

Saabir laughed once, and shook his head.

"Well, then, whatever her name is. What does she look like?" He passed his hand over his face, and through his hair matted with sweat.

Saabir shook his head again, this time with a slight smile, and said, "No." Then he hoisted his gun higher on his shoulder, and said, "She is man. Man."

"She's strong like a man?"

"No. Eyes. Eyes of man. See?" Saabir belatedly recognized the irony of the word, smiled, and then pointed at Marc very deliberately, and with the same finger slid it across his throat.

"Josephine," Saabir approximated, and smiled again, while Marc involuntarily brought his fingers to his Adam's apple.

"Eat," Saabir said, and rose to go to the door to fetch food from wherever it was prepared for him, probably in one of the low houses near this one, but someone knocked before he got there, and Saabir slipped outside where he overheard what sounded like an urgent conversation between Saabir and who he guessed was Azhar.

Then Saabir burst through the door and walked over to where Marc was still sitting on the mat, and reached down and grabbed him under each armpit and pulled him to his feet.

"Hey-hey," Marc said. "Just tell me what you want me to do." But Saabir was already standing behind him, slipping the blindfold over his eyes and yanking it hard, and tying the rope around his wrists so there would be no risk of the knots loosening. Saabir then pushed him toward the door, and outside; mingling with the bright, damp smell of the morning was the exhaust of a car, throttling low in what he knew was the narrow road that ran a few feet away from the house, and Saabir was pushing down on his head like a television cop—despite a rising sense of fear Marc laughed at the thought—and then he was inside and Saabir slammed hard into the driver's seat and the tires slipped for a half second before they went speeding away.

Marc clenched his teeth as they drove. He reasoned they were not taking him away to execute him, since clearly they had been taken by surprise. Still, this kind of flight was cold comfort, and he could feel his pulse in his bound hands. He guessed someone had learned where he was being held hostage, whether that was a Pakistani agency contacted by the American embassy, or some other terrorist organization, or, as the woman suggested, an angry family who had lost someone to a drone missile. They were banging over rough patches of road, and he hadn't eaten anything, and he'd read somewhere that you couldn't get carsick unless your eyes were open, but within fifteen minutes his stomach was turning over, and he groaned, and lay across the seat to try to steady the impact of the rocking car, which was almost impossible with his hands tied behind him. Saabir said something to him in Urdu, likely that it was better for him to lie down, anyway, in terms of them being observed, but if Saabir had been ordering him to sit up he wouldn't have found the strength.

He wished he could fall back to sleep, which had been the elixir for this kind of nausea when he was a boy, facilitated by the pale yellow tablet of Dramamine that was actually intended to knock him out, he learned, when Claire as a small girl suffered from the same kind of carsickness, and, on particularly long drives, Lynne would sometimes have her take half a pill just to curb her restlessness. When she was a baby, she'd hated the car seat, hated it, had howled in protest to the point of exhaustion during long drives, and once when he'd yelled at Lynne, who had given up, "Can't you shut that kid the fuck up?" she'd said, "How would you like to be strapped into a big blue box on wheels with no way to understand why you're not allowed to move, or play, or sit in your mother's lap? She's pissed off because it doesn't make any sense," which had never occurred to him before, but now, lying on his side with the smell of exhaust seeping through the floorboards, he fully understood.

His father slammed the brakes hard while pulling to the side of the road, threw open the van door, and led him out into the woods. He stood next to Marc, his arms crossed, and hissed, "Well, goddamn it, throw up. C'mon, throw up, for Christ's sake. We're two miles away from camp, and you couldn't wait. So throw up."

Under the blindfold, he opened his eyes. For a moment, he thought his father was behind the wheel, or that he himself was driving, and Claire was in the backseat, and he was hissing at her. He must have fallen asleep, gratefully, and his stomach had settled and the road was smoother. He started to sit up, but Saabir said, "No." The pit in his belly was drilled deeper by hunger, but at least there was no nausea.

They drove for what seemed like another hour, leaving what must have been the main road, and then over another route that was rough with sudden drops, but his carsickness didn't return. At last, Saabir pulled over and turned off the car. He sat without speaking for a full minute, likely surveying the landscape, and then pushed open the car door, and Marc heard the passenger-side door pushed open, too; he'd been unaware that another person, likely Azhar, was there for the entire ride, but it made sense that Saabir wouldn't be driving alone. The air smelled dry and warm, leaning toward hot, and in the absence of the car engine there was virtually no sound. Marc was afraid to leave the car.

Saabir opened his door then and said, "Up," and Marc slowly flexed his knees and rose to his feet. He felt Saabir's hand in the small of his back as Saabir led him along a path where Marc had to lift his feet so as not to stumble. He could hear the wind in what sounded like low trees or shrubs, and something skittered away in front of them. If he were to be executed, this would seem the perfect place; his body would never be found.

They reached a spot on the path where, under the blindfold, he could tell the light was dimmed, and then Saabir stopped. He unknotted the blindfold first, and when it fell away Saabir was standing directly in front of him, his hand on the trigger of the gun, and a rock wall was rising behind him. Above, the sky was pale blue with no sun; they seemed to be in a mountain range, and, if they had been keeping him on the outskirts of Karachi, it was likely the Kirthar Mountains, one of the few places he'd thought he might visit when he'd committed to the corporate office in Pakistan because of a supposedly beautiful national park.

"Marc, Saabir is going to untie your hands. But if you turn around to look at me, he will kill you. Do you understand that?"

Marc nodded. He was surprised that she'd been in the car and he hadn't sensed her presence, and felt his skin prickle at the sound of her voice, and then a brief sense of relief. Saabir moved behind him and unknotted the rope, and Marc folded his shoulders in like wings and felt the blood return to his forearms and fingers. It was good to breathe the fresh air of this place, and he filled his lungs with the dry, slightly sweet fragrance. He took a closer look at the rock wall in front of him, and on it was a scrawled image of what looked like an antelope with long, curved horns. Next to it was a dim handprint.

"Petroglyphs," he said. "Is that what you called them?"

She didn't answer him then. It was difficult to gain a perspective on where they were when he couldn't turn away from the wall. It seemed ridiculous, without the blindfold, to not simply shift his stance and look at her. Saabir took a few steps to one side and sat down on a small, flat boulder, his gun resting on his lap. From his pocket, he took a pack of cigarettes, withdrew one, and lit it with a lighter. The smoke smelled good, and distantly familiar. Marc heard her footsteps on the stones behind him.

"Yes, that's right," she said. "This one looks like an ibex."

"So you knew this was here?"

"Well, we didn't stumble on it, no."

Saabir lifted the cigarette to his mouth. He was watching the woman closely.

"Why do you suppose so many of them come with handprints?" Marc asked.

"The obvious reason. A signature in the time before written language."

"A handprint is more intimate, I think." He realized he was more curious about her appearance away from the room.

"I'm coming around to your right, so I want you to slowly turn to your left, away from the wall."

He heard her moving in a half circle, and he mirrored her, glimpsing, he thought, a length of dark-blue garment before he came around and saw the valley below their perch on an overhang. There were a few dry grasses, almost gold in the sunlight that reached them there, and farther on a grove of low, green trees around a source of water that was hidden from him, and beyond these, in the distance, dry, slightly pink mountains with deep, dark grooves he knew were likely expanses of low evergreens or shrubs that were shielded from the sun and wind.

"This is . . . It's an incredibly beautiful place," he said, and he was surprised that his eyes filled. "So desolate."

"Sometimes, from here, you can see herds of wild goats. I don't see any today, though. It's been a long time since I've come here."

Saabir was looking off into the horizon, and then glanced back to where they stood. He put his cigarette out on the rock and stood up, stretching his back. A large bird darted out from a crevice in the rock, and reflexively Saabir's hand went to his gun, but then he relaxed it, and when the bird flew into the light its shadow briefly flitted across Saabir's face. He smiled faintly. The bird soared high above the valley.

"I don't imagine this was an organized field trip," Marc said to the woman.

"No. There was word that someone was coming for you. We don't know who. Azhar stayed back and made sure there was no sign of your presence. When they find nothing there, we'll be able to take you back. They won't search there again soon."

"Someone might say something."

"I know; that's always a risk. But it comes with a price, so it's unlikely."

"Sometimes, I wonder if it's only three of you. You, Saabir, and Azhar. The four of us now."

She didn't say anything to this.

"Why here?" he asked.

"If you have to run, and you know you haven't been followed, then why not here? It's a place Saabir has known since he was a boy. And I'd told you about the petroglyphs."

"How do I know that Saabir didn't make those himself?"

Every time they said his name, Saabir, who had sat back down on the stone, glanced over at them.

"We need to stop mentioning him," she said. "Why would you want to believe that, anyway? We could have hidden in a Lyari slum. Instead, we took you to this beautiful place with this ancient art. Maybe it should mean something to you."

"Pardon me if I'm not grateful."

"You may never see anything like this again."

On the distant hills, clouds cast shadows that mottled the land, and seemed to slide into and emerge from the stony valleys.

"It's hot."

"A cool day for this time of year. We'll need to leave before midafternoon. Claire would have loved it here," she said.

He shook his head. "Claire lived her entire life in the city.

We sent her away to an expensive sleepaway camp when she was a kid, and she had a counselor call us within a day because she was terrified of the bugs."

"I'm not talking about Claire, the child. I mean Claire, the woman. She would have stood here like her father, with her eyes wet."

"You can't see my eyes because I can't see you."

"But you can see Claire now. And this place is closer to the one she imagined when she first dreamed of opening the hotel. With Jack."

"This exercise—" He looked out again over the hills. "Inside that tiny room, it almost makes sense. There's nothing else to see, to think of. But out here, it seems ridiculous. It's ridiculous that I don't turn around and look at the person I'm talking to. It's what anyone would do."

"Tell me a story about Claire."

"What if I lie to you? What if I make one up?"

"That's fine, too."

Marc laughed at this. He wished he could ask Saabir for a cigarette, who had lit another, and was watching him thoughtfully, as if he, too, were waiting for Marc's story.

"Do you mind if I sit down?"

"No," she said. She said something to Saabir, who nodded. "I'm leaning against the wall behind you."

He imagined the figure of a woman with the petroglyph near her head, as if posed for a photograph. He knelt and folded his knees. Nearer the ground, the air was slightly cooler and smelled of some kind of exotic herb. He breathed the scent in.

"I told you a lie already," he said. "At least partly. It's true that Claire was terrified of the bugs at that camp. But later—it's not that she changed her mind, exactly. Around the time she turned sixteen, well, that was when she started getting into trouble. She began stealing things. Things of no worth, you know? A plastic gold bracelet. A pair of canvas loafers that she wore out of the shoe store. Nothing that would have cost her more than five or ten bucks, and she had a job working at an ice cream shop. And we'd have given her money for anything she'd asked for. When she was caught, she told us that stealing these things was symbolic. She said she never stole anything of value because that might hurt people, and someone might lose their job. She told that to the judge, too, and said, when she took things, she imagined the hands of a poor kid in Vietnam running a scarf through a sewing machine in some dimly lit warehouse where he could never hope for better. And she stole the scarf so Americans couldn't profit from that poor kid's work. A girl after your own heart, I guess."

"Ha. You think you know my heart?"

"Would it matter if I did?"

"Would it matter if you knew Claire's?"

He wanted to say, *At one time I did,* but instead he shook his head and waved the thought away.

"Anyway, it was petty theft, and the judge sentenced her to

this kind of weekend excursion for wayward kids. She had to go on a three-day canoe trip down a river up north, you know, buildings fires, pitching tents with others, steering the canoe through some pretty substantial rapids, making meals at night. No cell phones. No technology. It was autumn, I remember, and the leaves had turned. It was a cold weekend, but it was supposed to be brilliantly clear. She hardly spoke to us in the two-hour trip to the campground, and when she got out of the car she walked away without saying good-bye. We had to register her without her help, and the camp counselor patted Lynne's shoulder and told her that it wasn't all that unusual for the kids who had no choice."

He stopped for a moment, and looked down at the base of the hills. "I'm guessing streams run through these mountains in the rainy season. There, along the deepest valley." But the woman didn't respond to this, and it seemed as if he were speaking only to Saabir.

"When we picked her up on Sunday afternoon, a perfect day, really, a sky deeper and bluer than this one, the red maples the color of apples the way they get up north, she literally bounded to the car. Skipping almost, like she hadn't since she was a little girl. She jumped into the backseat, and the first thing she said was, 'Mom and Dad, it snowed! Last night at the camp-fire. We were sitting around, and the counselor was trying to tell this pretty lame ghost story, and then these snowflakes started to fall from the sky! Not like a lot of them, or anything.

But for a few minutes. We all put our faces up, and let the snow fall on them. They melted right away because we were warm from the fire. One kid, Jesse, grabbed the bag of marshmallows and made a little snowman out of them. He used M&Ms for eyes. It was amazing, because you could see the underside of the leaves in the light from the fire and these dark flakes falling down.'"

He stopped there. His chest had tightened when he'd approximated her words and voice, and the tone of both was for a moment suspended in the air.

"Her cheeks were flushed," he continued. "I mean, like in a kid's book, apple-red like the leaves. She smelled—a little like this place. Like dry leaves and a campfire. And for the first half hour of the ride back, she sat up on the backseat and told us about the trip down the river, told us how one kid had fallen in and she was the one to extend the paddle and help pull him back into the canoe. How afterward, all the kids were brave and funny. One boy had stood up in the back of the canoe after riding the rapids, ripped his shirt off, and did a hula dance. One of the girls had stepped out of the canoe and rock-hopped to where a blue plastic bag was snagged on a fallen limb, and stuffed the bag into her pocket, and said, 'Too pretty for that here.' And then Claire told us, 'We sang songs. We sang songs, and actually meant it. I mean we wanted to. A counselor had a guitar, and, like, we sang hippie songs like one by Joni Mitchell called "Circle Game."'"

Now, a lyric of it spun through his head. He could barely remember the tune.

"For a minute, I thought she'd actually sing it. But of course she didn't. And of course, Lynne and I were silently delighted, and I was already composing in my head the grateful letter I would write to the judge. After a while, Claire settled back into the seat. I thought she might fall asleep like she had when she was little, but she kept her eyes on the passing landscape."

Near his knee was a small stone, and he picked it up and gave it a short toss. Saabir watched it slide under a shrub.

"And then, closer to home, when it was almost sunset, we were still outside of town, and we were passing a farm where a line of cows was headed back to the barn. It was idyllic, really. A Norman Rockwell painting of goodness. I looked into the backseat, and I could see Claire's face. And she was staring at the cows, and then when they were gone, she stared into a dried cornfield that hadn't yet been harvested. And her eyes were narrowed, and I was astonished to see her crying. And then she said, 'But that was bullshit. None of it was real. None of it. I can't believe the things a beautiful place can make you believe.' "

The three of them—Marc, Saabir, and the woman—sat in silence then. A cooling breeze came up the hill and through the trees, and he remembered a time when he was young when he'd visited an old friend who lived in the mountains in Oregon, and how late at night the wind poured through the firs with a deep, sweeping whisper, and he'd thought if he could hear that sound long enough it would have scrubbed his soul clean.

"I wonder if Saabir would be willing to share his cigarette," he said.

The woman spoke to him, and Saabir rose from his stone seat, his knee popping, and strode over and handed Marc the half-smoked cigarette. It tasted vaguely of Saabir's mouth, some subtle, unknown spice, and reminded him he hadn't eaten. Marc took a deep, long drag, and resisted the urge to cough. He hadn't smoked in twenty years. He exhaled and handed the cigarette back to Saabir.

"Thank you," Marc said. Saabir moved a few steps away behind him, so for the first time, all he could see were the mountains and the valley.

"You know, I'm sure it sounds like I told that story intentionally. Because we're here, in these hills. I didn't. Before the moment those words came out of my mouth, I wouldn't have remembered what Claire said on the way home."

With neither Saabir nor the woman in sight, under the isolating sky, it felt as if he were talking to himself.

"I don't understand how she could feel so much despair at age sixteen."

Here, maybe, he thought, had she grown up in poverty, had she seen too much suffering, but not back home. She had been partly right about beautiful places. Sitting here, now, the sun beginning to emerge from behind the cliff face warming his back and brightening the horizon, he could see the beauty, he could observe it and remember how, a few minutes ago, his eyes filled with tears, but it didn't penetrate, it didn't fill spaces taken up by other things, even the memory of Claire, temporarily transfigured by beauty, bounding toward the car. She was sixteen. Why hadn't she been living closer to her skin? Then at nineteen. He closed his eyes and shook the image of her away.

He heard Josephine take a few steps toward him, and as the sun shone from behind the wall, he could see her shadow cast near his own. He could see its narrow shoulders and perhaps its cloaked head.

"For the first few minutes Claire could think of very little to say to the woman, as she sat quietly beside her in the tiny truck," Josephine said.

Marc flinched at the mention of Claire's name. Would Josephine take up her story even out here, standing behind him, with the low desert wind sighing through the mountains?

7

Claire was used to making small talk with the guests at the motel, but had been traveling alone on the highway for so many hours that any question or observation was eluding her. She kept stealing surreptitious glances at the woman, who was, she now realized, maybe older than she looked, maybe in her late twenties, lines at her eyes and the corners of her mouth, but her expression held a subtle sense of mischief that conferred a kind of boyishness. The woman—Genevieve, she reminded herself, an unusual name—picked up the scarf she'd worn over her head in the sun and wiped some road dust from her face, and then took a corner and rubbed it gently over each eye; Claire had never met someone whose eyes appeared so deeply gray, so impenetrable, and they were by far her prettiest feature.

"So what's in Chicago?" Claire finally asked her.

"A boyfriend. An ex-boyfriend. He says it's the best city in the world, and he wants to show it to me and have me live with him there for a while. Probably, he's lonely. Or wants some company in his bed. But I've never been, and I'll have a place to stay for a few months."

The woman smiled and shifted her gaze from the road to Claire's face, and asked, "So who's in Michigan?"

"My father," Claire said.

The woman nodded and looked out the windshield, squinting. She pushed her sleeves up over her shoulders, and then ran a hand over each arm. The light hairs there were golden in the sun that came through the side window, and didn't seem to match her raven head. Claire guessed the woman colored it.

"Wow," she said. "It's so good to feel the air coming through."

Claire smiled at her. "You could've gotten heatstroke."

"Well, I'm used to it. It's always hot here."

"There's an extra pair of sunglasses in the glove box, if you want."

"No, that's okay. When I'm not driving, I like to see the world as it really is."

Reflexively, Claire looked out the top of her sunglasses. The sagebrush and distant plateaus were bleached pale in the sun.

"Your father," the woman said. "He's probably sick, isn't he?"

Claire remembered the man at the sandwich shop in the national forest, and wondered if everyone along this highway was trained to read minds.

"Yeah, he is," she said. "How did you know?"

"Well, you got a baby, too, right?" The woman leaned over and picked up a tiny rag doll that Lucy had tossed from the car seat weeks ago and had become a permanent feature of the floorboards.

"Yep. A little girl. She just turned three."

"What's her name?"

"Lucy."

"Lucy," the woman repeated. "Like Lucille Ball. *I Love Lucy.* Or the woman in the country song who left her husband with the crops in the field."

Claire smiled. "I have to admit, when she was born, we never thought of that song. It's my maternal grandmother's name."

"It's a nice old-fashioned name."

"Like Genevieve," Claire said.

"Yeah, I guess so." The woman looked out the window and seemed to watch the barbed-wire fence line that went on forever.

"Anyway," she said, her voice vibrating like a fan blade before she turned back toward Claire. "I figured you wouldn't be driving all this way without your baby or husband if you were just going to spend some time with your dad."

"He's in the hospital," Claire said. "Congestive heart failure. I guess he's had it for a while."

The woman nodded. "So how many years has it been since you've seen him?"

Claire couldn't help but cast a look at her.

"You said *I guess.* That means you didn't know about his illness before he called you on the phone."

"He wasn't the one who called," Claire said. "It was a woman I never met. My parents are divorced."

"I see. He must be pretty sick."

"I think he is. But to answer your question, I haven't spoken to him in around fifteen years."

The woman nodded and looked out the windshield. She pulled a strand of hair that was blowing around her face back behind her ear, and then suddenly pointed at a telephone pole. "Look, a hawk! It's perched right on top there." It lifted into the sky just as they passed.

"That's a long time," the woman continued. "My own father died a few years back. A stroke. He was still pretty young. I didn't have to drive across the country to see him, but I still didn't make it in time. I mean, he was still alive when I got there. But I don't think he recognized me. He only had one eye. I mean, after the stroke, he had one that still worked. It just sort of kept moving back and forth across my face, searching for something. I was holding his hand when he died. I'd never seen a person die before."

"I'm sorry," Claire said. It struck her that she had never seen someone die, either, and that of the people she had known, except for a boy from high school she'd heard was killed in a car crash, she had come closer to dying than anyone.

"It's something you're not ready for. I mean, it happens in its own time, out of your control. All the things I remembered about him. They didn't crowd in till afterward. I wanted to say, 'No, wait, Dad! I'm not ready.' But I don't imagine he was ready, either. It was just his body. His body didn't leave him any choice."

"How old was he?"

"Sixty-seven. He and my mom had me when he was older. The last of three kids. Two brothers and me."

"Do you miss him?" Claire was surprised at her own direct-ness, but the woman seemed so unselfconscious.

Genevieve shifted her eyes to Claire's face. Claire felt the awkwardness of being looked at while she had to keep her own eyes on the road. Finally, Genevieve said, "Not much more now that he's dead than I did when he was alive. My mother was the one who raised me. Raised us. My father worked hard as a sales-man. It's not that he was mean or stern. He was just away. The strange thing is—"

She stopped and looked out the window at the road.

"So we're on Interstate 80, right?"

"Yeah. I'm hoping to make Salt Lake City by tonight."

"That's a long haul, but I bet we can get there. Like I said, I'll be happy to drive."

Already the woman was saying *we*. They were headed around a bend with a high, bald hill and a few clumps of bushes toward the top.

"We'll see how it goes," Claire said. "So you were saying?"

"So I mean, we're going to take this trip together. All these hours here in this little truck. Nevada, Utah, Wyoming, Nebraska, Iowa. The landscape is pretty sometimes, but it's mostly bleak. And there will be long stretches of miles and miles that neither of us will remember. But some things will happen along the way, and we'll talk sometimes like we're talking now. And then you'll drop me off in Chicago, and we will probably never see each other again. But when you look back, you'll remember those things that happened and these conversations separated by all the quiet highway hours."

"Okay."

"Okay. So when someone dies . . . So when my father died, what happens is like you have Interstate 80 stretched out over a lifetime. But all those hours, all those weeks and months where nothing was happening, where you were living your life without even thinking about him, those spaces fall away, and the memories you do have slam into each other, one after another, and they're moving too fast to stop. It's one thing if you're someone like me. I mean, it's true that even thinking back to your father asleep in his chair can hurt a little once he's gone. But I didn't have that many memories of him. A time we played catch because I wanted to make the softball team. Or the time my mother was in the hospital and one morning he had to brush out my hair before I went to school. You remember how sometimes he pulled too hard, and your eyes watered, and your scalp stung, but it was your father brushing out your hair, which never happened before, so you didn't say anything. But, like I said, there weren't that many things I remembered, so they didn't pile up. But my poor mother. She got through the funeral okay, with all the people I hadn't seen for years, or had never seen, taking her hand and telling some little story of her husband. I wish they hadn't put him in a casket for everyone to see. But afterward, when the people left, and we went home, and I was standing in the kitchen with her. I was saying something about how nice everything had gone, and when I turned to look at her she was standing at the sink, clutching the edge of the counter. She had her eyes closed tight, and she was saying, 'Oh. Oh. Oh. Oh.' Just like that. All the empty hours and the stretches of loneliness she used to confide in me about, they all fell away, and everything else was slamming into each other. And she kept saying, 'Oh. Oh. Oh. Oh.' I could see how they were banging into her rib cage from the inside, and there was nothing I could do but wait till they stopped."

They had rounded the long bend, and now the Nevada desert lay out flat again. Claire saw how she was gripping the steering wheel tightly, and then releasing the grip, a rhythm she realized had persisted through the woman's story. The woman had turned away and was looking out the passenger window.

"That's so sad," Claire said.

The woman shrugged her shoulders, and when she spoke her voice was again buffeted by the air streaming in.

"It is, I guess. But that's the way it works. I don't know how it will be for you, with all of these years passed."

"Well, he hasn't died yet," she said. "How's your mom now?"

But the woman didn't answer this question. She was resting her chin on her hand, her elbow propped into the empty space of the window. Her eyes were closed.

Claire thought about her own father. She was now as close to his age at the time she last saw him as she was to nineteen. Closer. When she'd left, she'd taken no photographs, no images stored on smartphones, and so her memory of him—sandy-headed, a wide, lopsided smile that warmed when he saw her, his waist thickening in the middle after too many corporate lunches— faded as soon as she conjured it like the flash of a camera after you close your eyes. For some reason, she could remember her mother more clearly, probably because to Claire she had always been so beautiful. Thin, pale, taut skin. Ageless. She'd still looked like a girl when she braided her hair some summer mornings be- cause she wanted to keep the back of her neck cool. But her father. Jack had asked about him, and no, she never had told him about the kiss, but she did tell him about some of the things she remembered. How sometimes he had a temper, and once smashed the picture window in their house with a hammer because his paint job had sealed it closed and he couldn't get it open to let the air in. Or how he could be kind, and took in two stray cats that had begun to beg for food, even though because of allergies he had to drink Benadryl almost every day to keep from sneezing. Once, when she was maybe eight years old, he'd taken her to the circus, and she hadn't wanted to go because a friend had told her

circuses were for little kids, and besides, she felt sorry for the ele-
phants, but they had gone anyway, and she'd liked the tightrope
act, and afterward she let her father carry her on his shoulders
as he hadn't probably for over a year. He'd found a long, painted
line in the parking lot, and started walking across it like a tightrope, wobbling as he tried to keep his balance, and she was laughing over the thrill of possibly falling, and she'd slapped her hands
over his eyes once when he'd lurched slightly out of control, and
he'd said, "Marc the Magnificent, who can walk the high wire
even with a blindfold!" And she'd kept his eyes covered, and he'd
laughed, and started taking baby steps so she wouldn't fall.

When she'd told Jack that story, he'd said, "So how can you
go fifteen years without seeing the guy? I mean, my old man is
as poker-faced as they come; I don't think I heard him laugh
more than a half-dozen times growing up, but if a few months
pass and I haven't heard from him, I'm picking up the phone."

"I didn't do it on purpose, if that makes sense," she'd told
him. "I don't think I was being deliberate."

None of the years since she'd last seen him had been easy,
and yet, as they accumulated, and the gulf between her and her
father and mother widened and deepened, she felt less tethered.
No, her life hadn't begun the moment she met Jack, but those
other voices over a gulf were muted, no matter how beseeching,
and that was somehow comforting.

The thought of this made her ease back on the accelerator
pedal, and brought the woman out of her daydream.

"Can we stop soon?" the woman asked. "I need to use the bathroom."

"Sure. There was a sign a couple of miles back. We could use some gas, anyway. Maybe a snack."

The woman volunteered to pump the gas while Claire went in and paid and bought a couple of packages of peanut butter crackers that were on sale two for a dollar. She was still conscientious about every penny spent. Gas and tolls would be bad enough, and she'd told herself she'd sleep in the bed of the truck on a rolled mattress if she could pull off in safe places. That might be more complicated with the woman hitching a ride. She walked back out to the truck and waited for Genevieve to use the bathroom. She stayed standing alongside the pump and stretched her legs. It was midafternoon and the sun fully overhead, making the tiny gas station and the shimmering landscape shadowless. When the woman climbed back into the cab, and Claire pulled onto the freeway, she saw that she had several twenties folded into her palm. She peeled off one and handed it to Claire.

"Here's for my share of the gas and snacks."

Claire glanced at her. "You don't look like someone traveling with that much cash."

"I'm not. I mean, I wasn't. The man left the cash register open when he turned away to give me the bathroom key, so I took it when he wasn't looking."

Claire laughed and said, "Right."

"You don't believe me?" She was staring at her with those gray eyes.

"What the fuck, Genevieve. Are you serious?"

"I didn't take it all. Just eighty dollars."

"How do you know he didn't get our license plate?"

"He didn't see me take it. He won't find out till later when he counts up the drawer, and even then he might not figure it out."

"I can't afford to end up in the county jail!"

"You wouldn't have. I'd have told them the truth if he caught me. You picked me up on the highway, and we've only known each other for a couple of hours. Hey, it was the only way I could help with gas and food."

"I would've covered you, for God's sake."

"That wouldn't have been fair. You don't have much money yourself, or you wouldn't be driving all the way to Michigan in this old truck. You've got a little kid back home still in diapers."

Claire checked in her rearview mirror for a cop car.

"If you want me to get out, I will."

"Out here, you'd fry inside half an hour."

"No, I wouldn't."

Claire shook her head. "Look. No more stealing stuff, okay? We're gonna sleep in the back of the truck unless it rains, so you don't have to worry about hotels. We're making this trip on the cheap, okay?"

Genevieve gave her a slight smile. "You sound so maternal," she said.

Despite herself, she chuckled at this. "That might be the first time I ever heard that."

"It's not a criticism. It kind of suits you. But you don't need to worry about me. Look, I took down the address, see?" She pulled a slip of paper out of her pocket and showed her. "The gas at that place comes from Exxon. And if it was one of the little links in their giant chain, I'd say screw them, they can spare the cash. But that old guy was an independent operator. He's probably had that little station for years. I'll send him the money when I get to Chicago."

"All right," Claire said. She sighed heavily, and relaxed her grip on the steering wheel. "Let's see if we can make Salt Lake City."

Claire handed Genevieve a packet of crackers, and she opened it and handed one to Claire.

"You ever swim in it?"

"What?"

"The Great Salt Lake. You ever swim in it?"

"No, I've never been there at all."

"You can float in it without moving. Just like the Dead Sea."

"Yeah, I've heard that. You've been to the Dead Sea?"

"Oh, no. But that's what they compare it to."

The woman finished her crackers and laid her head back against the seat. After a while, she hummed a tune intermittently; Claire smiled, and then leaned forward, as if this would get them into Utah faster. She would have liked to call Jack and ask him what he thought of her new companion. Years running a motel had made him less wholesome, but he still had the farm-boy honesty that wouldn't allow him to take a cent without returning it sometime. He'd get irate when a towel came up missing after a guest had checked out. "Like no one has enough towels at home, especially the raggedy ones we give 'em at this place? That's stealing just to steal."

Genevieve was right about the view from the road as they moved through Nevada. These desolate landscapes could be beautiful, but not at the peak of the day. She looked over at her. Genevieve's eyes were closed, and she seemed to be dozing lightly. The sunburn had started to show on her high cheekbones. A strong face, she thought, but fair eyelashes that looked much longer now that she was asleep. A few beads of sweat showed on her upper lip. Her mouth was full, kissable like a starlet's, and it didn't fit her other features.

She may have felt her looking at her, and she opened her eyes and sat up quickly.

"Sorry. Must have been more tired than I thought."

"No rule against taking a nap."

"I'm supposed to be your shotgun."

"Out here, there's not much to be afraid of. Maybe an animal crossing the road."

Genevieve nodded, and rested her head and squinted into the bright light that poured through the windshield when they took a curve. She pulled the scarf back out of her pocket and wrapped it around her eyes.

"Better than sunglasses," she said, and Claire smiled. After a minute, she started humming a song quietly, the notes bounced around by the wind.

"The radio's broken, or I'd turn it on," Claire told her.

"That's okay." Genevieve licked her lips, and, as if in response, started humming again.

"What song is that?" Claire asked.

"It's an old Joni Mitchell tune. I mean, maybe sixty years old now."

" 'Circle Game'?"

"That's right!" Genevieve said. "My mother used to play that song on the CD player when I was little. I'd sing it sometimes when we were alone on the playground. It was perfect for the merry-go-round. I think she thought I knew what the lyrics meant, but I was just singing the words."

"It's funny."

It was odd to talk with her with the scarf wrapped around her eyes.

"What?"

"I learned that song at a campground when I was maybe sixteen years old."

"Why's that funny?"

Claire laughed uneasily and ran her hand through her damp hair. "I was at that camp because I stole something."

"Really? So they sent you to sing-along camp when you did something wrong?"

Claire laughed at this. "Yeah, something like that. I was stealing things because I was angry at the way the world operates. Useless things like a cheap bracelet or a hair ribbon. Stuff made in China because of the kids working in factories over there. But it's weird that you'd sing that song right after you took the money."

Genevieve pulled off the scarf and stared at her.

"I'm going to return it."

"I know. I know."

"So what was it? A Christian camp? Did they talk about the Ten Commandments?"

"Ha. No, nothing like that. My father wouldn't have gone in for that. It was one of those team-building camps. For kids who were troubled. We canoed down a river in Northern Michigan. It was so cold it snowed that night when we were sitting around the fire. I loved that little campground. And being on the river with those other kids."

"It sounds so nice."

"It was just the one weekend. Then back to real life."

Genevieve nodded and then asked, "Mind if I ask you a question?"

"What, are you kidding? You already know more about me than almost anyone I've met since Jack and I moved out here."

"Not this place, though, right? You never told me where you were driving from."

"No, California. Not far from the eastern border."

Genevieve nodded again, and seemed to be thinking about this. It struck Claire that what she'd said was true: for three years they'd been running the motel, and they were on a first-name basis with half the population of the small town. But maybe because it mostly lay on either side of a highway where almost everyone was passing through, no one asked about anything other than what was happening in the present. "That little Lucy," Joan, the woman who stocked the produce section at the grocery store, would say. "Look how she's motoring around. She's got her dad's sturdy legs." Or Larry, the manager at the Shell station, would stop by and say, "Noticed the *r* was out on your *Shadyrest* sign. Now it says *Shadyest.* Might want to get Jack up a ladder to fix that." But after the first few months, no one asked about where they came from or why they were there.

"It's pretty out that way," Genevieve said.

"It can be. Not so much on our stretch of road."

"So how old are you, anyway, Claire?"

"Almost thirty-five now. Is that the question you wanted to ask?"

"No. Or partly, I guess. So you were sixteen when you went to that campground. And now you're thirty-four. So you said it was fifteen years since you talked to your father, which means you were eighteen or nineteen the last time. Only three years after the time on the river with those other kids."

"That's right. Nineteen. Good math." She was amazed, a little, at Genevieve's quick and extraordinary grasp of detail.

"So what happened between nineteen and thirty-four? I mean, I know you had Lucy. What's your husband's name?"

"Jack."

"And you married Jack. But he probably came later, right?"

"I was in Nebraska when I met him. We had Lucy just a year later."

"Okay, so how'd you get to Nebraska? What happened between nineteen and Nebraska?"

"I—" She realized she was about to say "I don't know," which seemed somehow accurate, given how out of the habit she was of thinking of those years.

"Because if you stopped talking to your mom and dad for all that time, it must have been something interesting."

"I didn't tell you I stopped talking to my mom."

"But you did, didn't you?"

Anyone she ever told about it found this least forgivable. She'd stopped speaking of it entirely, and when a motel guest saw Lucy come around the front desk, and said something like, "What a doll! Her grandma must be tickled," Claire would nod and say, "She is."

For a few seconds, she let the sound of the tires on the highway become her answer.

"It's nothing to be ashamed of," Genevieve said.

"I don't know. That's not what most people think." The words came tumbling out. "You asked me what I was doing before Jack. Well, I had a few problems. The biggest one was drinking.

But I don't want you to think"—she wasn't sure why she suddenly cared what this woman thought of her—"that the drinking was the reason I stopped talking to my mother and father. It wasn't like that. God, I remember one night waking up next to a man. I lifted my head off the pillow, you know, and I didn't know where I was, and I had to stare at his face for, like, a full minute while he slept before I could vaguely remember him from the night before. He had his shirt off, and I could see the tracks in his arms. Say what you want, but I never did heroin. Maybe everything else, but not that. He woke up while I was looking at him, and he sat up in bed right away, with his back to me. It was obvious he didn't remember me, either. The first thing he said was, 'Better call Mom to pick you up.' Maybe he thought I was under eighteen, and that's why he wouldn't look at me. So I said to him, probably because I was angry, 'I haven't spoken to my mother in five years.' And that's when he turns and looks over his shoulder. Gives me what amounted to a long glance. And he says, 'What the fuck's wrong with you?' He's sitting there with tracks in his arms next to a hungover girl he can barely recognize from the night before, and he's asking me that."

In the middle of her story, Genevieve had turned her gray eyes on her.

"So don't tell me it's nothing to be ashamed of," Claire said. "The whole fucking world thinks it is."

She was surprised at her anger and the tightening of her throat.

"If Lucy ever did that to me—" But she stopped there.

The right tire caught the shoulder, and she steered back toward the centerline.

"Sorry," Claire said.

"But you said you named Lucy after your mom's mother."

"I did. I know I did."

"So you'll be seeing your mother for the first time in fifteen years, too?"

"I was almost killed," Claire said.

"What?"

"Nothing. Nothing. Yes, fifteen years. But I talked to her on the phone before I left California. She bawled her head off. But she was still proud."

"Proud of what? Being abandoned?"

She looked over at Genevieve, and then wiped her eyes with the back of her hand.

"Yeah. I guess that's a good way to put it."

"It's a deeper kind of pride than if she came out here and glowed while she watched Lucy stacking blocks."

"Why do you think that?"

But this, Genevieve didn't answer. Ahead in the road, emerging from the illusion of reflection on the pavement, was a crow perched over some carrion. It flew up and cawed as they approached. The woman was strange, and maybe fascinating. Claire reminded herself that she'd robbed the gas station.

"Do you think your father will be proud, too, in that way, when he sees you?" Genevieve asked.

"I don't know. If he's conscious, maybe. I doubt it."

"He probably fell in love."

She shook her head and smiled.

"Genevieve, how would you know that?"

"The woman who called you. I bet that's his wife. Or his longtime lover. Did she say anything?"

"Not about that. But she obviously knew him well. And she'd obviously worked hard to track me down."

"He fell in love with her. Maybe a few years ago. I can't say that your mom was probably as lucky, judging from her pride."

"You know, there's no way you could know that. There's no way I could."

"I'm sorry, Claire. I'm not trying to offend you. I just like stories. I like thinking about stories. And yours is pretty interesting, you have to admit. I like thinking about what happens to people."

"I'm not offended. It's just a little weird that your guesses seem on target."

"I'm just observant. I get it wrong every now and then, but most of the time I'm right. You think about most people's lives. They aren't that different from each other, even though people think they are."

Claire nodded. She felt a kind of heat generating from high in her stomach, and it worked its way into her face.

"I have to admit, I like the thought of my father falling in love."

"He was alone for a long time."

"Genevieve."

"But he was. Your wife leaves you. Your daughter disappears. For a few months, right after that, he fell into a woman's arms who thought he was charming and funny. She lived in an older suburban neighborhood where there were high oak trees, and maybe sometimes he spent the evening there and they watched a movie with her little boy. But at night, while she lay sleeping next to him, after autumn came, the wind would blow the acorns down from those high oaks, and he would lie with his head propped up on his elbow, listening to them hit the sidewalk and the road, everyone's cars parked in their garages, the wind in those drying leaves, and the unrhythmic, hollow plunk of the acorns, and they would remind him, then, of you disappearing, of the loss, and how he never predicted it, and he knew that he couldn't go on sleeping in that neighborhood or with that kind woman, where the truest thing that ever happened was at night when those acorns fell randomly from the trees."

Claire looked over at her. Genevieve's voice was hypnotic. She remembered being a small girl and wondering what her father was thinking when he lay in the mornings with his shoulders turned away, seemingly looking out the window.

"You make it sound like that's what actually happened," she said. "It's funny, because when I was a kid, he did lie in bed with his head propped up like that."

"Most men do," Genevieve said. "Doesn't Jack?"

Claire nodded. "You make him sound so lonely. My father, I mean."

"Maybe. But maybe he's just thoughtful, you know? And he knows the difference between being lonely and alone. But he is alone a long time after he breaks it off with the woman. Many years. Don't get the impression this is because you never called or tried to see him. I'm not saying there isn't a hollow in his heart where his memory of you is nestled like a sleeping rabbit. He knows you're out there. But he's bought a house on a lake a few miles out of town."

Claire almost said, "Which one?" before remembering this was Genevieve's story, and she'd probably never been to Michigan.

"It's a tiny house. A small screened porch facing the water, a living room, a kitchen, and one bedroom, a spare room upstairs, but a big garage, where he can work on projects for remaking the house to his own tastes. There are other cottages on the lake, some owned by people who only use them in the summertime, and in the evening, during those summer evenings, your father props up a lawn chair and sits where the edge of the grass meets the water, just in front of a large willow tree, and he watches some of the children from these vacation homes go tearing down a long pier, and leap into the water."

"You know, his mom lived on a lake like that. My grandma."

"Did she? Anyway, he's friendly with his neighbors without making friends. They'll ask him to watch the dog when they are away, and he'll amble along the lane that circles the lake, keeping the dog leashed until they get to the small public access with the tall reeds—the lake isn't large enough to allow anything other than small fishing boats—and then he'll let the dog hunt minnows in the shallows, or he'll toss a tennis ball into the water and watch the dog's dark head pursue it out past the lily pads. Winters, the lake freezes over, and he's one of the few people who continue to live there, and Saturday mornings he watches the ice fishermen trudge out through the snow, and hears the sharp thrust of their augers as they chip away at the ice come across the lake with the rays of the winter sun."

The thought of ice and snow briefly cooled the inside of the cab. Claire felt herself being pulled into the story.

"And that's how his days go. For most of those years you were gone. I mean, if you think about it, Claire. These years raising your baby. It's not all that often—maybe Christmas, maybe the Fourth of July—you sit back and embrace everything that's happened. But most of the time it's day upon day, like it is for everyone, like it is for your father. What's his name?"

"Marc."

They were coming upon the Nevada/Utah border, and a town called West Wendover. Past the buildings, there was a vast stretch of flat white land, then a distant range of mountains.

"So one summer," Genevieve continued, "Marc lays a wooden floor because he thinks maple boards will warm his house in the winter months. And another year, he tears down the wall that separates the little kitchen from the living area, so that when he turns away from the stove he can look directly out onto the lake. He'll have a friend over every now and then to admire his handiwork, but his friends are as plunged into their own lives as he is into his, and so this happens less and less often. In the summer, early mornings before going to work, when the lake is so calm that the clouds are perfectly reflected, and the houses along the shore offer perfect versions of themselves in the water, he begins the habit of taking a small rowboat across the lake, all the way to the opposite edge where the remnants of an old farm still stand, and where an old-timer who had a cottage on the lake for forty years tells a story of hoisting his daughter onto a grazing horse, bareback. So he thinks of you. He thinks of your mother. After the lake freezes, when the cold is tolerable and the roads clear, he takes slow runs around the lake. He loses weight. For an older man, he's strong. He realizes he's trying to make himself strong, and all these years seem like a preparation. He is aware he is preparing. For the onslaught of old age? he wonders. Something else, maybe. Maybe something that will never come. He loves his little house, where now he's planted a small vegetable garden. He bears his isolation."

8

Two days had passed since the drive to the mountains. On the way back, once they were again in the outskirts of what he now knew was the city, Saabir had pulled the car over, and Josephine had stepped out without a word. For a night, Marc was taken to a different house, more pleasant, scented with what may have been incense, and where a small family may have lived—he heard their voices but saw no one other than Saabir and another man who stood guard with utter disinterest. He overheard Saabir arguing with someone he assumed was the father in the house, and the next day he was transported back to the room with the half-dirt floor and the high window. "Home," he'd said to Saabir when he removed the blindfold, and even Saabir couldn't help but give him a wry smile.

But he hadn't seen Azhar in several days now, and since he

seemed a reluctant participant in whatever group Josephine was a member of, and because he seemed gentle, and had children, Marc worried that Azhar had been caught in some sort of crossfire when they'd driven out of the city.

So Marc asked, "What happened to Azhar?" after Saabir had blindfolded him and tied his hands and he heard the woman come in and sit down.

"Azhar's with his family," Josephine said. "You will see him again."

"Was he hurt?"

"So much concern for a terrorist, Marc?" She had returned to her tone of the first few days.

"He told you I called him that?"

"He mentioned it."

"I like Azhar. But he sits watching me with a gun over his shoulder."

"I know," she said, and she was suddenly no longer his interrogator. "It doesn't suit him. Like many people here, his family needs the money."

"Does Saabir have a family?"

"Of course."

"I mean a wife. Children."

She hesitated a moment.

"He has a son."

"And a wife?"

She seemed to turn her head toward the door.

"It's best if you don't ask too many questions about Saabir. His wife is dead. Let's leave it at that."

They sat quietly for what seemed several long minutes. He knew this was likely because of the intimacy of the storytelling during their past few meetings, which had perhaps surprised both of them, as if they somehow had become unintentional lovers who now had to bear the morning sun on their faces. The last time he'd felt such an awkwardness was the morning he woke in his home after Lynne had told him she wanted to separate. It was as if their years together had moved out before he had, and left him with nothing to say.

"How long do you think it'll be safe to stay here?" he asked.

"It's never been what I'd call *safe*," she said. "It's probably less so now. By now you know it's almost impossible to predict what might happen on any given day. What I've learned—"

She stopped there.

"What you've learned?" he pressed. She shifted in her chair, perhaps uncrossing and recrossing her legs. He realized he now was attempting to imagine her legs.

"I'm not going to tell you it's thrilling to live with a knife at your throat. I don't live that way, or at least I wouldn't describe it like that. But in our little crucible, on some days, when something unexpected happens, you could say so much is revealed about others so fast. Sometimes it's something about someone's mother or someone's home. Sometimes it's about fear or something else that's primitive."

"Like petroglyphs?"

For a second, he imagined he could hear her smile.

"Older than those," she said. "Living this way—as someone who didn't grow up here, who had someone else's money, and who is fighting for a cause. It's exciting for a long time. Even after the worst of everything it's exciting. But you get tired of others' blood . . ."

Again he thought of Azhar. "Blood on your hands, Josephine?"

"Don't ask me that question. It's not a relevant question today, and you know it. But I don't mean literally. I'm talking about something else. Like the other day, when we were driving away. Your heart was pounding, wasn't it? You might have thought you were about to die, and it's possible right then that you were. I thought I could hear your heart in your ears. And as Saabir was driving I could see the artery in his neck throbbing with tension. That's the kind of blood I mean. The blood that seems indifferent to anything other than escape, or flight, or some unwanted embrace that pushes it toward another generation."

"All right, Josephine. I get it."

"You think I'm overstating it?"

"Not really."

"You have no idea what I've lived through here."

For the first time she sounded almost angry.

"You could tell me."

At this, she stayed silent for a while. He had spoken with more tenderness than he'd intended.

"Is that why you gave me the little house on the lake? Those quiet years? The summer rowing across the pond?"

"That was Genevieve."

"Genevieve. Josephine. Any difference?"

"It's important you don't confuse the two."

She had told him the story of Claire and Genevieve's journey across Nevada while he sat at the base of the cliff with his back to her, and as her shadow, shrinking as the sun rose, moved a few steps one direction, and then another as she spoke, and Saabir burned through cigarette after cigarette, the smoke and the smell of the sparse trees on the rocky outcroppings heavier in the warming early afternoon. Sentence by sentence he was pulled in, not into the life of the Claire he knew, but the Claire he could barely have recognized. And had Josephine not stepped out of the car somewhere on the way back to the city, had he not been taken to a different house and had an additional glimpse of his own vulnerability, he would have asked her to stay to tell him more of that story.

"I'm not sure why that's important. Are you saying Genevieve's not like you?"

She laughed briefly, but chose not to answer him directly.

"I don't want you to think I'm being held here like you, against my will, though as I've already told you, I'm not free to travel," she said. "But I've spent years here, as a woman, in a place where the rules and roles for women are well defined and Americans are not exactly embraced."

"So you are American?"

"You know, I'm tired of the tone of these questions. You have no power here, and you know it. But if there's something specific you want to know about me, then ask. Yes, I'm American. And no, living here isn't exactly *The Sheltering Sky,* if you've read it. But there are times it's reminiscent."

"Honestly, I wasn't aware of my tone. And I haven't read it, of course."

"I think you're still carrying on as if the strangeness of this place is outside you, and you might endure it, and someday go home. It's a different thing once the strangeness is inside you. I bet Claire understood that at the moment she was killed. But when she doesn't die, like in our story, I don't know what she understands. We'll see, won't we?" She seemed to think about this for a moment. "And would I like for my own life a house on a lake where daily I could row across a pond and watch the little whirlpools spin away under the oars? Yes. Of course yes. At some point, everyone wants to have that for as long as they can hang on to it."

"It doesn't seem like many get that here. I wouldn't know, but life seems a hell of a lot less innocent than it does at home."

"This is my home now. And I think the man rowing across the lake in our story, he's not looking for a return to innocence. He's looking for something, but not that."

"Josephine," he said, lowering his voice as it dawned on him. "After your lover was killed. Did someone—what happened to you?"

She sat entirely still, the room silent, and then he heard her move forward on her chair.

"Let me see your hand." He extended it toward her. She bent it at the wrist and said, "Spread your fingers." After he did, she set the base of her palm against his, and then pressed against it with her entire hand. He could feel her fingers extend well above his own, and the tiny spaces the creases in them made, and her palm was cool and dry. He felt the intimacy of his effort to see her through the pressure of her hand on his. And then she tightened her fingers around his, squeezing, and he could feel the strength in them.

"That shouldn't necessarily be a complicated question, should it? But for me, it is. I've kept others from hurting me when I could."

She pulled her hand away.

The evening deepened as they continued to sit for a time without speaking. Outside, he occasionally heard voices, then a door closing and someone laughing. He remembered the table he'd seen days ago with the three place settings, and he had wanted to sit down there with that small family. And then the call went out for the evening prayer—he wasn't sure how far away the mosque was, but it was surely equipped with loudspeakers for the muezzin's voice to carry this far. Odd that a man's singing, with no instruments to support him, calling people to gather, could sometimes sound like a mournful plea for company.

"When I was seventeen," Josephine said, "a girl in my high school took an interest in my mortal soul. I think of her every time I hear that particular muezzin. He sounds like a woman, don't you think?"

"Before I came here, if I'd heard him, I would have been sure of it." He was feeling a sympathy for Josephine that he couldn't have explained.

"Years ago, I used to wonder if they tried to. Sound like women, I mean. I'm not sure why I wanted to think that. Jibril laughed at me when I asked him about it."

"Jibril was the man you traveled with?"

He imagined she nodded, sensed that she did, which meant that she had forgotten his blindfold because of the memory.

"The girl in my school," she said. "She was tiny, really. One of those young women who somehow managed to be short and thin at the same time. I towered over her. She wasn't particularly popular with the other kids, but she had that kind of sunflower face, round and always turning toward the light, and her brightness was appealing, so most of the kids forgave the Bible she hauled around with her schoolbooks. She didn't push it most of the time, but once she invited me to a concert in a small, open-air stadium in a park. I didn't believe in God then, but because she was sweet, and I considered her a friend, I spent the evening there with her. It was Christian rock, which I didn't have much patience for, but it was played well enough, and the lead singer would occasionally tell stories in between songs. In the middle of one of those stories, an ambulance went by with its siren blaring, louder and louder as it neared the venue, and the singer broke off his story and asked everyone to bow their heads, and as he was saying a prayer for whoever it was who was hurt or dying, my girlfriend took my hand. It was the only thing that reached me in the entire show."

Beneath the blindfold, he could see the two of them sitting at the concert with their heads lowered, but he still couldn't imagine Josephine's face, and for a moment he saw it as a featureless oval from which a voice emerged, and he tightened his eyes against its opacity.

"I don't know why I'm telling you this. I guess it's because of the one time I heard her sing, and how she reminded me of that muezzin. She had a boyfriend who went to a different school. The same church, apparently. They were serious about it in the way only seventeen year olds can get. He'd given her a ring. Anyway, our last year of school together, we took a trip with the other kids from our class to an amusement park that was a few hours' drive away, and we came back after nightfall. She was sitting with a boy who'd always liked her. I didn't make anything of it. I slept most of the way back. But when we got off that bus, she asked if I could give her a ride home, and when I looked over at her after she pulled the car door shut, she was crying, and was pulling her knees up to her chest. She said, 'I don't think he'll forgive me,' and, given the way she sometimes talked, I thought she might have been talking about Jesus. Maybe she was. I asked her what had happened, but she only shook her head. I was surprised to see that sunny face so dark, and it's possible part of me enjoyed that. She started rocking back and forth in the seat. I told her that whatever it was, she was taking it way too seriously. But she shook her head, and started humming. I didn't recognize the tune, but assumed it was a hymn. And when she started singing the words, her voice changed. Since she was so small, when she spoke people compared it to a Munchkin's. And her singing voice still had something of that quality. But it was overlaid with something mournful, something deeper, and resonant. She sang it all the way through, and when I pulled into her drive, I looked at her and said, 'My God, that was beautiful.' But she only nodded and wiped her eyes with her palm and said, 'Thanks for the ride.' She looked like an old woman when she walked hunched over into the porch light and pushed open the door to her house."

After Josephine finished speaking, she let out a long sigh.

"Anyway, when I hear that muezzin, I think of that girl. He's probably fifty years old, but his voice has the same quality. Of someone singing beautifully in the hope they'll be forgiven."

Her words hung in the air, and he cleared his throat.

"Or because they know they never will be," he said.

"Maybe that, too."

She stood up then, walked to the door, opened it, and said something to Saabir. He seemed to protest, but she insisted, and then pushed the door closed again.

"Saabir won't be standing guard for a short time, just so you know. He understands more English than you probably realize."

Marc heard her settle in the chair across from him.

"So I've been thinking about the stories you've told about Claire," she said.

"Yes?"

"Well, almost every one you've told was when she was slightly older. At twelve when she cut herself. Fourteen when you kissed her. Sixteen when she stole and went camping. Every story a time when she was on the verge of something. Or you were."

"Those are the stories you remember. Those are the ones that collide, like Genevieve said about her mom." He caught himself thinking about Genevieve as a living, breathing person.

"I know," she said. "I remember. But you've never described her as a small child."

Reflexively, he tried to recall an image of her at that age, but most of what he remembered he knew were photographs that Lynne had stored in albums that, at various ages, he'd find Claire occasionally leafing through.

"She was—" But he stopped himself, since he was about to resort to the words anyone would use: *beautiful, so bright, so sweet, precious, precocious,* when in truth, more and more, what he understood was the slow, cold creep of the word *was.*

"This," he started. "This story—" he said again, and swallowed down whatever was attempting to rise. "It's more Lynne's story than mine. I mean, she was the one who told it to me. About Claire. I'm not sure why it occurs to me, other than it's partly about a woman who wanted a child. But maybe it's because of the story of your friend. How it's about something that happened, and after that how things never felt the same again."

"Like all stories."

"I guess. Claire was probably about five years old. The summer before her first year of school. Kindergarten. And Lynne, at that point, well, she'd stopped working when Claire was born. And because soon Claire would be in school full time, she'd finally be able to go back. By then—well, it's not like she'd had her fill of child-rearing, but maybe it was something close to that. Like a lot of mothers, she missed the world of adults, and that summer she was pretty much at her wit's end trying to find things to do that would keep Claire entertained until school started. One day she took Claire to the park, and Lynne had a friend with her. A woman she'd known since college who was back in town for the week. The park had a pond, almost as big as a small lake, really, filled with lily pads and a few ducks and geese, probably domestic ones that the township brought in. We took Claire there a few times a year. They even had those machines, you know, where for a quarter you could buy a few pellets of food so the kids could feed the birds.

"Anyway, Claire had fed the ducks and was sitting between Lynne and her friend. Beth, that was her name. The sun was beating down, and there was no wind, and the smell of the pond was probably rank. Claire's cheeks would have been flushed red, and her hair was still strawberry-blond at that age, probably curling in the humidity. And according to Lynne, Beth, who'd been married for a couple of years now, was telling her she would be unable to have children. That's not a great tragedy in this age, but the woman had wanted babies as long as she could remember. She had been the kind of little girl who loved playing with dolls, and, when she got older, would save every one she ever owned and keep each in a proper place on the shelf in her closet, hidden away so her friends couldn't see how much she still loved them. So she was crying when she was telling Lynne about it. Whatever the problem was physiologically, it was with her, and not her husband, who also wanted kids. Lynne said Beth was having trouble stifling her sobs, but that when she glanced down at Claire, she was looking at her own feet, bobbing them up and down to a tune she must have been hearing in her head. Oblivious, Lynne thought.

"There was a rule at the park that any dog had to be on a leash. With the kids running around, and birds, it made perfect sense. But that afternoon, some guy materializes out of nowhere with his dog at his heels, and throws a ball into the pond, and of course the dog dives into the lily pads to retrieve it. The ducks and geese on the water, pretty well fattened on all of the pellets the kids were constantly feeding them, squawk and flap awkwardly in the other direction, trying to get away. A woman stands up from a nearby bench and hollers, 'Hey! Where's the goddamn leash?' But the guy just kind of shrugs his shoulders while his dog paddles back to shore. And of course, the second after it drops the ball and shakes the water from its hide, it takes off after one of the geese, one of those white ones, you know, that you used to see on a farm, so it's not much of a chase. The dog has it by the neck within a few seconds, gives it a few shakes, and of course it's dead. The other geese and ducks are honking and quacking from the other side of the pond, flapping their wings, raising their bills and shaking their heads. And the woman from the bench is shouting, 'You fucking asshole! Now see what you've done? That poor thing!' And the whole time Lynne is watching from the bench with Beth, when she suddenly remembers that Claire is sitting beside her, witnessing everything, and she pulls her off the bench, and the three of them head back to the car."

He could feel the blindfold was damp because of his effort at telling the story. Josephine was listening noiselessly.

"Apparently, Lynne didn't try to explain anything right away, and Claire fell asleep in the car on the way back to Beth's hotel. She woke up when Lynne parked in front of the lobby and Beth opened the door to the backseat of the car to give Claire a hug. As they pulled out of the lot, Lynne looked at Claire in the rearview mirror. She seemed to be watching the storefronts they were driving by. So she said, 'Claire. Do you understand what happened back at the pond?' 'Yeah,' Claire said. 'Beth can't have any babies.' Lynne was so surprised at this that she stared at her in the rearview for a moment too long, and had to hit the brakes hard to avoid hitting the car in front of her. Claire lurched forward in her car seat, but was okay. 'What about the dog and the goose?' Lynne asked once she was moving forward again. 'The dog was chasing the goose,' Claire said. So Lynne said, 'That's right. It was.'

"And she left it at that. She thought that was as much as Claire had understood. So Lynne went on driving, Claire watching out the window as she turned the corner into our neighborhood, and onto our street. And just before she pulled into the drive, Claire said, 'Mama. Someday I'm gonna die, aren't I?' "

He heard the last words resonate off the walls, and swallowed down hard again, and felt his skin prickle at Josephine's observation of him, and then a flush of anger at his helplessness.

"I can't keep talking this way. Hog-tied and blindfolded like this."

"I'm sorry, Marc."

He pulled hard at the knots.

"Don't be angry," she said.

He threw his head back and laughed. *"Don't be angry?* Are you fucking kidding me? I feel like I'm in a zoo. Like I'm a lab specimen."

"We're only talking."

At this he strained hard at the ropes, his feet set against the floor for ballast, and his muscles taut. He let out a low cry at the effort, but he felt something inside coming loose, and he was afraid of it, so he stopped. He was breathing heavily.

"I'd give anything to get out of here right now. Sell the house, the car. The whole fucking Pepsi corporation. You can have it. Use the money for rocket launchers."

His wrists burned from the ropes. He felt defeated, and then laughed, as if there were any other way to feel since the moment he was captured.

"Something funny?"

"Oh, yes. There's a ton that's funny. This zoo. You as my zookeeper. Training me to jump through hoops. You could sell tickets. Pathetic little penny-ante carnival."

"You need to settle down. Saabir will be back soon."

"Maybe he'll do me the favor of lopping off my head."

Josephine stood up then, and walked around behind him. He heard her kneel to the floor, and she unknotted the ropes so that, for a brief instant, he could have pulled away, and then she re-knotted them again tight against his wrists.

"It won't do for others to see that you were fighting against these restraints," she said. She stood up again, but instead of sitting back down, she put her hand on his shoulder and her mouth near his ear.

"You chose that story to tell, Marc. Don't be angry with me for making that choice."

"Don't be angry?" he said again. "For Christ's sake, Josephine, look at me. You just retied my arms behind my back while I sit here blindfolded. I'm your fucking hostage."

Someone knocked at the door, and after she opened it, she said something to probably Saabir in Urdu. He recognized Azhar's name in a sentence, and after the door latched, Saabir untied the ropes and removed the blindfold, and Marc saw Azhar standing in front of him. Saabir held the blindfold up by a corner; it was nearly soaked through, and he said something to Azhar while grinning. In the narrow light of the room still lit by a lantern, Azhar's face looked grim, and he seemed to favor the shoulder that wasn't bearing the weight of his rifle.

"Walk," Azhar said weakly, almost at a whisper. Saabir gestured with his hand, as if Marc should get up and join Azhar. Marc's chest tightened.

The night was clear, with no moon, but the lights from the city dimmed the stars. In the air there was still the persistent smell of smoke, and more distantly sewage, but also a coolness that seemed familiar. He tried not to think of Claire. Of Lynne. Azhar led him once around the perimeter, and this time, when they passed the window of the house next door with the tables and chairs, it, too, was lit by a lantern, and a young, thin man with a beard was sitting over a cup of tea. He didn't raise his head as they passed.

A quarter of the way back around, Azhar put his hand on Marc's shoulder, but when Marc started to turn to face him,

Azhar stopped him. Marc heard the click of the safety being released on the rifle. A few seconds passed as he listened to Azhar breathing with some difficulty as he shifted his weight, and then Marc felt the end of the barrel of the gun at the base of his neck. His feet and hands tingled with the rush of adrenaline, and after this first flush he turned cold.

"Azhar," he said quietly.

The gun barrel was steady on his spine, though Azhar seemed to be holding it up with effort. He said something to him in Urdu. Then he said. "Sorry. You want live? You want?"

Azhar pulled the gun away from Marc's head, and he heard him latch the safety. He grabbed Marc's shoulder, and turned him around. Marc was sweating hard under his arms and along his inner thighs. The gun was back on Azhar's shoulder, and with Azhar's back to the night sky, Marc could barely make out his face. But he looked like he was in pain.

Azhar raised his hand palm down as he had before to indicate his children.

"They kill," he said. "You live? They kill." Then something in Urdu. He turned Marc around again, and walked him the rest of the way around the perimeter. By the time they reached the window, the man in it was gone and the light turned out.

When they went back into the room, he saw that Saabir had laid out Marc's bedroll, and he used his gun to indicate to Marc that he should lie down. At the gesture, Azhar turned and left, though Saabir uttered a few words in his direction before he closed the door. Marc lay with his back to Saabir, as he'd been instructed each night for reasons he never understood, since once the light was out he was free to roll over.

He tried to imagine Azhar walking through the dark streets along the outskirts of Karachi, and what his wife must have thought when he came home shaken, the gun slung over his shoulder. Marc was beginning to understand how his own life was putting innocents at risk.

Unlike most nights, Saabir wasn't going to sleep at the same time Marc was. He heard him sit down in his chair.

"Saabir," Marc said. "Did something happen to one of Azhar's children?"

He didn't answer right away, and Marc had no idea if he'd understood the question.

"Hmmmm," Saabir said. "Children." He did his best to pronounce the word. "No."

Saabir shifted his feet, tapped them once, and then stood up and picked up the broom, and Marc listened to his sweeping, in a slow and deliberate rhythm that allowed Marc to close his eyes. He remembered the feel of the gun at his head, how his body had gone cold, but how indifferent he'd felt to Azhar possibly pulling the trigger. He wondered if Josephine had instructed him to make the threat. He could still feel the spot where the barrel had rested, and he dreamed lightly there was an insect crawling along his hairline. When someone knocked on the door, he reached back to push it away.

He knew it was the woman even though she didn't speak to Saabir. She'd pulled the chair over almost to the edge of Marc's bedroll. Saabir picked up his broom and began sweeping again.

"Josephine, did something happen to Azhar's children?"

"His children are fine," she said. "Azhar's gone home."

"When we were out walking, he—" But he stopped himself.

"He what?"

"He seemed afraid of something."

"I know. He has a family. He is afraid. I don't have to tell you not to turn around, do I?"

"No."

Saabir's strokes with the broom grew longer, slower. Marc couldn't imagine there was anything left to sweep. He heard Josephine take a long breath, and then release it.

9

In the time that she and Jack had owned the battered little truck, Claire had never slept in its bed. Jack had done so several times, when he'd traveled some distance to pick up supplies for the motel. "Not too bad," he'd said after the first time he'd tried it. "Back was a little sore in the morning. It'd be awfully snug for two people." And now she was lying on her own back, shoulder to shoulder with Genevieve, the ridges in the truck's bottom pushing into the mattress along her rib cage. The bed smelled vaguely of rust, dirt, and mildew.

"Sorry about the accommodations," Claire said.

They had driven to the outskirts of the city, near the Great Salt Lake itself, and in the last light of the day found a primitive campground that was mostly abandoned. A small camper was parked in one spot, and someone had managed to pitch a tent in the dry, hard ground, but no car was near it.

"Are you kidding?" Genevieve said. "Without you, I might be sleeping in a truck stop a few hundred miles farther from Chicago. I've slept in worse places."

"It's funny," Claire said. "Did I tell you that Jack and I run a motel back in California?"

"No, you didn't."

"Well, we do. It's a pretty run-down little place. We've fixed it up some. Lucy knows every nook and cranny of every room. But one of those motel rooms would look pretty good right now."

"This is fine," Genevieve said. "I'm used to sleeping under the stars."

Both of them were looking at the sky.

"Look," Genevieve said. "You can kind of see the Milky Way."

Before they'd climbed into the truck bed, the air was so cool that Claire had put on a sweater, but now she was hot under the blanket, and she sat up and pulled the sweater over her head, and as she did her pajama top came up off her shoulder. She flung the sweater at her feet and pulled the pajama top back down. Before she lay back, she felt Genevieve touch a spot on her left shoulder, and she jumped.

"Sorry," Genevieve said. "But what's that?"

"A scar," Claire said.

"I know it's a scar. But I could see it even in the starlight. It doesn't look like—well, it doesn't look like it was made by a scalpel."

"It wasn't. It's a long story, Genevieve."

After waiting a few seconds, Genevieve said, "When someone has a scar like that, I don't think there would be many short stories."

As they'd crossed into Utah, Genevieve seemed to lose interest in telling the tale of Claire's father. Maybe it was because once they'd left Nevada, they were closer to their first destination. Claire had taken plenty of road trips, and knew that when people talked while traveling, if they talked at all, once they were on the verge of arrival, they started thinking of their homes, or began to imagine the ocean, or the embrace of a brother or sister, so they would often fall silent. But the story of her father. She knew that had she seen him throughout the course of these years, had she come at Christmas and once over the summer, as other grown children did, Genevieve's vision of who her father had become would have seemed bizarre and even laughable. But the void of years made most anything imaginable, and it struck her how through that time she had dreamed so little for him. The metronomic quality of his days that Genevieve had described, of his rising in the morning to a little boat on a lake, of his lying down at night with lights winking across the glassy surface, and the quiet anticipation of the slow shift of the seasons that's magnified over a body of water—to imagine her father this way, less troubled by her disappearance, was, oddly, a deeper comfort than she would have guessed.

Claire settled back into the truck bed and looked into the sky. She didn't want to take up Genevieve's comment about her scar. She was missing Lucy. Tonight, outside the diner, she'd talked to her briefly on the phone. "We miss you, Mama, but we been so busy!" Maybe a line Jack or his mother had told her to say.

Now, Claire closed her eyes; they ached from the hours of driving in the sun, and she thought she might let Genevieve take a turn at the wheel tomorrow.

"It was a long time ago," she said finally. "I was someone completely different."

"People say that, but I don't know how often they mean it," Genevieve said. Anytime either of them moved on the mattress, the truck bed amplified the sound.

Claire shifted to her side and propped herself up on her elbow. Genevieve was lying with her eyes closed, her skin tinted blue, her high cheekbones catching a bit more of the light from the sky. Claire thought that Genevieve, like most people, looked ageless away from the light of day. She had picked her up fewer than twelve hours earlier, but a quality in her face tugged at something planted deeply into Claire's memory.

"I always liked it when I knew someone was watching me when I was trying to fall asleep," Genevieve said.

"Sorry," Claire said. "I didn't mean to stare."

"No, I'm serious. I know it creeps out some people. That someone would be looking at their unconscious face. That maybe they'd be drooling or snoring. But I always liked it. It felt like someone was protecting me. Watching over me."

"The boyfriend from Chicago—the one you're moving in with. Is that what he did?"

Genevieve smiled. "You asked that question because that's the kind of question I've been asking you."

"Gives you a little jolt, doesn't it?"

"I guess," she said. She was still smiling. "But yeah, he did. I remember one time. We were renting this little two-room shack out in the country. It was December, and a front had gone through the night before, the first strong one of that winter, and we got like ten inches of wet snow. And even half-asleep, you know that's happened, and you wrap yourself tighter in the blankets and try to sleep further into the morning. When I finally opened my eyes, he was sitting up in bed, looking down on me. And I don't know what it was about the way the sun was shining through the clouds, but it was still snowing, and when the light came through the window I could see the shadows of the heavy flakes falling over his face and bare chest."

Claire could see her eyelashes fluttering, and a crescent of white beneath them.

"He was just a boy then, really."

Claire lay back down. Genevieve seemed to have a capacity

to create a kind of longing in any story she told. After they were quiet for a while, Claire heard in the distance a scratching or sniffing in the dirt, an animal out in the desert.

"Do you hear that?" she asked.

"Yeah. It's probably just a coyote, or something like that."

But then she thought she heard footsteps, and the sniffing and scratching came closer, and by the time she raised her head, her heart pounding, she saw a dog pissing on the tire of the truck and a large man standing behind it.

"Can I help you?" she asked, which she immediately regretted, because her politeness had been a reflex from encountering strangers at the motel. Genevieve, who was nearest to him, had sat up in the truck bed.

"Well, you can start by paying for the campsite you're sitting on." His face was difficult to make out in the darkness, but Claire could tell he was looking them over.

"This is a campground you have to pay for? Sorry, when no one was here, we thought it was free."

"Well, we have a tent over here. And my camper. It's posted right outside the pull-through, along with envelopes to drop your money in. Plain as day."

Claire was beginning to feel angry that the man had emerged after nightfall.

"So you train your dog to piss on the cars that haven't paid?" Genevieve asked.

"Sorry 'bout that. He doesn't know any better. It's just your tire." He rested his hand on the truck bed, and Genevieve reached out and took hold of his wrist and pushed it back toward his side.

"Whoa!" he said. "Excuse me!"

"This might be your campground," Genevieve said. "But it's not your truck. Keep your hands off."

"Look, I'm not trying to cause problems here."

"Then why didn't you wait till morning?" Claire asked.

"People drive off without paying. They get up at the crack of dawn, and drive off. Usually I take down people's license plates just in case."

The dog whimpered once at his heels, and offered a single bark, and the man said, "Settle."

Claire was in her pajamas, and had locked her wallet in the cab of the truck, and she started to climb out of the truck to retrieve it, but Genevieve said, "I got this." She had slept in the clothes she'd been riding in all day, and she reached into one of her pockets and pulled out the twenties that she'd stolen from the gas station.

"It's fifteen, not twenty," the man said after she handed him the bill.

"Then give us our change," Genevieve said. He smiled, and reached into his back pocket and pulled out a small clip of bills and peeled off one and handed it to Genevieve.

"Tell you what," he said. "It's unusual for people to pull into a campground and sleep in an open-air truck bed. Could have pulled off most anywhere under a nice, bright light and saved yourself the trouble."

"We thought this was most anywhere," Claire said, but he ignored her.

"It's pretty unusual, too, to find two women sleeping in the back of that truck. Nice-looking women. Don't know where you're heading to, but I wouldn't recommend doing it again out along these roads."

"I see," Genevieve said. "What year is this?"

The man shook his head. His face was round and heavy. Claire could see him better now in the starlight—middle aged, fat, like the bad-guy sheriff in an old movie.

"If you lived in this area long as I have, you know the year it is don't matter much. At least not out here in the wilds. Not for two women alone."

Genevieve snorted at this. "This isn't *the wilds*. You're ten miles from the city."

"You'd be surprised, miss."

"This isn't the wilds," she said again. "I know them better than you do."

He stood staring at them for a few seconds longer before he smiled, said, "Good night, ladies," and walked off toward his camper. Claire hadn't seen the dim light coming from its curtained windows till now. The dog followed him into the back.

"Aren't you the bold woman?" she whispered to Genevieve.

"Taking hold of his hand like that and sticking it back in his pocket. Calling him on his little story."

"I hate bullshit," Genevieve said, without whispering.

Genevieve tilted her head up to the sky, sighed heavily, and then lay back down with her shoulder turned away from her. The night was rapidly getting colder, and the warmth from Genevieve's body was comforting. For a few minutes, she'd forgotten why she was out here—this journey to visit her father who might very well be dying—as if the trip had emerged whole cloth from some other realm, and Genevieve was her best friend on some unplanned adventure. She was sleepy. She resettled herself on the mattress.

"It's weird," Genevieve said.

"What is?"

"That dog. I had a dog when I was a kid that looked like that one."

"Yeah? Nicer than this guy's?"

"No, not really. We were out living in the country, and my dad wanted a farm dog, even though we weren't on a farm. She was a black Lab, about the same size as the one that peed on your tire. She liked to chase birds, and you could hardly blame her, since she was bred to do it. My dad insisted on keeping her unchained to roam the yard and ward off strangers, and she'd catch a crow or starling from time to time, and my dad would stroke her head afterward and tell her she was a good girl. Then one day she got out of the yard and into a neighbor's chicken shed, and killed something like forty laying hens. That was the end of the dog."

Claire felt something run through her, as if this were a parable she should remember, but she couldn't name it.

"I always wondered," Genevieve continued. "Killing forty hens like that. Would you call that violence? When the dog goes after that many chickens? Or was it violent when my dad left the dog unleashed when he knew that dog killed birds?"

Claire was trying to figure out how they'd gotten here.

Nearby, there were the sudden ticking wings of an insect, and the dog barked once.

"That was supposed to be funny."

"You're a very strange person, Genevieve. I mean that affectionately."

"Sure you do," she said.

In the morning, Claire was wakened by the man in the camper pulling away from his site and out onto the road, and once she could no longer hear his truck, she climbed out of the bed and pulled on fresh clothes under the still-rising sun. She glanced over at the tent pitched a few yards away, but it now appeared that no one was in it. Once she was dressed, she tugged on the blanket that Genevieve had pulled up to her nose and said, "We should hit the road."

She sat up and stretched, and then held a hand over her eyes. "Look, you can see the lake."

"Yeah," Claire said. "It looks pretty bleak out there."

"We should go for a swim."

Claire glanced out toward the water.

"I don't know, Genevieve. I was hoping to make Nebraska today."

"We can," she said. "No problem. But when are you gonna have another chance to swim in the Great Salt Lake?"

Claire looked at her and smiled. "You got a swimsuit in that tiny backpack of yours?"

"No, but I have a change of clothes. I can swim in these."

When they pulled into the parking lot outside the swimming beach, the stench of the lake was powerful, a briny odor overlaid with the smell of sulfur and something rotting, briefly reminiscent of family visits to Lake Michigan when Claire was a child, and she'd find a narrow piece of driftwood to poke at the remains of an alewife. Worse, when they stepped outside the cab, they were set upon by flies. The lake itself seemed flatter than any she'd ever seen, with the distant mountains and the expanses of bleached salt.

"Boy, can't wait to take a dip in that fresh water," Claire said.

Genevieve smiled. "Once in a lifetime, Claire. Someday you can tell Lucy about it." She slapped at the back of her neck and took her hand away, and in the center of her palm was a dead fly. Claire was waving others from her hair.

"This must be what gets people in the water," she said, and started running toward the beach, Genevieve following.

"Those clothes will be caked in salt!" Genevieve called after her.

"So will yours!"

The water was cooler than she'd anticipated, and so shallow that she stopped running after she was no more than knee-deep. Genevieve caught up to her. There were others at the lake, some walking the edge of the water, a few children scattered among the stones and salt-sand, picking through tiny objects they'd found. Farther out, here and there across the water, people were lying on their backs without swimming, testing the claims they'd heard in elementary school geography. Off to their left, a big man was floating with his belly above the surface.

"Check it out!" Genevieve said.

She was already lying on her back, her clothes loose and floating away from her skin so Claire could see the outline of her body underneath, and it seemed to shift dimensions in the light breeze. She was smiling, and under the sun her teeth looked thin and translucent. Claire sank into the water, the deep cool immediately exhilarating, and before the water reached her chin she could taste its salinity. She lay back and floated with her body parallel to Genevieve's, the water gently lapping along her legs and arms. She spread them out like she was making a snow angel.

"This is amazing," Claire said.

She tilted her head up. Mostly submerged as she was, the lake now looked beautiful. There was a rocky island not far off that seemed tinted with rust in the still-early-morning sun, and beyond it were two boats with bright red sails. Away from the flies, the mountains looked bluer and cooler.

"I bet it's incredible in the winter," Genevieve said. "There'd be snow on the mountains, and the sky would be deeper blue. And no bugs. Except of course you couldn't swim."

As they lay back, a waterbird flew directly over them, its thin, bent legs trailing the slow beating of its wings. Claire followed it on an imaginary line that split the sky as it moved toward some distant clouds in the west already piled high. They seemed suddenly ominous, and a fear took hold of her, and she stood up.

"Gonna get out already?" Genevieve asked.

The big man who had been floating with his belly above the water was wading toward them.

"It's the guy from the campground," Claire said.

Genevieve slapped the water as she got to her feet and stood next to her. Their clothes clung to their skin, and Claire could see Genevieve's narrow hips and small breasts. She knew she was similarly exposed. But as the man walked up to them, he was averting his eyes. His own belly was thrust well over his low-slung swim trunks where a tightly drawn string was digging into the flesh at his sides. He stopped about ten feet away and looked toward the beach.

"Morning, ladies," he said. "I just wanna say I'm sorry about last night. I shouldn't've come over after dark asking for a fee."

"Thank you for the apology," Genevieve said flatly.

The man nodded and still wouldn't look at them. He turned sideways to face the shore.

"I come out here most every morning in the summer and fall," he said. "You see folks like you, visitors, you know, floating on the water. Me, I come out because it's the only time a man my size feels light, you know? Buoyant. That's the word I mean."

He cleared his throat and licked some of the salt from his lips.

"You ladies have a safe trip, wherever you're headin'." He walked away without looking at them, and when he'd moved off a good distance, he slid into the water again, his face turned up to the sky and his eyes closed.

Genevieve touched Claire's shoulder and said, "Let's go."

They had driven into Wyoming by noon, stopping for coffee and blueberry muffins in one of the small towns. Claire had knotted their wet clothes to a rope she'd strung behind the cab of the truck, and so far none had flown away. Mostly, they hadn't talked, but as they entered the tunnels outside Green River, Claire yanked off her sunglasses.

"Wow. Can't see a damn thing," she said.

Out of the hot sun, the tunnel cooled the inside of the cab

and filled it with exhaust fumes, and they both rolled up their windows. When they emerged, Genevieve was squinting in the bright light.

"Nice while it lasted," Claire said, and cracked the window again. The bluffs and rocks along the highway were dramatic, but bled of color in the middle of the day.

"Getting closer to getting there, aren't we?" said Genevieve.

"Still a long way yet."

"Nebraska will seem closer. Flat. More like home for you."

"I guess that's true. It was my home for a while."

"It's funny. You leave on a trip like this only with your destination in mind, and only thinking about getting there, and what it will be like, and then along the way you start enjoying the road, and you wish you had another day or two of solitude with nothing to do but drive."

"Yeah, I know what you mean," Claire said. She had made it through the morning mostly without thinking of her mother and father.

"You think I'm being impulsive?" Genevieve asked. "Moving to Chicago like this with a guy I haven't seen in a year?"

"I don't know. It's not like you're trailing a moving truck behind you. It'd be pretty easy to change your mind."

"He's lonely," she said. "All those people in Chicago to remind him."

"Seems like all those people would make it a little less lonely."

Genevieve looked at her and smiled.

"Maybe," she said. "But not when he stops to watch couples walking along the lakeshore holding hands." She still hadn't rolled her window all the way back down, and she leaned her head against the glass pane. "I wonder," she said. "The guy back at the campsite. He was kind of lonely, too."

"I don't know about that, Genevieve."

"No, seriously. I have some sympathy for him now. Going down to the lake every morning. Floating on the water like that. Wanting to feel *buoyant,* like he said. I think he meant boy-ant. B-o-y. Like he felt when he was a boy."

"That doesn't make him lonely."

"No, I know. I bet if two women pulled into his little campground tonight, and slept in the bed of their truck, he'd walk over and then do the same thing. Maybe loneliness becomes something else once night falls. Or after you've been lonely for a long time."

"I don't know, Genevieve. He seemed a little creepy."

"Maybe he was a little desperate," she said.

"You can be both."

"I'm not trying to excuse him. I'm trying to explain him. Loneliness can be a pathology."

"All right, Professor." Claire realized Genevieve had two ways of speaking—one when she talked about herself, and another when she talked about others. But Genevieve smiled at this, took her head from the glass pane, and rolled down the window. She sat up straight.

"But it wasn't that kind of loneliness for your father, I don't think."

"Genevieve, we don't need to—"

"It's a long drive," she interrupted.

Claire tightened her hands on the steering wheel. They were passing a small lake where a deer was wading among the reeds in the water, and Claire glanced over as it lifted its head.

"Okay. All right."

"Do you think it's different, falling in love when you're older?"

"It was different when I fell in love with Jack."

"I don't mean that. You're still young. Your dad's over sixty. He falls in love with a woman he meets in the supermarket."

"That's certainly romantic."

"It's because he isn't looking, Claire. He only goes there once every two weeks because he doesn't need much. And on the lake where he lives is a little store that sells bait, some lettuce and tomatoes in the summer months, and some canned goods. More expensive, but he feels a loyalty to the old man or the local kids he hires who are usually behind the cash register. The woman at the supermarket is standing in the self-checkout lane, and he is waiting to go next, since he always checks his own groceries through because of his impatience with the cashiers and baggers who sometimes chat distractedly while scanning things."

"I remember that about him," Claire said. "His impatience."

"Is that right?" Genevieve said, and smiled. She sat back and let the wind through the car windows blow the hair away from her long neck. Claire already felt completely pulled in.

"She is staring at the checkout computer, holding a plastic bag of yellow delicious apples in her hand, trying to figure out how to scan it through. She's aware of your father's impatience, and smiles apologetically at him, and she tells him that she never buys apples, she just needs something that reminds her of summer. She's wearing a full-length wool coat, since it's a cold February in a cold winter, and she is pretty, maybe a few years younger than he is, her eyes made up, her hair cut short but over her collar, her earrings silver, catching light as they dangle alongside her neck. He tells her you have to punch in the code, that it's on the little stickers. 4-0-2-0. 'What, are you the store manager or something?' she says, smiling. He laughs lightly at this and tells her, 'I've been through this checkout line a few times.'"

Genevieve stopped for a moment, and turned and looked at the passing landscape.

"What was your father's name?"

"You asked me that already. It's Marc."

"That's right. And what was the name of the woman who called you on the phone and told you your father was sick?"

"Kathleen."

"Kathleen. She asks him out to coffee, which surprises him. She sits across from him at the small, round table, the late-winter sun streaming through a window, warming them. She does most of the talking, not because she's particularly chatty, but because, during these years of solitude, he's grown used to not talking to anyone, particularly women, other than his sisters."

"He does have sisters," Claire said. "Two of them." She again had the sensation that, as they headed east, they were driving back through the past.

"He's the kind of man who has sisters," Genevieve said. "Kathleen can tell that, too. But your father's unaware of it. He's watching Kathleen's face. He sees how she's penciled over her eyebrows, blackening them to match her deep, dark eyes, and in the bright light, through her makeup, he sees the tiny fissures in her skin, around the corners of her mouth, beneath her eyelids, and he's touched by her effort to conceal them. She has been married, she says, divorced now for five years, and he asks her why she still wears a ring on her left hand, and she tells him she got used to it, the weight of it on her hand, and when she takes it off, it feels like her finger will float away. 'I guess it's cost me a few dates,' she says, and laughs. She has two children, both grown, both married, a son and a daughter, but no grand-children yet. One lives in Detroit, the other in Pittsburgh, and she tells him she's accustomed to seeing them only a few times a year. And then she asks Marc about his own kids.

"The question takes him by surprise. He realizes he hasn't talked to anyone but longtime friends for several years, and they already knew the story of how Claire disappeared."

Claire felt her skin flush hot. Genevieve hovered over those words for only a few seconds before going on.

"Your father only smiles, searching for a way to respond, and Kathleen says, 'No children, then, Marc?' And he coughs once, runs his hand through his hair, trying to figure out what to tell her. 'No, I don't think so,' he finally says. Kathleen laughs at this, and tells him if he didn't know for sure, he must have been some kind of ladies' man when he was young. He likes the lilt to her voice, its suggestive wink, and he likes its depth, which reveals her years. He says, 'No, hardly. I don't mean it like that at all.' But Kathleen doesn't pursue him on it. She says, 'Well, I wouldn't be surprised. You're a very nice-looking man.' "

Claire pulled past a semi, and Genevieve stopped speaking as the roar of its engine poured through the windows. Claire's throat was tight, and she had to remind herself that this was only Genevieve's imagination working on her.

When they passed the truck, she asked, "You really think he wouldn't even tell her about me? That I was never his child?"

But Genevieve wouldn't look at her, and only put a finger to her lips as if to say "Shhhh."

"So, they start seeing each other," Genevieve continued. "And because they are older, because they both recognize the limits of love and its ultimately modest satisfactions, within a year they start living together, though they haven't married. She sells her home in the little complex she always found somewhat sterile, and moves in with him in the lake house. It takes several months for Marc to remember what it's like to habitually wake up next to another person, to feel the rhythms of her night-time rituals, of her sleeping, how she brings a glass of water to her bedside and wakes each night to have a drink, how she shifts onto her back and sometimes something catches deep in her throat, and she coughs. He thinks of the woman he slept with after he first left your mother, and wonders how this is different. For one, he loves Kathleen, and for another, she's sleeping in a place that has been his home for almost fifteen years. When he lies awake, listening to the sounds on the water—small waves rocking the boat along the dock, a distant splash when a fish jumps out of the lake—they're deeply familiar, unlike Kathleen's breathing. But he knows the chief difference between now and then is his age, and how each passing year of solitude has ebbed from an advancing need for company, in part to share a present with this woman he found charming and lovely, but mostly against the ravages of the years to come."

Claire wondered at how Genevieve could speak so fluidly, and how the Wyoming landscape they were traveling through was piece by piece supplanted by her father's house at the lake.

"After a couple of months, Kathleen's daughter phones and tells her that she's pregnant. The baby is born the following February in a winter that's been even more brutally cold, the small lake frozen with a full foot of ice that the fishermen have to auger for several minutes before they can open up a hole they can drop their lines through. Each morning, before driving into town to the office, your father lights a fire in the small wood-burning stove to keep the house warm, and Kathleen has taken a few days off from work to prep the house for her grand-daughter's first visit, even though she'd flown out when the baby was born. Your father marvels at how she has made the house her own home. It's early March, but still no sign of spring. On the morning before their arrival, a Saturday, he wakes with a start from a deep slumber before the sun has risen. He gets out of bed, pulls on socks that he's left by his nightstand against the cold of the floor, and walks out to the stove and fills it with wood. As he strikes the match, he realizes that what has wakened him is the recognition that he will have to hold this infant girl in his arms, and it will be the first time he's held a baby girl since Claire was born."

10

The wind through the flue of the chimney makes the flame flicker, but he has become an expert at lighting these simple fires, and a minute later the slivers of bark along the split wood are popping and crackling, sending shadows against the walls of the room because, after he woke, he'd turned on only the light above the kitchen stove, and he didn't even need that to navigate the rooms. He closes the door of the already warming wood burner, stands and brushes the bits of bark from his hands, thinks about starting the coffee, but doesn't want to make more noise that might wake Kathleen, since it's still an hour before sunrise, and he wants to sit alone for a while with the memory of Claire as a small child that is visiting him more sharply than it has in years.

He had been delighted when he'd learned of Kathleen's

daughter's pregnancy, and Kathleen had been effervescent, and inclusive, saying, "Ready or not, Marc, you're gonna be a grandpa." He had sidestepped the impact of that claim, had still not told Kathleen about Claire, which had never been his intention. But if he did not intend it, then what was the reason for keeping it secret? His sisters, along with the few friends he still had from his marriage to Lynne, showed discretion on the rare occasions where they were in Kathleen's company, though he was sure they assumed Kathleen knew about his daughter.

The rooms in the house are warming, and he pulls off the blanket he is using and sits back against the chair. In the year he's been living with Kathleen, he's grown heavier, surrendering his morning rows across the water last summer and fall so he could lie next to her in the early-morning hours. And for the most part, it's been too cold to go out and run in the winter months; he's grateful that it's March, even if the wind over the ice didn't feel like spring; there was more daylight now, and by late April he was hoping to see expanses of open water across the lake. He remembers how one spring he took the boat out and navigated the remaining patches of ice, how he'd managed to wedge it between two miniature icebergs, and had to climb out of the boat to free it, his weight on the ice letting the water rise to his knees, and he'd lost his balance and was lucky to tumble back into the boat without risking hypothermia.

Has he stopped missing Claire? He remembers how, at a year and a half, she used to reach for things, a wooden block, a leaf, and turn it in her hand while she gazed. He remembers her wide eyes when she was born. But when he thinks of her now, it is less about memory, less about the recollections of her childhood—he had almost no artifacts from that time, because Lynne had claimed them, no crayon drawings, no school pictures, no ribbons or gold-starred schoolwork—than it is about wonder over who she'd become; the bitterness he used to feel about her willingness to cut him out of her life so completely is replaced by additional wonder over her capacity to do it.

Outside, some light has returned to the sky, and the lake ice reflects it dully. There will be no visible sunrise: another gray winter day. As the room warms further, the smell of furniture oil deepens, since Kathleen had rubbed each piece yesterday evening, the finishing touches before her daughter's arrival. She phoned her once a week, usually Sunday mornings, followed by a shorter phone call to her son. He can see she carries them with her like charms, particularly those evenings when her work as a real estate agent has left her rattled, or those mornings when she wakes up and her joints ache, or the time she said to the mirror, *My face is gray.* Her family is a lean-to against what she worries are her growing limitations, and at last a solace against finality.

He wonders if he should have searched for Claire further. From time to time, in those first years of her absence, he'd track down a phone number or an address, but he wouldn't have described it as a relief to hear her greet him anonymously over voice mail. He remembered how he'd called Claire by mistake the night she was attacked, how Lynne had left a voice mail on his hotel phone after those weeks he'd fled to Pakistan, of all places, and when he'd pushed the number for speed dial, after the phone rang, it was Claire's voice that said *Hello,* and for a split second the nightmare of Lynne's message had lifted before Claire said, *You have reached . . .* After that, after she was out of danger, it had been okay for a few months while Claire healed. Then she'd disappeared. Those times he was able to track down her number, he tried not to sound despairing in the messages he left: "Claire, I'm not asking to know where you are. I'm not even asking to talk to you. But please, let me know that you're safe. Even if it's a one-line postcard. Here's my address at the lake . . ."

But after five years, he'd stopped trying at all. He assumed, if she'd died, news would have ultimately traveled back to him. He knew she was living somewhere, and in the long years when he would row the boat across the lake, particularly the cool September mornings when a mist hovered over the water, he'd imagine that with each stroke of the oars he was pushing into the fog where Claire lived. As the director of a homeless shelter, maybe, ladling soup into bowls held by children whose mothers had fled a dangerous home, or as a mother herself of three children, packing lunches in the early morning because she couldn't bear the food they were served at school, or as an expatriate, sipping coffee in a European café while she thumbed the edges of an underground newspaper for whose revolutionary whims she could no long muster enthusiasm.

She would be thirty-five years old in July.

The sky is brighter, and he can see smoke rising from the chimneys of the few houses on the lake where people live year-round. Kathleen is beginning to turn over in bed, slowly waking, and he pushes himself out of the chair and makes coffee. *Claire, how could you?* He's not thought that in months. Often, after she left, it had become a reflexive rhetorical flourish, usually unassociated with his memory of her. If he had a flat tire on his way to an important business meeting, he'd say through his teeth, *Claire, how could you?* If the Tigers lost in the bottom of the ninth, he'd holler at the television, *Claire, how could you?* Another bombing in Afghanistan. *Claire, how could you?* He'd caught himself saying it aloud only once in Kathleen's presence, and when she'd asked, "Who's Claire?" he'd told her one of his colleagues who had screwed up a proposal. She'd walked over then and rubbed the back of his neck and said, "Let's not start railing against ghosts just yet, okay, sweetie?" That moment was the closest he'd come to telling her the truth.

The smell of coffee invades the air. Outside, he hears his neighbor's feet crunching in the snow, and then the rattle of a trash can. From the bedroom, he hears Kathleen move again in the sheets. She's in that space between sleeping and waking where images of a dream collide with the coming demands of the day. She's yet to remember her daughter is visiting. Then she does, and he hears her pull the blanket away. He still loves the sound of her feet on the cool wooden floor.

"Well, look at you," Kathleen's daughter, Joline, says to Marc. "You're a regular Dr. Spock."

"A Vulcan?" her husband, Tom, says.

Kathleen laughs, and Joline punches Tom lightly on the shoulder.

"*Doctor,* not *mister,* sci-fi boy."

Marc had taken their coats when they came in, though everyone is still standing near the entrance of the house. He had met them both on only one other occasion, and that was in Pittsburgh, where Kathleen's entire family had gathered, so there had been opportunity only for small talk. Joline had been unselfconscious about the baby from the moment she stepped through the door, extending her arms to her mother with the swaddled little girl balanced in both hands, as if she were a nurse. When Kathleen hesitated for just a moment, Joline had said, "C'mon, Ma. You know you want it."

Now it is Marc's turn. He is surprised at how easily he has settled the baby into the nook of his arm, using his free hand to support her tiny head. He peers into the baby's face; her skin has patches of red, probably from exposure to the cold, and her eyes and nose and mouth are scrunched together in what appears to be a concerted effort at sleep. "Well, hello there, little Lulu," he says to her, hearing his voice crack.

Joline says, "Little Lulu. I like that. I mean, I love the name Laura and all, but it's a woman's name, and I've been racking my brain trying to come up with a nickname. I don't like Laurie. Or Lor-lor. Or the Lorax. Lulu might just work."

Joline is watching Marc closely, less, it seems, because she doesn't trust him with her child, but for another reason he can't discern. Perhaps, for her mother's benefit, she is trying to know who he is. Partly because he feels the weight of her stare, and partly because he wants to, he raises the baby toward his face and breathes in her scent: milky, sweetly animal, with a faint, underlying pungency. *Claire, how could you?* he thinks reflexively, but a current runs through his heart, and he pushes the words away.

"Don't tell me she's loaded up her drawers already," Joline says. She is still watching him. He's struck, then, by how pretty Joline is, despite their long drive, despite the trappings of motherhood, a bag slung over her shoulder, a loose blouse that can be unsnapped for breast-feeding. She has a narrow, pale face, and her hair, which she must have brushed out before they came in, hangs to her shoulders, and her large gray eyes are full of something under that wit she seems to use to meet the world.

"No, no, not at all. It's just—well, there's nothing like the smell of a newborn baby."

She smiles at him then and turns her head slightly. Tom has edged away toward the kitchen, and is peering in where Kathleen has already set a beautiful table: four Wedgwood plates that she'd brought when she moved in, polished silverware, and a spring bouquet of tulips and hyacinths that seem to almost pulse with color, surrounded as it is by the winter landscape.

"I'll tell you something that comes close," Tom says. "The smell of whatever you got cooking in here."

"Oh, those are meatballs," Kathleen says. "Turkey meatballs. We're trying to watch our calories here."

"Don't apologize," Tom says. "I go by the smell, not the kind of meat." He laughs to himself. "Sorry. That sounded kind of crude, didn't it?"

"Lunch will be ready in about ten minutes," Kathleen says. "Tom, if you want to take your suitcases upstairs to the spare room, feel free. We set up a little space heater. It can get cold up there at night."

Marc is still holding the baby, bouncing her on his arm slightly. She stirs, pushes her hand outside the blanket, and opens her eyes once, then closes them. Joline walks toward him, and he lifts the baby to her because he assumes she wants her back, but Joline brushes by him and strides into the living room. He follows her in. She's looking out the front windows.

"God, this is so beautiful," she says. "So desolate."

Because of the wind, or the lateness of the season, no one

is out on the ice. At its edge, the branches of the willow tree are waving wildly; most everything else seems brittle. Occasional gusts of snow move over the lake. A small bird careens between branches and finally takes shelter in a low, leafless bush.

"It is," he says. "And cold. Maybe all of us should be bundled up like this little one."

"Little Lulu?" she asks.

He laughs and says, "That's right. Little Lulu."

She looks out the front window again.

"The light's brighter now," he says. "Even on days like this, you can usually see the sun through the clouds. It'll melt the snow off the branches, and you can watch it fall away in chunks."

She smiles back at him. "Why did you decide to move here?"

The question surprises him. Not *when,* which he would have expected, but *why.* When he doesn't respond right away, she turns back toward him, and he looks down at the baby. She is awake, and her dark eyes are slowly taking in his face.

"I'm not sure, really. It was the end of a difficult time. And I spent a number of years on a lake when I was a kid. It's peaceful here. If you came back six weeks from now and looked out this front window, you'd hardly recognize the place."

"Well, maybe I'll do that," she says, grinning, it seems, almost flirtatiously, and she walks toward him and holds her hands out for the baby. He stands close to her and transfers the child to her arm. She exhales as she takes her, and he thinks her breath has the same scent as the baby.

"Where did you learn to hold these little runts? You're such a natural."

"My sisters' boys."

"I see," she says. "The doting uncle."

Kathleen calls them in to lunch.

"These meatballs are amazing, Kathleen," Tom is saying. "They taste almost like falafel."

"That's high praise, Ma," Joline says. "Tom considers himself the Sultan of Seasoning when it comes to Mediterranean food." The baby is asleep again in a portable bassinet near her feet. Marc has put on some Miles Davis that plays quietly under their conversation.

"You need those spices when it's just turkey," she says. "Marc loves this dish, so we have it pretty often. He lived in the Middle East for a while."

Tom says mid-chew, "Really? Which country?"

"Pakistan."

"Whoa. No kidding? What was in Pakistan?"

Marc says, "I'd say *lived there* is something of an overstatement. I was there a little over a month around fifteen years ago. On business, mostly."

"What business?"

Kathleen says, "Marc worked for Pepsi back then. They have corporate offices in Karachi."

"In Pakistan? I wouldn't have guessed that."

"A lot of American companies there," Marc says. "Even more today."

"Still not a top vacation spot, though," Tom says.

"Not for Americans, no."

"Only a month?" Joline asks.

"Well, it was supposed to be for half a year."

"Really? Why'd you come home so early?" Joline is looking at him with the same tilt of her head and slight smile.

"Homesickness," he says. And Kathleen reaches under the table and squeezes his knee, since he'd told her the reason he'd returned was because he couldn't bear the weight of his separation from Lynne in such a strange land. She tries to shift the focus of the conversation.

"I wish Jonathan and Diane could've come." Kathleen's son and his wife. "He hasn't even met little Laura yet. I guess it's a lot to ask to drive that far through the snow for just a night or two."

Tom and Joline exchange a glance. Joline pokes a fork at a few grains of the rice dish left on her plate.

"Ma, there's trouble in paradise for Jon and Diane right now."

"What do you mean 'trouble in paradise'?"

"Jon's a bit restless. I don't know. Maybe it's a seven-year-itch kind of thing."

"He's having an affair?"

Miles Davis chooses then to stop playing, and Marc stands up to put something else on.

"Where are you going?" Kathleen asks. Tom slices another meatball in half, and outside another gust of wind fills in the suspended moment.

"Just going to put on more music."

"Why? We don't need a soundtrack for this conversation." He's rarely heard her tone sound so arch.

"Ma, let him. Put on something with words, Marc."

He walks over to the console and chooses some old Dylan as Joline says, "I don't know that he's having an affair, but let's just say he's distracted by someone."

"Who?"

"I don't know, Ma. Someone he kept seeing at a coffee shop."

Dylan croons, *Mama, you've been on my mind,* as Marc sits back down. Joline directs her eyes at him for a half second, and mostly under her breath says, "Jesus. Great choice."

"Why hasn't he called me?" she asks.

"He knows how much you like Diane. And he hasn't even told her about this yet."

"Is it because they can't have kids?"

"Christ, no. Jesus. I don't think they ever wanted any kids, anyway."

In the ensuing silence, Tom slides the half meatball into his mouth and chews noiselessly. The fork makes no sound when he lays it on the tablecloth.

"This," he says, "might be a good opportunity for me to check the Michigan game. Care to join me, Marc?"

Marc watches him stand and smile, and then Joline says, "No, you stay," and he thinks she means Tom, but when he turns to her she's looking directly in his eyes. "Tom can tell you the halftime score."

Later, he wonders why she asked him to sit and listen as she and Kathleen talked it through. He'd contributed nothing to the conversation, had absorbed the occasional glances that Kathleen gave him, who seemed to search his face for understanding of her son. Joline was sure that her brother and his wife were heading for divorce.

When Kathleen asked her why, she said, "I don't know, Ma. Once you walk down that path, I think it's hard to walk it back. Some people can have affairs, and then just accept them as part of the long journey to the grave, maybe even a kind of protest against it, and forgive themselves. Not Jon. I feel sorry for him. And Diane. But I'm gonna support him. He's not Dad. He's not only like Dad. He's like you, too."

After that, the baby had woken, and before lifting her out of the bassinet, Joline had unabashedly unsnapped her blouse and her nursing bra and exposed her breast. With the baby latched on, Kathleen stood to clear the dishes, her face pale.

Now, Joline says, "Thanks for staying," while Kathleen loads the dishwasher in the kitchen.

"Why'd you ask me to?" Marc says, though in truth she hadn't asked.

"She needed you here, I think. She's told you about my father?"

"Some."

She nods. "You remind me of Jon a little."

"Why?"

She pulls the baby off her breast, re-snaps her blouse, and then switches her to the other side. "There you go, little one," she coos, and she closes her eyes and hums a few bars of a song. "Because you know what it's like to hide a secret sadness."

Then Tom comes in from the living room and says, "Indiana thirty-seven, Michigan thirty-four at the half."

Toward evening, as he'd predicted, the wind dies down, and Tom wants to take a walk out onto the ice. The wind has formed a frozen crust over the top of the snow, and when they step across the yard toward the willow tree, Tom's shoe catches the edge of one of his footsteps, and he stumbles, and Marc has to grab hold of him. He tweaks something in his shoulder breaking Tom's fall, and while Tom brushes the snow from his knees,

Marc works his arm to loosen the muscle. The pain lingers in his chest.

"You all right?" Tom asks.

"No problem. The old shoulder socket isn't what it used to be."

"Sorry about that. How the hell do people walk across this stuff, anyway?"

"Snowshoes. Cross-country skis. Or you get used to it. It'll be easier out on the ice. The wind helps keep the snow levels low, and the lake has more exposure to the sun."

Marc lets Tom lead the way. He walks well out toward the middle so they're standing under the dark-blue dome of the sky, the clouds filtering the remaining light after sunset. Marc realizes he hasn't come out this far all winter. Tom holds his arms out and spins in a circle, and it's easy to see the kid in him.

"This is kind of amazing," Tom says. "It's like you're at the bottom of a huge crater."

"That's true especially this time of the day."

With the wind down, there's a dampness in the air that smells like spring.

Tom asks, "So, uh, how was the table talk earlier?"

"Not particularly pleasant."

"Yeah, I figured that was the way it would go. Sorry you missed the game."

"I admit, I was surprised Joline asked me to stay."

"She's that way sometimes. I don't understand it, and I don't try to explain it. She probably thought you being there would soften the blow."

"Probably."

The air is damp enough that he can briefly see the mist from Tom's mouth when he laughs.

"You know, even Kathleen will get nowhere with Joline if she sticks up for Diane at Jon's expense. She takes no prisoners when it comes to shielding him."

"Why's that?"

"Don't get me wrong. Diane's a fine woman. You met her?"

"Just the one time in Pittsburgh."

"That's right. Then you know. She's beautiful. Not hard at all to stand on the beach with her in her bikini during family vacations. Sorry, but true. Otherwise pleasantly, smartly suburban. Content, I think. This will rattle her, but I doubt it will tear her apart."

"Yeah? Be best if it worked out that way. Wasn't so lucky myself."

"That right?" Tom looks up at the sky and spins in a circle again. "But you say a word against Jon in Joline's earshot, that March wind you had wailing out here this afternoon? Be like a June breeze."

"I gathered they were pretty tight."

"You gathered? Sometimes I don't know where one begins and the other ends."

"No kidding?"

"No kidding. You got sisters?"

"Two."

"Close?"

"When we were children, sure."

"This is a different story. She made it clear early and often who the principal man in her life was and would be. I got it. I can roll with it."

Tom again looks up, and arches his back with his arms spread. He closes his eyes and smiles.

"What's he like?" Marc asks. He is remembering Joline had said Marc had reminded her of her brother.

"Who, Jon? A little aloof, you know? Brooding. Not without a dark sense of humor. Good-looking, too, like every damn cousin twice removed in that family."

A shadow passes over Tom's face, and he opens his eyes. He straightens his back and looks at Marc with a thin smile.

"Thanks for walking me out here. It's quite a place. A little center of the universe."

"Thanks. I've always thought that myself."

Tom stares back at the house where the windows are shining a deep yellow.

"Jesus, it looks like a Christmas card."

He takes a single step toward it, and then turns back and looks at Marc.

"I don't think I'm made for this," he says.

"For what?"

"For fatherhood. You got no idea how it changes things."

And then Tom walks back toward the house, trying to step lightly so his shoes won't break through the crusted snow.

Marc's unable to sleep. The nights he can't aren't unusual anymore, and have become more numerous since Kathleen has come to live with him, though he knows this one is not about the rhythms of growing older, but about Tom and Joline sleeping upstairs, the baby between them. And about Kathleen, who is walking the difficult balance of her sadness over her son and her joy over her granddaughter, two rooms that have opened inside her that she doesn't yet know how to fill. And, if he's honest with himself, it's about Claire's ghost, which he imagines with its face pressed to the house windows, outside in the cold, wanting in, wanting to hover over the infant girl and the sleeping mother and father.

He takes another sip from his cup of tea, lifting it to his lips with his left hand, and he sees the liquid in the cup tremble as if it's frightened, a response to a slight tremor in his arm that he's begun to feel over the past half year and about which he's told no one. The heat from the wood-burning stove envelops his chair, but he knows the other rooms of the house are cooling, and he's lived in them so long that he feels them as his own extremities. He remembers how, as a small boy, he would sometimes wake late in the evening, and walk into the living room where his father would be sitting on one end of the couch, smoking a pipe. Once, Marc had stood for what seemed a long time, watching his father take a pinch of tobacco from a pouch, and then tamp it into the pipe with his forefinger. He'd popped the cap of his metal lighter, and then worked the tiny wheel near the flint, slowly, as if he were contemplating it, and when he finally had flicked it to ignite the flame, he'd stared at the small fire for several seconds before bringing it to the tobacco in the pipe and the pipe to his mouth. He drew on it to make sure the tobacco burned, two spurts of smoke coming from the corner of his mouth, and then took the pipe from his mouth and turned his wrist to glance at his watch. Now, Marc glances at his own watch, and wishes he had the rituals of pipe smoking to fend off his loneliness, and he understands that his father had checked his watch not only because he was calculating how much sleep he was losing, but because he wished to wed his rituals to the increments of time passing, which, at an hour of desperation, were the only things that made it bearable.

He hears the slight creak of the floor upstairs, and, because he knows the house so well, figures that Joline has risen to change the baby's diaper. But then she walks out of the room, and he hears, without turning his head, her descend each stair, and counts each till he knows she's reached the bottom. He shifts in his chair and looks at her. She's wearing a white gown with rows of some kind of floral pattern that is difficult to discern in the dim light, and she stands with the baby in one arm, turning at the hips to rock her though the baby seems sound asleep. She stares at him for a few moments, and he sees again the depth of her gray eyes, and then she walks over and sits down in the chair adjacent to him.

"Couldn't sleep?" he asks. He reaches for the pipe, then, realizing how deep his reverie about his father had been, picks up the cup of tea instead.

"Not well," she says.

He lifts the cup toward her and says, "I'd be happy to make you some tea."

"No, thank you. Thanks for asking, though."

He takes a sip and looks at her over the rim of the mug as she stares at him, sleepy-eyed, but levelly. He has to look away. She glances down at the sleeping baby, pulls a corner of her flannel blanket away from her mouth, and then looks up at him again.

"So I was up there sleeping. Dreaming," she says.

He does not like to hear about people's dreams, or interpret their subconscious stories from the fragments of memory and desire that arrange themselves according to a substructure that, to his mind, is no more illuminating than patterns of crystal in a stone. Kathleen loves to recount her dreams, and he is not surprised her daughter would, too. So he asks, "What was your dream?"

She looks once at the woodstove, where only an ember or two still burn visibly through the small door, then out through the front window into a starless night where the whiteness of the snow has always seemed to capture some light from a source he could never discern.

"You were in it," she says, and waits to observe the effect of that statement on him. "But a lot like you are now, how you were all afternoon and evening, really. Passive. A bystander. A man standing in a bus shelter overhearing an argument between lovers."

"I don't know you," he says. "I don't know your family's history. It's not my place to offer insight or advice when there's trouble for your brother, who I've barely met."

"What about Kathleen?" He is surprised she uses her mother's name.

"She and I will talk later, I suppose. Tomorrow, after you leave."

She nods, looks down at the baby, and rocks her once or twice on her arm.

"I always wanted a sister," she says. "And in the dream I had one. An older sister. And it was strange, because I had memories of our childhood. I could remember in the dream how she would want to dress me up as her own daughter, and she'd have me sit at a tiny table where only I could fit, and she would make in her toy oven, you know, a small tea cake that she'd sprinkle with powdered sugar and serve to me on a plate like she was a waitress at a fancy restaurant. Then she'd pour a mug of warm water from a little teapot that she said was very hot, and tell me to be careful."

She looks up at him, and then out toward the lake again.

"It's so dark out there. You'd think it would make it easier to sleep," she says. "Anyway, in the dream, I had that memory, and others, but I also knew I'd never met my sister. And then the little room where she was giving me a tea cake transformed, and we were here, only the lake wasn't frozen, or pretty and small like this one, but a kind of ocean or sea, except you could see to the other side, like a lake, and you were sitting in your chair here and my sister came in right through that front door."

She points toward it, but he doesn't need to turn his head to look.

"And then she walked right up to where I was standing, like where I was standing when we were looking out at the wind blowing the snow off the trees this afternoon. She was taller than I was, and she didn't say anything until she took my hands. Then she only said, 'Joline, I've missed you so much.' And she squeezed my fingers and pulled me closer to her, and lowered her head and kissed me on the mouth. She let her kiss linger there, and when she pulled away I saw you watching us, only you were crying."

She looks over at him, but he's unable to meet her eyes.

"I woke up then, and knew you were down here, sitting up."

He stares into his cup, and catches a slim reflection of his glasses on the liquid surface.

"Marc. What was your daughter's name? She was your daughter, wasn't she? Not a son?"

He feels his face go hot, and his eyes water. But he manages. "Yes."

"What was her name?"

"Claire."

"Claire," she repeats. "That's a pretty name. Is she dead? I'm sorry. I mean, did she die?"

He swallows hard, and his voice sounds outside of him. "I don't know, Joline. I don't think so. But I don't know for certain."

He expects her to ask why, but she doesn't just yet, and only nods, staring at the floor, her eyes glassy. She remembers the baby, and blows very gently into her face.

"I don't want her to get too warm." His own hands are cold.

"How did you know?" he asks her.

"Well, the dream," she says. "But when I first came in. And I handed Laura to you. You didn't hesitate. And—well, there's something you can see when a man holds a baby. Or at least I can see. It's like the light in the room changes if he's had a child of his own, like it's, I guess, refracted by his memory as it gets close to his skin. Some men look happy, some look sad, depending on their experience since the time their kids were babies."

"How did I look?"

She has been gazing at the baby's face while speaking, but now she looks up at him and seems to be taking him in.

"Like you do now," she says. "Like a hostage. How old is Claire?"

"She'd be almost thirty-five."

"And how long has it been since you've seen her?"

"Fifteen years."

She shifts forward in her chair then, and holds the baby to her chest and rises to her feet; she takes the few steps over to him noiselessly, and when she stands over him, her hair frames her face in the darkness so he can't see it, and she lowers the baby into his arms. He takes the baby as she wakes and turns her head, opens her eyes, and briefly looks into his own, and then closes them and settles in. He feels her warmth at his chest. Joline walks back to the chair and sits down.

"I can see it again. Even with the lights out. You're captive."

He shuts his eyes against the emotion.

"Why haven't you told my mother?"

"I don't know why, Joline. I really don't."

"How close were you and Claire?"

He thinks about it, thinks through the images of her he can hold in his mind; he can no longer discern how the edge of a memory is altered by the time since. He loved her curiosity when she was only three, and she'd be running down a sidewalk when a bird lit on a wire overhead, and she'd stop almost midstride to look, her straw hair falling to one shoulder as she cocked her head sideways, her lips parted in thought, and the color in her cheeks rising with interest.

"You have so much to look forward to," he says to her, and coughs to keep something from rising in his throat.

"What do you mean?"

"I mean yes, we were close, when she was still small."

"What happened to her?"

"She was injured. Hurt. She'd been stabbed, and we thought she'd die. But she recovered. It took months, but she did get well. And then she left a little note for her mother and me, and disappeared."

He can smell the sweet, slightly musky scent of the baby again, and reflexively starts to raise her to his face, but he resists. Joline has been sitting with an arm on each rest of the chair, as if she were piloting something, but now she crosses her arms over her chest.

"You can have her back if you're getting cold," he says, but she only shakes her head. She takes in a slight breath, as if she's about to say something, and then decides against it. But the air between them, if possible, has gone even more still.

"I have another child," she says. "Fathered by a different man."

She turns her head and looks into his face, her eyes dark.

"How old are you, Joline?"

She smiles slightly. "What a strange question to ask. I'm twenty-nine."

"I'm sorry. You just seem so young."

"Only a few years younger than your daughter."

"Does Tom know?"

"He's not the kind of man who would want to."

"And your mother?"

She shakes her head.

"Why are you telling me?"

"I'd think that'd be obvious."

He looks down at the baby again. "What happened?"

She watches him holding the baby, and he realizes that unwittingly, he's been rocking her slightly.

"I was so in love with his father. The baby's father. I was only twenty-three, and I know you'd probably laugh if I weren't sitting right here in front of you when I say that I believed then that I knew all there was to know about love."

"I wouldn't laugh."

"Well, I might. Not that loving Tom has deepened those waters. I guess it's made them wider."

"I think I understand that."

"Yeah?" she asks, but isn't waiting for an answer. "My brother didn't like him. And that mattered to me, of course."

"Tom told me that your brother mattered to you more than anyone. More than any other man, anyway."

She looks away. "I guess that's true. But he did not like him. He thought he was dangerous. Or reckless, I think, was the word he used. And that turned out to be true, you know, but I don't mean because I became pregnant. Probably I wanted that. Secretly I wanted that. To secure some part of him. And I don't mean to keep him in a place, or to keep him with me, because that was something I wouldn't do. Or couldn't do."

He watches her thinking about this for a few moments. It is strange that, while her bringing the baby into his home had brought Claire near, he was having a conversation unlike any he'd ever had with his daughter.

"Did you give the baby up for adoption, Joline?"

"Yes." She turns toward him then, but seems to be looking past him back into the night. "It was a challenge to keep the pregnancy hidden from Kathleen. And Jon."

"That was something the father wanted, then."

"No. No, he didn't want that."

"Well, then, did he run away?"

"No. It's funny. As reckless as he probably was, he didn't know how to do that."

"What do you mean?"

"Well, he was reckless, but not irresponsible. He took risks, but that was because he was young, and he believed in his— I don't know what to call them. He believed in his little crusades. When he found out I was pregnant, he was overjoyed. I don't think he'd once thought of being a father, but when I told him, and even I wasn't sure I wanted to keep the baby then, it's like you could see his face fill with the possibility, like he was already pushing a five-year-old boy on his bicycle down the sidewalk, and telling him he was about to let go."

"So what happened? What do you mean by *little crusades*?"

She shakes her head, and looks away, back toward the kitchen, and the way the remaining light strikes her face makes her look older.

"I shouldn't have used the word *little*. It just seems that way now, now that I'm, you know, living this suburban life with this husband and a newborn baby. It's like that was something that was inevitable all along."

"It's still not inevitable."

She gives a short laugh. "Now you sound like him."

"Who?"

"My child's father."

"What was his name?" But she shakes her head again.

"That was one of his 'go-to' phrases. *Nothing's inevitable.* And he meant the way people live as if tracks have been laid in themselves, or through them, is what he said, and so they have no choice but to follow them. But he meant it politically, you know. He was a Marxist. He believed revolution was possible. I think he missed the point."

Marc looks down at the baby again. Her eyes are open now, but she still seems to be sleeping, since they are the only parts of her moving. She is swaddled tightly.

"So what was the point?" he asks.

"I mean the way he believed tracks are laid in you. They're not political, or they are only after the fact. I fell in love with him. And I was happy at the time, before I met him, you know, having graduated college, and getting a good job. But after I met him— on the street where he was wearing a dark wool jacket, and directing protesters who were staging a walkout for higher wages. I mean, to tell you the truth, I never thought twice about that. About the rights of workers, the rights of the poor. Just abstractly. And I wasn't thinking about it when I stopped to watch for a second, and he turned, suddenly, as if he knew I was there, and when he saw me—he had this kind of scruffy beard, and curly hair, and an earnestness or resolve that slowly disappeared into this beautiful, warm smile, and he was only taking me in, you know? He was taking me in, and it wasn't about me picking up a sign or chanting for a cause. He was seeing me. I thought he was seeing me."

She glances at the baby, and then pulls herself up in the chair and tucks her legs under her, so she is sitting higher, her back erect.

"I miss that. I still miss that. That sense of being seen. By someone you hadn't even come to know yet. I know it sounds naïve."

"Not really."

"No? I'm not so sure, Marc. Something primitive led me there. Something that happened before I could find the words to describe it."

"Why didn't he want the baby?"

"I told you, he did. It was me that didn't want him. He was killed. By an angry union worker in a truck. Manslaughter. He wasn't trying to hit him, just get him to move. And he wouldn't."

"I'm so sorry, Joline."

"It's not about his death, Marc. It's not about his death. He doesn't matter anymore, except in memory. It's about what became of me. It's about what became of that little boy, who would be six now. It's about Laura, who has a brother she may never know."

She pushes herself up from the chair then, and walks over to him, and he lifts the baby, who has fallen asleep again, toward her arms, but she shakes her head and stands next to the chair, looking down on him, her face obscured again by her hair. He feels a tightness in his chest, like his heart is catching on a rib, as she places the palms of her hands over his eyes.

"Keep them closed," she says.

She pulls her hands away and places them on the arms of the chair, and even with his eyes closed he can sense her shadow over him as she lowers her head toward his. When she kisses him, his head moves slightly, involuntarily, and she brings her hand to the side of his face, but the kiss itself is gentle, lingering, her lips warm, tasting of something both of them had eaten earlier in the day.

Then she says, "What do you think happened to Claire?"

He is still absorbing her kiss.

"I don't know. I've thought of a thousand things. Why did you kiss me like that?"

But she smiles and shakes her head, and then takes the baby from him.

"Good night, Marc."

The next morning, she is again the young woman who first came through the door, and he has slept later than he usually does, and she and Tom and Kathleen are finishing their coffee and English muffins when he walks into the dining room, the suitcases already sitting at the front door.

"Hey, sleepyhead," Joline says, her eyes bright. "Up late?"

"Yeah, a little."

Tom says, "I took the liberty of starting a fire. Hope I didn't overheat the place."

"It feels nice and warm," Marc says.

Kathleen's expression is difficult to read.

"They have to leave a little earlier than planned," she says. "Tom has to work on a project for tomorrow morning."

"A call came in before you woke up," he said. "Not the big deal they're making it, but gotta put a little Sunday-evening time in."

They sit with Marc at the table for maybe fifteen minutes out of politeness. The baby is awake, and her occasional coos, her wide-eyed accidental smiles, her clutching of Kathleen's pinkie finger, occupy both Kathleen and Joline, and neither gives him much more than a glance. Tom has pushed his chair away from the table and leans back and watches with an expression of halfhearted amusement. *It gets better, kid,* Marc wants to say to him, but doesn't.

At the back door, while Tom brushes away the snow blown onto the windshield, Marc stands with Joline and Kathleen while they say good-bye. Kathleen gives her a long hug, and Joline lets her mother hold the baby one more time.

"Don't worry, Mom. We'll be back before you know it. Or come down and visit us before the real estate business cranks up."

They chat a bit more while Marc carries the suitcases to the car. Tom lifts them into the trunk but leaves the lid up and glances at Marc with a half smile.

"So I understand you and Joline had a little late-night conversation."

"She tell you that?"

"No. I woke up and saw she'd taken Laura down with her."

"Yeah. She let me hold her for a while."

"She likes it here. The baby, I mean. Joline, too. It's peaceful. We're in an apartment on a busy street. Weekends get pretty rowdy with the college kids. We'll have to move once Laura starts walking."

Tom lifts his hand to the lid of the trunk.

"So Joline tell you her life story?"

Marc glances into his eyes, and then shakes his head and looks down at the ground.

"No? Well, she's pretty free with it. I know more of it than you probably think."

Tom slams the lid of the trunk, and then puts an arm around Marc and gives him a fast hug.

"Thanks for having us out. I'd like to come out again soon."

"You're welcome anytime."

Joline walks with Kathleen out to the car. For the first time that morning, Joline looks fully into his face, and then she reaches for him and gives him a tight hug, the warmth of her body coming through even her winter coat. She pulls away slightly, with her hands still at his waist, looks at him, and then hugs him again.

She turns away for the baby without saying anything to him, and then gives her mother a kiss on the cheek and one final good-bye before walking to the car, settling the baby in her car seat, and joining Tom inside. They wave as they pull away.

Back indoors, the day brightening the rooms with a pale March sun as they both clear the dishes from the table, Kathleen says to him, "I guess it was a nice visit. Yesterday was a little hard."

"It was good to have them here," he says. He knows they will speak about it later, and perhaps Kathleen will call her son, Jon, and tell him about her conversation with Joline and ask about his marriage. And then afterward, Kathleen will come out of the bedroom and sit in the chair where Joline sat last night, and they'll talk it over for a while. "She's an interesting young woman," he says.

"Interesting?" Kathleen lifts an eyebrow and gives him a half-cocked smile.

"Yeah, interesting. There's a lot to her. She's her mother's daughter, isn't she?"

Kathleen waves her hand at him and goes on loading the dishwasher. And after that, they are quiet for a long while, returning to the rhythms of their winter Sundays on the lake. They read the newspaper and drink coffee. Kathleen watches a gardening show while knitting, the quiet tapping of her knitting needles a comfort that Marc recognizes stretches back into childhood, when his own mother used to knit Christmas scarves for him and his sisters. Marc looks through a magazine for a new boat he might buy when the lake thaws, makes a soup for them that afternoon, and splits a little wood for exercise, though they have plenty to last them through the cool nights of spring, and he stops anyway after fifteen minutes because of the ache in his shoulder. He watches the birds at the feeder, and again thinks about taking up sketching, especially for the stark contrasts of the whites and blues and blacks of trees and houses and ice in the winter. The later afternoon feels warmer, damp, and still, and he thinks for a while that Claire's presence has gone away with Joline and the baby, but as the sky dims with sunset he feels that chill again.

Because of his restlessness, he tells Kathleen, "I'm going for a little walk out on the ice."

"Wow. Twice in two days. I don't think you were out there at all before this weekend."

"You might be right."

"You want me to come with you?"

"No, that's okay. You look comfortable where you are." She is sitting in her chair with a book, her legs folded up in a way that makes her look young.

"It seems like it's nicer out there today."

"Yep. Warmer. Spring's almost here."

His footprints from yesterday alongside Tom's have deepened with the slight melting that had occurred in the afternoon, though the thin crust of brittle snow has returned now that it is almost nightfall and colder. He listens to the pleasant and familiar crunch of his boots on the ice as he makes his way to the place he and Tom had stood. His conversation with Tom at the car had unsettled him—he wondered what Tom may have overheard last night. Marc looks up at the sky, and it is the same cobalt blue as yesterday, though lingering from the sunset is a shade of warm orange. He glances back at his home and sees the windows lit. He touches his fingers to his lips and remembers Joline's kiss. Her mouth had been so warm. He still can't understand why she'd given it to him.

He remembers a time, years ago, when he'd walked out onto the ice to watch the sunset. He'd learned from all his seasons here to watch for cloud formations that would lead to bright colors, and that evening the sun had turned the sky a brilliant blood orange, and the ice and the snow and even the cottages along the shoreline were drenched in it. Alone out on the lake, he'd wanted to call out to someone to come and look, come and see, but the only other person on the ice was a fisherman at least fifty yards away, and they'd given each other a brief, awestruck wave and together watched the sun descend. At the time, he had seen the orange sky as perhaps a sign, construed for him alone, and he'd remembered Claire, thought then that soon he might hear from her. But he'd been wrong.

This time of the evening, it's easy to imagine the lake before any home had been built on it, and he squints so as to obscure the cottages with the trees. Now he stretches his arms out and spins once as Tom had last night. Even that single circle makes him slightly dizzy, and he has to catch himself with a half step to stay on his feet.

When he walks back into the house, he hears Kathleen in the next room on the phone. He assumes she's talking to Joline, or perhaps she'd called her son, Jon. Marc settles into his chair, and warms his hands by the stove. He's reading a book when Kathleen's phone call abruptly ends, and she comes into the living room and stands in front of him.

"What is it?" he asks. She doesn't look angry, but her eyes are narrowed, as if she's trying to see into him.

"Joline told me she kissed you last night. On the mouth."

He feels his stomach drop.

"She did. She kissed me. She asked me to close my eyes."

He has no idea why he offers that detail, but he can't bear Kathleen's gaze.

"She told me you have a daughter."

For a moment, he's petrified.

"Marc, look at me. She said her name is Claire."

11

When Marc woke, he first remembered Josephine's story of Claire and Genevieve driving down the highway, and asked himself, *Did that happen?* The phrase returned to him when he lifted his head and watched Saabir rise from his mat over the threshold of the door. *Did that happen?* Much as the phrase *Claire, how could you?* returned to the version of Marc in the story that Genevieve told. That Josephine told, though he knew her name wasn't Josephine. He found himself wondering again if she was a woman at all.

He laid his head back down, and Saabir glanced over at him and said, "Up. Time to eat." Saabir finished rolling his mat, set it neatly in a corner of the room, and opened the door and walked out to get the food.

Did that happen? Marc with an imagined live-in lover who had discovered he had an estranged daughter. It was the blindfold he had to wear as Josephine spoke, he thought, as much as anything. As a boy, he had played the game with other children that began with the question, "If you had to choose, would you rather be blind or deaf?" and he'd chosen blind because he couldn't imagine not hearing his mother's voice when he asked her a simple question, such as "What are we having for dinner tonight?" But now he wondered how reality was shaped for those who couldn't see, who had to trust those who could for the naming of things, for the laying out of the world. An image returned to him of Joline holding the baby that late winter night, an image that was not real, and how the baby, too, would have to trust others for the naming of things, no less helpless, ultimately, than any child. Than he was himself when blindfolded. Than Claire had been. Had been, because she was dead. She was killed. Yet those words, even as he almost whispered them to himself, still seemed unreal, more inverted because of the stories Josephine had told, and suddenly he saw Claire at age six, playing with magnetized letters on a metal board, creating random arrangements of imagined words—*czelim, erintel*— until she turned the board toward him and the letters read *She is dead. She is killed,* and he woke again with such a start that he immediately sat up on the mat.

And yet, still, in the imagined house on the frozen lake, he held to the mystery of her disappearance, to Kathleen, who may share in that mystery, and the possibility Claire was out there; he thought he would have given his life, here, in Pakistan, so that she and Genevieve could go on driving east.

He felt cold, felt he wanted to hold Joline's baby to warm himself. He tried to stand up, and had to catch himself against the wall because he was suddenly light-headed. The walks around the perimeter of the building had done little to maintain what he considered the already waning strength of his limbs. His head cleared as he heard the muezzin call for the morning prayer; he remembered the story Josephine had told about the girl in high school.

When Saabir came back through the door, his gun strapped to his shoulder, he brought a bowl of mashed fruit and cereal, and then motioned to the chair. Marc walked over and sat down; Saabir cupped his hand under the bottom of the bowl without holding the rim as he held it out to Marc, as if it were a kind of offering, and along the edge of his forefinger Marc saw a faint spattering of dark fluid.

"Azhar," Marc said, looking up at Saabir, who was still standing in front of him. He remembered Azhar's despair the night before as he rested the barrel of his gun against the back of Marc's neck, but, likely because of the storytelling, last night seemed a week past. Saabir was smiling, his mouth slightly open, his eyes in the rising morning light dark and beautiful.

"Today, no Azhar," he said. The phrasing seemed ominous.

"What do you mean, no Azhar?"

But Saabir had learned enough English to turn the sentence around.

"You know Azhar?" Saabir asked him, his eyes still on his face. "Do you know Azhar? Marc?"

That was the first time Saabir had used his name, and Marc could no longer hold his gaze.

"You know Karachi?" He took the gun from his shoulder and tapped it three times on the ground. "You know here. Here. Room."

"What happened to Azhar?" Marc asked again.

Saabir shook his head and smiled, pulled the gun back over his shoulder, and tapped his temple with his fingers, as if he were signaling for Marc to think.

"You have a son, Saabir? A boy?"

Saabir's eyes narrowed, but he looked more troubled than angry.

"Josephine told me."

"Josephine," Saabir repeated.

"And a wife who died."

He half expected Saabir to reach back and strike him, and he did lift his hand, but instead he brought it to the side of Marc's face and rested his fingers for a few seconds on his cheek, and then patted it slightly.

"Girl," Saabir said. "Marc's girl. Died."

Marc felt the familiar cut in his diaphragm.

"I want to see Josephine," he said.

Saabir took his hand away and stepped back and smiled, and Marc belatedly recognized the irony of his statement.

"Eat," Saabir said. "Josephine after."

But it was long after. When he'd finished the cereal, Saabir walked him around the small perimeter of the two buildings; rarely did he see anyone in these slow, ten-minute walks, and he realized now this was likely by design; he might get a glimpse of a long-limbed boy through a narrow space between buildings when they came around to the door again, but he was always at least fifty feet away, and never turned his head to look at him. And there was the man he saw in the next building the one time, and the empty cups of tea. But when he was inside the room, he often heard people passing by. Many must have known about him now, but he was unable to hold that knowledge as comfort. He was thinking less and less of Lynne, and more of Josephine, and Claire as a woman, and himself as a lonely man who Joline had said was a hostage, as if this were a destiny no matter if Claire lived.

Through the extended afternoon he sat up on his mat and thought of them. The day was particularly warm, and even sitting still, sweat dripped from his face and into his lap. Saabir alternately sat staring at his feet, or sweeping up only the dirt that his broom raised, or stepping outside, Marc assumed, to escape for a minute or two the rising suffocation of the room. Saabir spoke only when he brought in his noon meal.

Marc understood that Claire seemed the least real of the

people that Josephine described. In his telling of his own memories of her, she had grown increasingly vivid, and the ache in his stomach as he spoke had slowly developed a knife's edge that only eased when Josephine began her storytelling. He still couldn't grasp its purpose. Could not get the point. Why should Claire seem less formed? Because he'd known her? Because he loved her? Because she'd died? Josephine had described her as someone who wished she could choose a day that her life would begin, and Claire's more distant memories, at least of her childhood, seemed to pass through her like a sieve, and only Genevieve's story of Marc at the lake house seemed to take root in her. And why should that concern him? It was all an invention. It was preposterous. There was something horrific about the entire construct. But Josephine's voice, deepening slightly as she narrated her tale, was the only thing that soothed him anymore, and any apparition of Claire if she had lived was better than—what exactly? *Don't let her die,* he thought. And yet, she was dead.

For the last two days, toward evening, a shaft of sunlight angled through the small upper window, and the beam now slanted half a foot above Saabir's head, and the rectangle of light on the floor seemed almost brilliant in the darkening room. He remembered a year after his parents separated, where he and his mother and sisters lived with his grandmother. On the wall adjacent to the dining room table, where each night he sat to do his homework, there was a small stained-glass window that would brighten near sunset on the few winter nights that were left undimmed by clouds. He had tracked the progress of the light across the glass for weeks, how a blue rectangle would brighten at a certain hour, and then a few days later, the yellow one next to it as the sun arced higher across the sky through the lengthening days. Even in June, when school was out, he'd find a way to escape his friends—their pickup ball games in the field near the well house, their cooling swims in the nearby murky lake—to sit in the chair at sunset, and his mother began to worry over him, asking why he would come in to sit alone after dinner when there was another hour of daylight to play outside.

He was waiting for something—though he was unsure of what, perhaps the return of his father, whose face he was struggling to recall—when, the last day of June, the sun found a particular sliver of the sky, and shone through the glass so that a patch of colored light was cast on his chest where he sat in the chair. In his mind, it was as if he'd stopped time, and he thought to call in his mother, but wanted to keep the moment for himself, and for five nights afterward on a brilliant stretch of sunny days the square of light traveled up his chest and was finally cast on his face, warming it slightly through the heavy panes of blue and yellow glass, until, two nights later, it disappeared altogether.

Now, he watched the rectangle of light travel up the far wall, narrowing with each minute, as if it, too, might in time bring a revelation. When it had become the width of a flashlight beam, he heard her knock on the door.

Saabir pulled the chairs so they were facing one another in the now familiar ritual, and Marc rose to his feet without being prompted and sat in one of them, and then Saabir bound his wrists and wrapped the blindfold around his eyes.

When she came through the door, the sounds outside were briefly amplified: someone's footsteps on the street, and what sounded like a cart with a broken wheel being dragged through a distant alley. He realized part of him had been waiting for the call of the muezzin and the sunset prayer, but it had yet to come. She said a few words to Saabir, and closed the door. He wasn't certain, but he thought Saabir was still in the room, and Marc listened to her settle her garments as she sat down in the chair.

"How are you tonight, Marc?" she said. He again felt her voice as soothing, and he knew that he would have trouble resisting it.

"Not much different from how I was last night," he said.

"Really? After everything we told each other?"

"I'm not always sure of the purpose of what you're telling me."

"I'm not, either, if you can believe that."

"Well, you rarely hesitate. You rarely stumble on a word."

He heard her shift on her chair, uncross and recross her legs.

"Has Azhar been killed?" he asked, and was struck by his tone of resignation.

She didn't respond immediately, and then said a few words in Urdu. Saabir was still in the room, after all.

"If I told you no, would you believe me?"

"To take away a father from his children, I don't care the cause—"

"Don't. Listen to me. I'm telling you no."

"What did you say to Saabir?"

"I told him that soon I would be asking him to leave."

"Can I see Azhar?"

"No. You won't see him again."

He opened his mouth to say something, but remained silent. She said a single word to Saabir, who responded with a word of his own that sounded half-spit, but he opened the door to walk into the evening. When he closed it, the call went out for the sunset prayer.

Marc asked, "When he leaves like that, and he hears the muezzin, where does he go to pray?"

"You're assuming Saabir is necessarily devout," she said.

"I asked him about his wife and child."

She was quiet for a moment, and then said, "The time is coming where we may have to move you. It may be far away, and I may not be the one speaking to you anymore."

"Why?" He heard the note of desperation in his voice.

"Because, as I've told you, I don't coordinate things here."

He felt hollow inside.

"Have you remembered another story you can tell me about Claire?"

Before an image could invade his mind, he said, "Josephine. Joline's story is your story, isn't it?"

"Shhhhh," she said. "Tell me a story you remember about Claire."

Something rose in him without the effort of recollection.

"The last—" He had to clear his throat against a tide. "It's strange, you know." Because he had to think past the story of the time of Claire's healing, and her leaving the note, and her running away, but this he didn't say. "The last time I saw her. It was like something out of a movie, if you can believe that. It was maybe a month before the phone call I told you about."

"When she said, 'You shouldn't have kissed me'?"

"Yes." He was quiet for a moment, thinking about that.

"Tell me about it."

"I told you already that the time of that phone call was just after I'd moved into an apartment. A month and a half. And when I saw Claire, I'd been in it maybe a week. It was early December, out in the street in the city, and it was late afternoon, but seemed closer to nightfall because of the shorter days. There were a lot of people out on the sidewalks, but it was colder than hell, and they were walking fast to get to their bus stops or into the stores. The light posts were already wound with those tiny white lights, and the display windows framed with ribbon. I don't know how it is for you to feel heartbroken, but for me, it—" He stopped for a half minute, and Josephine didn't speak. "For me, it made the world more alive. Closer. Raw. I remember feeling this cynicism. At the orgy of buying going on in those streets. And the next second, I remember almost weeping at one of the shop displays where a gold ribbon was strung above a child mannequin's head like it was a halo. I thought it was so beautiful. Before I saw Claire, I was standing near a bell ringer. Someone working for the Salvation Army, an old woman. She did not seem right all the way, you know? There was something fixed in the smile on her face, and her eyes seemed vacant. She was probably half-frozen. But a few people were dropping in coins. And I remember standing there, imagining how cold those coins must feel in people's hands, and how much colder they were sitting in that kettle, and I was fingering a dime and a quarter in my own pocket, and not feeling particularly charitable, and then suddenly wanting to empty my wallet for the strange woman. The coins in my hand were cold, too, and I said to myself, 'Well, I think I'll give my coldness away,' and I remember thinking—like it was an epiphany, and it wasn't—that the source of all charity was not a human warmth but instead a need to distance yourself from the cold, and then my eyes glazed with it, and despite myself, I saw a beautiful woman coming around the corner across the street."

He could feel himself sweating, and he could hear himself

breathing in the odor of it. Each time Josephine came to see him, he was increasingly aware of the smell of his body, which had grown worse even though he washed up in the mornings with the basin half-full of stale water.

"I wonder if you'd wipe my face," he said to her.

He heard her stand up. He thought he heard her lift a corner of her garment, and she started with his forehead, and, with a light touch, worked around the circumference of his face, then under his eyes, and down his neck before she sat back down.

"Thank you."

When she turned back to her chair, her clothing moved the air over his skin.

"So, like I said, my vision was blurred. But, like everything else that afternoon, her beauty seemed vivid. Striking. I wanted it closer, and ran my coat sleeve over my eyes, and saw that it was Claire. And I thought I was losing it, then. For a few seconds, I thought I was falling apart, hallucinating, and I was terrified. But it was her. And she *was* beautiful, but not in the way I'd first seen. She was walking with her arms wrapped around herself against the cold, no gloves, in a navy-blue coat. She had a wool cap over her head, but I could see her red hair falling to her shoulders. Her eyes were focused on a spot on the sidewalk always a few feet ahead of where she was stepping. I guess I was transfixed. Her expression from that distance—I thought it was troubled, but why wouldn't I? She looked pale, but she was always pale. And then a man walked into that space in front of her, and she glanced up at him, and she smiled with—well, people call it a radiance, but it was actually that way—and then I saw her mouth the words *Excuse me,* and she reached up and tapped the man's shoulder as she passed. And it was only then, after she touched him, that I thought to say her name. My jaw was tight with the cold, and I probably said it barely audibly at first. By the time I said it with a shout, she was already heading around another corner.

"But she heard, and she slowed and looked back. I couldn't tell you if she saw me. From that distance, you can't tell when someone's eyes meet yours. But she kept on going. There was a lot of traffic on the street. By the time I'd crossed over, she was gone."

He heard Josephine stand up again, and again she wiped his forehead, and ran the garment in precisely the same motions she'd used earlier, as if it were a ritual she'd been observing for months.

"Thank you," he said again. But he was feeling the knife edge in his gut. She was sitting in silence in front of him. He was under the blindfold. Claire was turning the corner. She was turning the corner. He called her name again. She looked back. She was turning the corner.

"I want to see your face," he said quietly.

She sighed, but it sounded more like she was blowing a candle flame to make it flicker.

"Marc, you know that will never—"

"I want to see your face," he interrupted.

"I'm going to tell you about Claire and Genevieve now."

"No," he heard himself say. "I want to see your face."

"Marc—"

But he was standing up. "I want to see your face," he said more loudly.

"You have to stop this."

He took a step toward her voice, and almost stumbled, and when he found his balance, she brushed against him but stepped away.

"I want to see your face!" He was shouting now.

"Marc—"

"I want to see your face!"

Then Saabir came through the door and put two hands hard to his chest and pushed him, and he sprawled across the floor, and he knew she had gone, but he was shouting, "I want to see her face!"

"No face," Saabir said. Marc rose to his feet and charged at the voice, but Saabir had moved, and he slammed into the wall.

"I want to see her face!"

"Who face?" Saabir said, mocking him. "No face."

He again ran at the sound of it, and Saabir caught him, wrapped him in his arms, and pushed him to the floor with his mouth to his ear.

"You die? You die now? Who face?"

But now he was shaking, shaking, and the sobs were working their way up through his throat, and he thought he would vomit. "Her face," he said. "I have to see it. Please, please let me see—" And he could not stop it then, saying over and over, "Her face, her face," and everything he'd ever known about her, about anything, was coming up: *"Dad, I don't want your help." "But if you just shift the paper this way—I don't want your help!" On Lake Michigan, she was lifted by a heavy wave and went under. "She's drowning!" Lynne shouted. "No, she's not; she's learning how to swim." He was a boy, and his mother was an hour late from the store, and he was alone in the house, and a panic rose in him. Later, she ran her hand through his damp hair. "What were you afraid of?" "That something happened." "That what happened?" But he could not tell. Claire was sprinkling brown sugar over the entire surface of her bowl of oatmeal. "You trying to make candy out of that, kid?" "Yep. I like candy." Lynne, so small when he first knew her, lay with her head on his bare chest and her nude body stretched out the entire length of him. "Do you think this will last?" "What will last?" "This. This. The incredible comfort of this. Me lying on top of you like this." At seventeen, Claire took a black-and-white photo of herself, and her expression, under black freckles that seemed overexposed, was a kind of amused confusion, as if she weren't certain the camera would work properly, and when she hung the photo on the wall, she said, "That's my all-time favorite picture of me." Just before she asked him to leave, Lynne had said something uncharacteristic, and she was holding a glass of orange juice when she said it, the sun pouring through the kitchen window. "Mornings shouldn't feel like this. Not morning after morning." "Like what?" "Like a shroud. This November sunshine feels like a shroud." Claire wanted to play the whisper game. "The whisper game? We haven't played that in like two years. Since you were maybe nine." "I know, Dad." It was a game where you spoke in the other's ear in the faintest voice possible to see if the other could still discern the words. The angles of her face were becoming more like a woman's. She put her mouth to his ear. "I like boys." He had heard her, but he told her he hadn't, so she repeated it again, with a half-suppressed delighted laugh at the end. "I like boys."*

And then he felt Saabir whispering in his ear, still lying on top of him, pressing him to the floor. But he had not used his gun. "Stop now, Marc? Stop now?" He felt himself trembling under him, and was cold, though he knew the room was still certainly too warm. "I get up," Saabir said, then something in Urdu. He used Marc's shoulder for ballast and pushed himself to his feet. Perhaps Saabir had dropped the gun, because Marc heard him checking it, releasing the safety, and then reengaging it. He heard him kneel down again. Saabir said, quietly, "Last time, Marc. Yes?" Then he untied Marc's hands and removed the blindfold.

Because Marc had been sweating so profusely, and had been pushed down onto the half floor with the hard-packed dirt, his arms were streaked with it, and he imagined his face was the same. Saabir was looking down on him, but must have felt no threat, because the gun was on his back. When Marc sat up, Saabir walked over and took Marc's bedroll from the corner, and laid it out along the wall where he usually slept.

Marc did not bother getting to his feet. His shoulder ached from the hard fall, and he crawled over to the mat and lay flat on his back. Saabir stood over and looked down on him. His expression was almost sad.

"No face," he said. "No Josephine."

And then he took the gun from his back and tapped the near wall with the barrel, and Marc knew he should turn to face it. Fortunately, the shoulder he lay on was the one that wasn't aching. He was still trembling, and his body smelled foul after the struggle. He felt as if something had spilled out of him, that he'd lost blood. The run of memories seemed bled out of him, too, as if pooling somewhere, part of him, but somehow now apart from him.

He did not expect her knock on the door, and he flinched when he heard it. Saabir pulled the door open, and he heard them exchange words that were increasingly heated. He slammed it shut and strode over to the makeshift bathroom, and then walked back to Marc and said, "Sit."

With difficulty, he pulled himself up, and Saabir stooped and handed him a cup of water and a damp cloth. He hadn't realized how thirsty he was, and he quickly drained the cup and took the cloth and wiped his face and hands. Saabir again took the gun from his shoulder, but this time held it in his hands for a moment. Then he tapped the wall three times. Marc turned toward it.

He heard Saabir step back to the door and let her in, and she pulled the chair close to his mat and sat down. The room was deeply quiet, with Saabir, he imagined, standing with his back erect at the door. Marc could hear her sitting nearby, hear her steady breathing before she began.

"That night, Claire was once again lying on the thin mattress of the truck bed next to Genevieve, staring at a starless sky."

"Josephine," he said. "Maybe it doesn't matter anymore."

She didn't respond immediately, but didn't go back to her story, either.

"Maybe it doesn't," she said. "Maybe not to you. But it matters to me. It matters to Claire."

"Claire is dead." Even saying that, there was still something hard in his throat he had to swallow back down.

"Marc, you could turn and look at me now. That would be the end, but our time will end soon, anyway. As soon as tomorrow. So you could turn and see my face."

He thought to ask if she would be the one to kill him, but he didn't.

"I don't want to see your face."

She shifted on the chair then. He imagined she was lowering her head.

"But you want to hear the story, don't you?"

"Yes."

12

Claire had found a place to sleep that she imagined was safer, the parking lot of a nearby elementary school that was hidden from the main road in a small western Nebraska town just over the border. She'd pulled in near a streetlamp, but she'd parked the car outside the circle of light it cast. Genevieve had been sleeping for the last hundred miles, through the dark, flat land where moths obliterated themselves in the headlights.

Her face had been turned toward Claire, since she slept curled up with her seat belt unfastened against the cool air that came through the windows. In the light of the dashboard, Claire couldn't decide if, sleeping, Genevieve looked older or younger than she was. She decided older, and over the course of several miles, she glanced over at Genevieve's full mouth, which she imagined again would be pleasing to kiss, and then at her ears, which were unmarked by any piercings. Her nose seemed delicate, almost like a child's. But mostly she remembered her gray eyes, a match for that kind of August afternoon where, out of nowhere, a cool, windless day emerges and a heavy bank of clouds sinks low. She thinks it's the kind of face that someone could look at for a long time. Not for minutes, or even days, but for weeks and years.

Now, after unrolling the mattress, as they lay again in the truck bed, staring at the blank sky, it occurred to Claire that the air was heavy with moisture.

"Do you think it might rain?" she asked Genevieve.

"I don't know," Genevieve said. "I guess we'll be the first to know, won't we?"

"I guess so." Claire tilted her chin up, waiting for a drop to fall. It wasn't surprising that she felt thick with a sense of expectation. The story Genevieve told about her father had carried to her a version of him that she couldn't have imagined. While it was true that images of her mother and father crossed her mind on occasion over these years, she had tried to sweep them behind her. It would be easy to close her eyes now and see the interstate stretched out before her, and to envision her father or mother hitchhiking as Genevieve had, only she would not pull over, and she would see them as shrinking dolls drawn into her rearview mirror.

But the tale that Genevieve was telling was something else again. She wondered about Joline, and whether she might be

someone Genevieve had once wanted to be. The immense still-
ness of those rooms in her story—and a winter landscape that
Claire hadn't seen in years—had expanded inside her as Genevieve spoke, and she felt the sad serenity her father had earned
begin to peel away under Joline's gaze. But the strangest thing
was how Claire haunted him. How Genevieve described her as
outside in that cold wind at the windows looking in, and how, as
Claire listened while driving, she was inside that infant daughter
gazing up at her father's face.

Everyone she'd ever loved had formed stories of her they had
translated as the truth, but she knew they were only founded in
those parts of her that she chose to reveal. But this was different. None of this had happened; all of it was Genevieve's invention, but because of this, she felt her presence in her father's
rooms, in Joline's baby, not as something to remind her father of
his past, but as someone who was waiting, just as he was, for a
revelation that might never come. It was not a story that you
could outrun, like you could a person, or a memory of someone
you once loved. If Genevieve disappeared tonight—if, while
Claire was sleeping, she climbed out of the truck bed undetected
and slipped down the highway—she thought the story would be
like a thick haze through which only slowly the other things of
her life would emerge, and the memory of the haze would cling to
those things for a long, long time.

She had called home too late to talk to Lucy. Even
though they'd eaten at a diner with a pay phone, and even

though Genevieve had long before that set aside telling the story of her father, Lucy had slipped her mind, while instead, she was thinking of the baby that Joline, in Genevieve's story, had given away. She'd promised she'd talk to Lucy each night she was gone, and she'd told Lucy that when she arrived in Michigan she might even get to speak for the first time with her other grandmother. But sitting across from Genevieve, who was describing the life she imagined she'd have in Chicago, she'd lost track of time. When she did call, and talked to Jack, Lucy was long asleep, and she explained to him, lying, that she had forgotten to anticipate the differences in time zones. "Well, it's later where you are," Jack had said, and Claire felt her face go hot. "But she's fine," Jack reassured her, though with perhaps an edge to his voice. "She fell asleep on my mother's lap practically in the middle of a sentence." Claire asked, "Does she miss me?" She heard Jack sigh into the phone. "Of course she does. She can't go ten minutes without saying, 'Mommy does it this way; Mommy does it that.' But she hasn't shed any tears yet."

That "yet" lingered with her as she walked back toward the booth, where Genevieve was pushing a french fry through the ketchup she'd poured onto her plate. Claire had thought fleetingly that this was a little like falling in love, how, those few times she'd experienced it, the people and habits in her life that had before seemed essential and stabilizing were now in the way, and she wanted to cast them aside to get a lasting and unobstructed view of the only one she loved.

Now Genevieve shifted in the truck bed, turning from her back to her side, and Claire felt the edge of her hand on her right shoulder.

"Can I ask you something?"

"You know you can."

"When was the last time you saw your father?"

Claire thought about it.

"Well, of course, I saw him when he'd come and take care of me. When my mother couldn't. Before I moved away. But there was another time, before I was—"

She found herself staring at the streetlight where moths were fluttering about, and she could hear them lightly bumping on the bulb; it was strange that that was the only sound she could hear—no crickets, no bullfrogs, though a creek ran through a dim wooded area behind the school—other than Genevieve's breathing.

"This isn't something I'm proud of. It was right before that awful year when I was hurt. I saw him on the street around Christmastime. I was on my way to meet my boyfriend. It was so cold, and I was underdressed, and walking fast. I'd talked to my mother a few days earlier after ignoring her calls, but there were so many of them I finally picked up, and she'd told me she'd left my father. I had a moment where I felt like I was falling. It was as if you went out for a bike ride and when you came home you saw that all the windows of your house were rearranged. But I shrugged that off. I wasn't thinking of either of them at that time. I thought I was headlong into my own life, and I didn't care then that I was a little out of control. I liked it.

"Anyway, I'd gone around a block and was heading down another. I heard a man shout my name, and I turned in his direction. There were a lot of people along the street, and cars passing, but I could see it was my father. He caught my eyes for a split second, or at least I think he did. It was hard to tell from that distance. But I didn't want to see him. I didn't want to talk to him. He always seemed wounded to me in some small way, and now, after my mother had just left him—besides, I wanted to get to my boyfriend."

Genevieve's face was bathed in the amber light from the streetlamp. There was a lit sign in front of the school that read, *Last Day of Classes: June 13th. Have a smart summer!* The parking lot was empty and the building dark.

"I spoke to him one more time before I was hurt. But the time I was—well, when I was attacked—that was when he was in—" She felt an icy realization pass through her.

"Genevieve?"

"Yeah?" She was still staring up at the sky.

"In the story you told. About my father. And Kathleen and Tom and Joline. And the baby. When they were at the table eating lunch. How did you know my father was in Pakistan?"

Genevieve's expression didn't change, but she did close her eyes for a second or two before opening them again and staring upward.

"It was kind of a guess. But I'll tell you how I guessed if you'll tell me something."

"How could you guess a place like Pakistan?"

"You wouldn't believe me if I told you."

"*You wouldn't believe me* seems like a funny thing to say after everything you've described to me."

"I was there for a while. Not for long. Six months or so."

"Why?"

"I'll tell you that story if you'll tell one to me."

"What story do you want to hear?"

Genevieve finally turned away from the sky, shifted onto her side, and looked back at the building. She said, "Can't you just see all those kids running out of here on the last day of school, with their backpacks stuffed with pictures and projects they'd forgotten to bring home earlier in the year? My mother would take me and my friends out for ice cream, and she'd sort through my pack, admiring everything I'd done. I used to love that. What's today, the sixteenth? It was only three days ago for these kids. They're already becoming their endless summer selves."

"Not endless," Claire said.

"No, but it seemed like it back then, didn't it?" Genevieve fell back against the thin mattress with her fingers crossed and under her chin. She looked like a child, and this didn't suit her. "You probably already know what story. The one about this scar." She reached over and found the place and touched Claire through her T-shirt. "Of the time you were attacked.

How it happened. And who you were with. And who did it to you."

"I really don't want to tell that story. I don't think I've ever told it to anyone. Even Jack."

"I know. That's why it's the one I want to hear."

Claire looked at Genevieve's face. There was a slight smile on her full lips, and she was staring at her without blinking.

"Just tell me part of it," she said. "The first part. Then I'll tell you the rest of Marc's story, and while we're driving you can tell me the rest of yours. Do you think we'll make Chicago by tomorrow night?"

"There's a chance. It's a long way. But maybe before midnight tomorrow."

"So this could be our last night."

"That's right."

"Then start telling me your story, Claire."

Claire rolled over onto her back and looked at the dark sky. With Lucy and Jack seeming so far away, Genevieve was now the only one who stood between her and this reunion. She tried to imagine standing at her father's bedside, his gray head on a pillow. Her mother's aging face.

"I was living in a tiny apartment in the city," she heard herself begin. "It wasn't, you know, a nice place. If you turned the lights on in the middle of the night, you'd see roaches scurrying under the spoons or saucers you left out. And in January, the cold came through the cracks in the walls, and you had to walk around in sweaters with your shoulders wrapped in a blanket. I remember one cold snap where we brought in a thermometer, and the temperature inside read forty-nine degrees. We took a photo and sent it with the rent check to the landlord, but of course he never did anything. We didn't expect him to. I don't think we were even outraged. Spring was coming, after all."

"Who's *we?*" Genevieve asked.

"I'm getting to that. It's my story, isn't it?" She smiled, and glanced at Genevieve, who nodded her head and smiled back.

"But I loved that little place. It was the first apartment I ever had, the first time I'd ever lived away from my mother and father. It was in this anonymous, square, yellow-brick building. I guess you could call it university housing, or something like that, because it was near a college, but the people who lived there mostly weren't college students. A man in his seventies lived in the apartment below me. He'd come up and knock on my door if I played music too loud, but never in a mean way. He called me *Clairekins*. He'd say, 'Clairekins, your music isn't so bad, but it's so loud.' He brought me a tin of cookies for Christmas. And there was a Vietnamese family who lived two doors down. They didn't hang curtains over their windows, and when you came up the walk toward the building, sometimes you could see them eating dinner, with chopsticks and everything, through their front window. I remember thinking it was so much better than TV. And a woman who lived on the first floor who'd set up a small patio outside her kitchen window. Each afternoon I'd come in from work, she'd say, 'Hello, beautiful!' which, at that age, surprised me every time. One spring day she asked me to sit next to her in a lawn chair and have a glass of wine. She told me she was married once, and that she lived in the country with her husband. And she said the thing she missed most was hanging laundry on clotheslines. She loved to see the wind billowing her sheets and her husband's white shirts, particularly when the sun was bright and they seemed to blaze like the robes of the holy. She used that exact phrase. *The robes of the holy.* I always remembered what she said about laundry. Did I tell you I used to hang my daughter's diapers on a clothesline behind the hotel?"

"Yeah, you did."

She thought about it. She realized she had her eyes closed. "Are you sure I told you that?"

"Uh-huh."

"Anyway, my neighbor and I had our glass of wine. And that was a time I was drinking a lot. With the man I was living with. I couldn't tell you why now. It's not like I was trying to numb myself. Or somehow overthrowing the memories of a painful childhood. It tasted good, then. And at night, you know? It made it easier. I was only nineteen. I was still used to thinking of my body as a child's in some way. I remember how we'd sit across from each other almost every night. At this small dining room table we'd dragged home from Goodwill. It had metal legs that someone had painted with a thick, green paint, and this For-mica top that was supposed to look like wood, and two matching metal chairs. It was probably patio furniture, but that never oc-curred to me then. We had a bottle of whiskey on the table be-tween us, and two shot glasses we'd found at Goodwill, too, mine with Betty Boop and his with a hunter's hat. Who would make a shot glass with a hunter's hat?

"Anyway, he started calling me Betty, and I started calling him Hunter, which I think he liked. His real name was Seth. He was young, too, twenty at the time, and not much more worldly than I was. So we'd sit across from each other, and our first shot glass we'd sip. We'd talk about our days, the silly details. At the time, he was working unloading trucks in the market district, and he'd tell me how he was shifting crates of lettuce when a chicken came from behind one of them, and his boss ordered him to capture it. Then he'd describe in great detail how he had to chase it around the back of the truck, and how they had to close the door behind him so he could corner it. Those silly kinds of stories. I don't know if they were even true. I was working in an Asian market that sold sandwiches to college students, and I was in charge of making them. I don't think my boss understood half of what I said, but he always smiled at me, and he paid me well, under the table."

She heard something scurry near a trash bin next to the school building, and flinched.

"It's nothing," Genevieve said.

"I thought the guy from Salt Lake was making another appearance."

"That'd be something, wouldn't it?"

Claire was remembering.

"So we'd sit at that table and sip that first shot of whiskey. And for a long time, each time seemed like the first time, if you know what I mean. Like we were friends, or on a first date. We'd talk about the chicken on the loading dock, or the sweet old man who came into the market all stooped over and ordered the same sandwich every day, or how Seth saw a falcon flying above one of the city's skyscrapers, or how sometimes I could wash the smell of onions from my hands, and sometimes I couldn't. And we'd sit at that table each night, and he'd say, 'Can I smell your hands?' and if the scent of onions was there, you could see his face—and he was beautiful in the way boys that age are. He looked feminine. I mean his face did. Narrow. An almost delicate, thin nose, and a shy, sideways smile. Wet eyes. But what I mean is that when he would smell my hands, this sense of relief would pass over his face. As if he were thinking, *Okay, now I know you. Because of the onions. Now you're familiar again.* And then he'd pour us another whiskey into each of our shot glasses, which we'd drink faster. Because what we were really doing was trying to get to each other's body."

Her skin was flushed warm with the memory, and her scalp was tingling.

"We'd have four or five drinks like that. One after the other, and somehow we'd know when it was the last one, and we'd look each other in the eyes before downing it in a single swallow. And then I'd reach across that metal table for his hand, and we'd pull each other to our feet. I'd feel the whiskey burning in my veins, in my throat and stomach, but, you know . . . it didn't hurt or make me sick because I knew what was coming. I knew that meant that we were going to the bedroom. It made me excited. By the time he pulled me down onto that beat-up mattress, I was almost panting.

"At first, it was the way it always is when you're young. I was so hungry for him. Any part of his body. I wanted my mouth on it, or I wanted it in my mouth. Of course, we were drunk. I remember once I was kissing his legs. His thighs, his thick muscles. And then I started kissing his knee. This will sound silly, but he had beautiful knees. And I guess I was trying to—see it with my lips, too, and my tongue. The way the bone was rounded and how if I opened my mouth at its widest I could almost hold it inside. I mean, it was his knee. And then the slope just below that that led to his shin. I followed that with my tongue. And the dimpled spaces on either side. And the filaments of hair there. After a while, I felt his hand on my head, and he said, 'You okay?' I probably had been obsessed with his knee for five minutes. But it would be his ears another time. Or the small of his back. Or his rib cage when he lay back naked with his hands behind his head."

She heard Genevieve's steady breathing beside her, but she knew she wasn't asleep.

"I knew I was troubled. I mean, not because of the sex, or even the drinking. My head wasn't right, and my mother and father and the doctor said I wasn't right. They worried that I was depressed, that I was bipolar, that I suffered from schizophrenia. I said stuff like, 'Look at the schizophrenic world. I'm taking its cues.' But the thing was, I knew. I knew it. I knew how I always felt the dark half of the world was screaming at my door. And then with Seth's body—for a while all that mattered was that. I endured the day to get to the table and sit across from him and drink, and then I endured the drinking to get to our bed."

Genevieve said, "For a while?"

"I'm getting to that. And it went on that way. He was taken with my body as much as I was taken with his. He would linger over my belly. He'd breathe in the scent of it, deep breath after deep breath. He'd lift his fingers to his mouth and get some saliva on the tips, and then he'd rub it into the crease behind my knees. And then he'd kiss those places. And all of this lasted for what seemed like a long time, probably into February. But, you know, even when you're that young, that level of fascination has to turn into something else. You can't live in that narrow space, even though I wanted to.

"At that age, I considered myself political. You know, angry at the hypocrisy of the world. There was the war in Afghanistan, and I'd go to protests, but there'd be maybe twenty people at those protests. Mostly older people carrying signs and waving at those who honked their horns in support."

She thought for a moment about the man at the rest stop eating his sandwich with his wife, and how he'd chided her for losing touch with her father.

"And I was outraged. Not so much at the world, you know, but instead that I had to live in it. But in that time with Seth, those first weeks, I would hear the radio. In the little market where I worked, we kept it on. I'd hear the reports at the top of the hour of civilian deaths, or drone strikes. And I'd shake my head, but I'd be shaking my head into a grin. Thinking of him. The way the winter light struck his chest that morning. Like that boyfriend you described with the shadow of the snow falling on him, remember?"

"Sure."

"Everything else seemed like a cartoon. Except then, you know, it shifted. Like it always does. We'd still do our little evening ritual. Sitting at that table and talking, sipping, and then swallowing those full shots of whiskey. And taking each other's hand. But when he was inside me, and we were making love, he started talking to me. I mean, I know that's what people do. I even knew it then. But it was the first time for me. And the things he would whisper to me were gentle at first—about how much he loved me, about how it felt so good, about the smell of my skin when I was excited—but then, after a while, the things he said became, well, there's no way to describe it but to say they got more violent."

Saying this made her pause for a moment. She listened to the moths battering the streetlamp. Not a single car had passed along the road that led past the school lot in the time she was speaking. She could distantly hear the cars along the highway a mile or so away, and their rushing past sounded like a faraway wind, but the air wasn't moving at all. She had to remind herself they were just over the Nebraska border. She was on her way back to Michigan.

"It's so ungodly quiet here," she said. "I mean, it's June. We're out in the middle of nowhere with trees and grass and this empty school. No crickets, no katydids. I'd love to hear an owl, or something."

"Maybe they think it's going to start to rain."

"I don't think everything goes quiet because of the rain."

"I guess not. But sometimes it seems that way once you start to hear it fall."

She turned her head and looked at Genevieve.

"You're right about that. It does seem that way." She couldn't see Genevieve's eyes in the shadow cast by her head, and felt herself wanting to. "Why don't the moths disappear if it's going to rain?"

"They're distracted by the streetlight."

"Ah. You have a kind of answer for everything, don't you, Gen?"

"Not really. What did you mean by *violent*?" Claire remembered Genevieve's questions the night the fat man had come to their truck when she'd told the story about her family's dog that killed the chickens.

"He would talk to me. He'd tell me the kind of things he would do to me. It wasn't particularly dramatic at first. About how he was going to tie me down so I couldn't move, and then how he'd gag me so I could barely breathe. Or how someday when I came home from the shop he was going to meet me at the door and knock me to the floor and tear off my clothes and take me from behind. Those kinds of things."

Genevieve, who had been listening the whole time with her hands folded under her chin, now turned away and ran her fingers along the edge of the truck bed, but didn't speak.

"But even then, I didn't think much of it. We were drunk, and it was exciting. They were fantasies, and I knew about fantasies. To speak them out loud—well, I loved words enough back then. They seemed new to me, too, at least when Seth was saying them. It was a kind of thrill—the words close to what we were doing in the bed. I don't mean close to describing what we were doing in bed. I mean close as in proximity. As if when he gave them a voice they were wrapped around us almost as tightly as our arms and legs.

"But then—I don't know. I don't know why. It got darker. We were drinking more. We'd finish half a bottle of whiskey between us. I think both of us were pushing to see what would come next.

"I'll tell you one story that I remember, Genevieve. I try not to think about it, not because it's horrifying, or anything, but because in some ways I've wondered how it affected what happened next. I don't know. I'm not superstitious, or anything. But when you are making love—when a man is inside your body, and you're wanting him to come inside you harder and harder—and then there are these words in the air that are so close to you, like I said, well, the words become more real, like a physical presence in the room. It was like they wanted a life of their own. And that's why I think I was hurt, that's why I think I was attacked. Does this make any sense?"

Genevieve was still turned away from Claire, propped up on an elbow, the top of her head silhouetted against the pale night sky. Claire couldn't see her face.

"Maybe. I'll let you know when you tell me what happened next."

"Well, like I said, I'll tell you one story. We were both really drunk. I mean way over the line. He was lying on top of me and had his face pressed hard to mine, and I could feel how his whiskers were chafing my face, but that felt good, too. I was staring at the spinning ceiling, that lone bulb turning in its socket, and I was trying not to feel sick.

"And that's when he started talking to me, though it was almost like he didn't care if I was listening. He told me we were downtown, late at night, walking hand in hand. We'd seen a movie, and we were going back to the car, and I was wearing tights and a short black skirt. And that the whole time we were watching the movie he'd been sliding his hand up the tights and under the skirt and fondling me, so the cloth between my legs was already damp. And as we were walking, he was holding my hand, only he was also using his fingernail to lightly scratch the skin on my palm, which is something he knew I liked. And we wanted each other, he said. So badly that even though we were only a few blocks from the car, we slipped into an alley between buildings that had a closed end. He told me how he pinned me against a wall, pushing me hard, first, so my head hit the bricks, and then he'd yanked my tights off of me, and lifted me up and then I'd wrapped my legs around him while he flattened me against the wall. He was pulling my underwear to the side so he could enter me, he said. And just as he was about to do that three other men turned into the alley and caught us there."

She stopped and found herself listening again. She imagined she heard footsteps, but it was only the story. Something like a soft pellet struck the asphalt outside the truck where they were parked.

"Did you hear that?"

"Yeah," Genevieve said. "I think it's a raindrop."

"Did you feel any yet?"

"A couple."

"Do you think we should go inside before the skies open up?"

"I don't think they're going to open up."

Just then a raindrop hit the roof of the cab.

"You sure about that?"

"No, but I think we can wait. Keep telling your story."

Claire lay flat on her back and waited to feel the rain on her face, and continued. "So Seth kept talking to me as he was pushing inside me. He told me that the men were drunk, just like we were. And he told me they were laughing when they came into the alley, but as soon as they saw how he had me pinned against the wall they went completely silent. They stood there watching me, he said, and that I was still breathing hard because I couldn't help myself, and he said he was frozen there with his body against mine, and he told me how the three men were standing there, and how you could see the veins in their arms, the same way that I liked to trace the veins in his arms with my fingertip, and even from where he was standing he could see in their veins their pulses quickening. And then he said he slowly let me down, let my back slide against the wall until I was on my feet, and he turned to face the men, but they were already on him, and one had slammed his head with a broken piece of brick, and almost knocked him out, and he was slumped down at the base of the wall opposite me, his head bleeding, and barely conscious, and the other two men were already on me. They'd forced me to the pavement between the alley walls, and they were holding me down on my hands and knees, and when I struggled to get away, one had slapped me open-handed hard against my face, and this had made me go still, and one of the men was holding my hair tight to the base of my scalp, and the other was tearing at my skirt and panties, and he told me, Seth told me, that they both entered me at the same time, one of them in my mouth, and one of them from behind, and that the man who had knocked him almost unconscious with the brick had taken hold of Seth's bloody hair and was forcing him to watch as the men did this to me. He told me how the men were getting more and more excited, how the stones and broken glass in the alley were cutting my knees as they thrust against me, and when he started to tell me how they were coming inside me, Seth himself came so hard that he knocked me off the edge of the mattress and onto the wood floor, and it was ten seconds before he could say, 'Sorry! Sorry! Sorry if I hurt you.'"

Genevieve was lying still with her head turned away. She could hear her breath moving in and out of her nostrils.

"I admit, I thought part of it was exciting. I don't remember if I came myself; we'd been drinking so much, and I don't know if I was excited because of what he was telling me or excited because it excited him. But it was only a minute later that we were back on the mattress with my head on his bare chest, and he was stroking my backbone with his fingers as gently as if he were sorting pearls. And a few minutes later he was asleep, and I could feel my head rising and falling with his deep breathing, and in a half dream I was seeing him as a boy kneeling at the edge of the water along a lake with a pebbled beach, and turning over small stones and holding them up to the sun, and I was wondering what it was inside of him that would want to be bleeding and half-unconscious while his love was raped in front of him."

For a full minute neither of them spoke. Finally, Genevieve said, "I wish I knew how to answer that, Claire."

"He was only twenty. A boy. In my memory, I can see him as a boy. And when we woke the next morning, our heads hurt. We'd drunk more than we ever had. And it was late February, but it was one of those winter-into-spring days, where somehow the temperature had risen overnight, and when I walked from the bedroom to the front window, I could see the mounds of snow melting into rivers that ran down the street, and there were people outside in the sun walking without their coats on. Seth came up from behind me and was holding me while we looked out the window. A boy was out on the sidewalk kicking a soccer ball. I remember it surprised me because I didn't think there were any families living in the neighborhood. He kept kicking it toward the front porch steps of his house, and it would careen off in different directions, and he tried to keep saving it from going into the street. I watched him for a while and then turned my head to look back at Seth. 'What?' he asked, but I didn't say anything. Then I told him I wanted to take a walk.

"So we got dressed then, and went out into the day. And Genevieve, it was one of those magical mornings. The kind you always remember even years later, maybe even when you're very old. The air had that fragrance, you know? That smell of moisture and warmth that I'd lived long enough to know was how things turned green. The patches of grass in the row houses down our street weren't winter dead anymore, and we could see bulbs pushing out of the ground where a few of the older people who still lived in the neighborhood had planted them. A man was walking a puppy, and I remember watching how it sniffed at every melting and fragrant thing, all those smells released by the cold, and yeah, there was some garbage, and yeah, dog shit in people's yards, but it didn't matter. I liked how everything seemed released, and we saw a couple walking up the street, on the other side, opposite to us, holding hands, and it was like we recognized each other, recognized ourselves as mirrors of each other, and the girl even smiled at me and gave a little wave.

"Near the main drag through that part of town, so many people were out. Some of them in overcoats, even though it was sixty degrees, but out of habit, you know, because it had been so cold. But also boys in shorts and basketball jerseys. And all the sounds were amplified. People's conversations, the roar of buses, the flap of pigeons near the library steps. And Seth and I, we hadn't intended to go to the bakery. It was too expensive for us, and we saved our money for drinking, though I don't think we ever said that out loud to each other, but the smell of bread that was hovering near the door—the proprietor had propped it open; it was one of the last original bakeries in the city, and he knew how to draw people in. He was old, and he ran the shop with his wife, and I think it was only a month or so later that they closed.

"Anyway, Seth and I went in. Several customers were inside. They still had people take numbers, and we took one, even though Seth had only a couple of dollars in his pocket, and that might have been enough for a single salt roll. When it was our turn, I smiled at the man behind the counter. He was short, Italian, and you could tell he was full of the spring day, too. He spread his arms as if he was offering everything in the glass case in front of him. Beside the loaves of bread were beautifully glazed cinnamon rolls and these almost shimmering nut rolls and muffins that seemed more blueberry than muffin.

"I remember saying to him, 'I'm sorry we're taking up your time, but we have almost no money. Would it be okay if you held up one of those beautiful loaves of bread, and I could just take a deep smell of it?' On another day, maybe he might have told me no, and asked me to leave, but he smiled at me, and said, 'Sure, no charge,' and he pulled a loaf from the rack and held it out over the counter in his gloved hands, and I brought my face close, and breathed it in. When I pulled my head away, I said, 'Thank you so much,' and he laughed, and I looked at Seth and said, 'What?' and he rubbed his finger across his own nose. 'You got a little flour there. You took a little too big a whiff.' I turned to the baker and said, 'I'm sorry!' but he was already sliding the loaf in a paper bag, and then setting it on the counter, and saying, 'On the house, my girl,' and when we walked out of there, he called out after us, 'Enjoy the bread! Enjoy your youth!' and Seth held my hand as we walked home, except when we were tearing away pieces of the loaf. It was so good. The sun on our faces. The warmth of that bread in our mouths."

She kept hearing drops of rain pelt the lot, but none had landed on her yet, and she couldn't see them falling in the streetlight.

"When we got home, and back up to the apartment, I stood at the window again, and I was nibbling at a crust of the bread. But I remember how it seemed, standing there, that by going back upstairs, I'd been removed from the day. And Seth came up from behind me again. And he wanted to make love, and of course we hadn't been drinking, and if we had made love, maybe that would have been the first time without it. But I couldn't. I couldn't. He kept telling me he loved me, which he usually didn't tell me in the daytime, in the morning, and I didn't want to hear it. I kept thinking of the men in the fantasy he'd described the night before when we were drunk, and the boy with the soccer ball, and the baker and his springtime gift to us, and I kept wondering why Seth wanted to be bleeding in an alley while I was raped, and why this man would want to give us this bread, and how there could have been no baker without the men in the alley, how the boy couldn't have kicked the ball without Seth being hit with the brick, and that wasn't literally true, I knew, but it was in my head, and the rest of that day I wouldn't let Seth come near me."

She stopped then, having slid into the space between re-membering that time, remembering Seth, and the place she was now lying next to Genevieve. She thought of how, sometimes, when it rained, a breeze would come up with the first wave of raindrops, and she often wondered why that happened, why everything would seem still, and then when the breeze arrived, she wondered if it was being pulled by the rain or if the wind was carrying the rain over her. But this night was airless, and the few drops that had hit the ground had now passed. She wanted Lucy. She wanted to see her sleeping in her bed at home in order to dispel the closeness of the night.

"So maybe you should stop right there," Genevieve said. "And tell me the rest tomorrow in the car. It's late, and we have a long drive."

"All right, Gen," she said.

"Are you okay?"

"I think I'm a little homesick."

Genevieve reached out and took her hand and squeezed it.

"I know," she said. "Sometimes it seems like the road was made for it. Do you want to hear a little more of your father's story?"

"I don't know, Gen. The closer we get, the less that seems to make sense. I'm going to see him for real in less than forty-eight hours."

"Don't you want to hear what happened next?"

She lay there, thinking about it. She had told Genevieve more than she'd ever intended. But she said, "I do. I do. I do want to hear what happened."

"The next stretch of highway is so plain," Genevieve said. "So dull. I'll tell you a little bit now, and I'll wait to tell you the very last part till then. Maybe we'll change the landscape some."

"Okay."

And then they lay quietly for a while. Genevieve had not let go of her hand. Claire was waiting for Genevieve to begin, but she could feel herself passing into the images that accompany first sleep, and she heard Genevieve humming a tune, like a lullaby. In the midst of that tune, Genevieve asked, "Did you lose track of Seth?" The question caught Claire off guard.

"Yes. Of course I did."

"Why *of course*?"

"Well, I lost track of almost everyone from that time. After I was—after I was hurt, I never heard from Seth again. It was strange, I suppose. My mother told me he had been cut, too, right along a cheekbone. I don't imagine that had anything to do with him never even trying to call. What do you say after something like that happens and you're twenty years old?"

Genevieve nodded, and kept her eyes closed, and finished humming her tune.

"What song is that?" Claire asked, but instead of answering, Genevieve shook her head and pulled back some strands of hair.

"After Marc tells Kathleen about Claire," Genevieve began, "filling in the details as honestly as he can, he and Kathleen sit quietly in the living room. He knows Kathleen feels in some way betrayed, though she didn't shed any tears and hasn't spoken of it. She has tried to read; she's taken up her knitting again, but has stopped and is now staring absently out the window, her fingers covering her mouth. Marc wishes she would say something, and resists wondering if she might leave him. He doesn't want to think about Claire. Instead, he steadies his mind on this enormous, new kind of quiet. And on this new kind of cold. Did the cold bring the quiet, or the quiet the cold?"

"I was thinking about something like that just a few minutes ago," Claire said.

"Is that right?" Genevieve asked, but didn't wait for an answer. "Of course it is the cold that brings the quiet. In the winter, things sleep. Hibernate. Most birds fly south. *The sedge has withered from the lake, and no birds sing.* Marc doesn't know where that line came from. Something he read in high school. But birds do gather at the feeder his neighbor puts out. He sees them in the morning sometimes pecking at seeds, sometimes driving other birds away. In winter, their calls seem more like claim than song. He hopes the cold that has descended on him and Kathleen isn't permanent.

"Yet, in a way, the quiet brings the cold, too. If it is a remote September day, a warm, last-of-summer day, and you are walking with some children along a lakeshore, and they're chattering, playing, dodging the lapping waves, and a small flock of gulls lands a hundred feet up the beach, and the children take off after them, chasing them into the sky as they screech and fly away, their calls receding into the sound of the waves, and the children are struck dumb as they watch what they accomplished, and everything is muted for a few seconds, so quiet, and then comes a chill—finger-light—running along your spine: then the quiet brings the cold. And reminds you of—what? Of the coming autumn? Of death? He'd read that some say when they're about to die, that what they want is more light, and some say they want more warmth.

"And then, despite himself, Marc remembers again the warmth of Joline's kiss. The way she'd told him to keep his eyes closed."

Genevieve stopped there and seemed to be listening to something in the night.

"Are you still awake, Claire?"

13

When he woke in the early morning before dawn, still facing the wall, his arms and legs aching, his shoulder throbbing, his first thought was, *Please don't let her die.* He had not recoiled from the story Claire had told—Josephine had told—about Claire's lover and his fantasy, though he recognized the destination for Claire was not Chicago, not Michigan, but telling the story of the moment of her death. And he was unsure whether he'd be able to bear hearing it, or, even more terribly, not hearing it. He was unable to measure Genevieve's intentions any more than he could measure Josephine's, as if they were somehow distinct, which Josephine had insisted. And how would it end, anyway? How could it, since Josephine had said their own time together would be ending soon? Anyway, Claire was dead. His memory of his collapse the night before pulled at the corner of his eyes. *I want to see your face.*

The room was already too warm. Slowly, he began to make the painful shift onto his back.

"Marc, I'm still here. Saabir's outside the door."

Rather than roll over onto his back, Marc slowly stretched his legs. She had not given him the invitation again, but he could easily have turned toward her and looked at her fully.

"Did you sleep at all, Josephine?"

"Not tonight, no."

"What have you been doing?"

"Sitting here thinking about our story, mostly. Watching you sleep."

She was speaking nearly in a whisper, most likely in order not to wake Saabir, though he supposed that's what people do anyway when they speak to each other in the middle of the night. Facing the wall, he could not discern whether light was beginning to come through the window. He closed his eyes, and recognized the comfort in having her nearby when he was unable to see.

"I smell bad," he said.

He heard her uncross her legs and shift on the chair, and he listened to the familiar resettling of her garments.

"It's something you get used to."

"I don't think I could ever get used to this place. This room. Pakistan. This world."

"Do you think, if you went home now, you'd get used to that place again, given all that's happened?"

"Part of me—" But he didn't finish the sentence, since he didn't want to tell her that he would be willing to stay here if Claire could go on living, even if it were only in Josephine's story. "I think it would take many, many days."

They were quiet for a minute or so.

"You know this is our last day, Marc."

He resisted the ache in his chest. "Where are they taking me?"

"I couldn't tell you if I knew. You understand that."

He nodded again. "Is it dawn yet?" he asked.

"Not for another hour or so."

He lay on his side, waiting. "What happens after today?" he asked. "To these stories we've told? What will happen to Claire then? And Genevieve? All of this for what, finally?"

"I don't know, Marc."

"All of this was your idea. You suggested at least twice that there was some purpose."

She cleared her throat. "I was sitting here thinking while you slept. Most every story you've told about Claire was an attempt to explain who she became, and what happened. Is there a story you can tell where you remember her as happy?"

He turned his shoulder toward her, because he realized this was likely the last story he'd ever tell of Claire, and he felt suddenly catapulted through the roof of the room, and he was looking down on the two of them from above with a dispassionate eye at the odd mechanics of the history of their conversation set in an inconsequential hovel on a street diminished by a sprawling city where millions breathed the heavy, foul air of the day.

"Are you going to kill me, Josephine?"

She didn't answer that question, either. He was warm and damp, and his clothes clung to him. She was waiting for his story, but it didn't seem impatiently.

He said, "Happy." And then he began.

"She was ten or eleven years old. I don't know why I remember this, particularly. I want to say we were in our backyard, but it couldn't have been, because I remember trees, oaks, a number of them, and our yard wasn't large. Claire had a friend over, her best friend at the time."

"Was this before the day she cut herself on the leg?"

He blinked twice at how much she'd come to know about Claire.

"Yes. Before that day. It seems a long time before, but it couldn't have been. She and her friend"—he hesitated trying to remember—"I think her name was Chloe. It was something close to that, anyway. She and Chloe had taken a sudden and passionate interest in birds. I don't think it lasted more than the day or so, the way it does for kids, who seem to wake up every morning as if someone thrust a new map in their hands. But this was the day for birds. They had one set of binoculars between them, and when one of them spotted what they thought was a blue jay or a cardinal in the higher limbs, the other would say, 'Let me see the binocs!'

"It was humid and warm, one of those late May evenings

when the leaves had recently broadened into bright green blades, and the wind was blowing lightly, and the girls kept mistaking the movement of the leaves for the movement of birds. Whoever wasn't carrying the binoculars around her neck was writing down the names of the birds in a tiny notebook. They were running from tree to tree, their *shushing* loud enough to chase away any animal, but the birds in that woods were used to children. Claire's hair was cut short at the time, and she could have passed for a boy, the way strands of it were damp with sweat at her temples and her eyebrows.

"I remember how it started growing darker under those trees, and when they were about to give up the search, a crow descended into one of the lower limbs, and gave out three loud caws. Claire had the binoculars, and she immediately trained them on the crow, but Chloe was so excited, she screamed, 'Look! Look! It's gonna caw again!' and it lifted off into the sky, calling as it flew away. And Claire said, 'Aw, Chloe. You scared it. You scared it away. You scarecrow.' They both laughed at this, but before their laughter could end in the usual fit of giggling, Chloe struck a pose she likely stole from *The Wizard of Oz*, crossing her arms and pointing in opposite directions, her back stiff as if her shirt was run through with a pole. I could see Chloe's shoulders shaking with muted laughter, and Claire flipped the binoculars so Chloe would seem tiny.

"Claire looked through them and said, 'That's a good Mr. Scarecrow. You keep those nasty crows away from your corn way out in your field.' Chloe laughed, fell out of her pose, and said, 'Now you try. Let me see you,' and Claire ran over and handed her the binoculars, then walked backward away from her, taking slow, long steps. Claire always had an amazing sense of balance when she was young that she was eager to show off. We thought for a while she might become a gymnast. So she stood about ten yards away from Chloe, and drew one foot up and pressed the arch to the side of the knee of the leg she'd planted on the ground. Then she held her arms out on either side at full length, tilted her chin up slightly, and for a few seconds, while Chloe peered through the binoculars, she closed her eyes."

His own eyes closed, as if he were still blindfolded; he was seeing her.

"She had—she had this smile on her face. A closed-mouth smile, you know, her cheeks and throat pink from running around that oak grove. This blissful look. And I can't tell you where I was standing now. I don't remember standing anywhere. I was close enough to see her expression, see her posed there so still, so still, as if she'd cast her own statue. But I remember, too, wondering how she looked through the binoculars Chloe was holding backward. I was seeing how she looked from where I was standing. That face flushed with color. I was wondering how she would look from far away."

Far away. He was holding still himself, still curled on the mat, but returning to the room.

"I don't remember going home. I don't remember walking

back inside after that evening. I doubt Claire remembered it at all."

He rolled over onto his back.

"What's going to happen, Josephine?"

She didn't answer, but he heard her let out a long breath, and rise to her feet. She walked over to the door, and he guessed she was listening, and then he heard her move over to the window.

"It's likely they will come for you at first light," she said.

He nodded again, and then she walked back to the chair, her steps sounding amplified in the silence of early morning.

"Why wait till first light? I never understood the tradition of waiting for dawn for an execution. Another night for the condemned to suffer his long thoughts."

She said nothing to this. He thought he heard her raise her arms and lower them again, for reasons he couldn't determine, but the same fragrance he'd occasionally smelled on her returned.

"Under that deep Nebraska sky, the moths still bumping the streetlight, while waiting for Genevieve to continue her story, Claire had fallen asleep. Now she turned over in the truck bed, her mind surfacing to the sounds of crickets."

"Josephine," Marc said.

"Shh. Listen," Josephine said. "It's all that's left to tell." And then she continued.

14

Claire sat straight up in the truck bed, and her sudden movement woke Genevieve. The sky had cleared utterly, and now was flooded with morning stars, and Claire looked east, the direction they would be heading, and checked the horizon for the first sign of dawn, but as yet there was none. Along the highway, the sound of the engine of a lone truck whined into the distance. She looked back toward Genevieve.

"Claire, you okay?" she asked. "Did you have a bad dream?"

"No. I'm okay."

"Did my story about your dad upset you?"

"No, Genevieve. I fell asleep."

Genevieve nodded, and lay back in the truck bed and closed her eyes. Only then did Claire look at her face, glancing from it back to the school beyond the lot where they had parked the truck, and she saw Genevieve's mouth open slightly, could see her eyes moving under her eyelids, and Claire knew she was sleeping.

If they didn't get started soon, they would need to stop before Chicago, probably just outside Iowa City, and she would have to lie for one more night next to Genevieve, who would by then know the rest of her story about Seth and the night she was attacked. And she wanted to tell Genevieve the story, could feel it welling up inside her, and yet was afraid to, and as Genevieve slept, Claire could feel herself trembling, though the June morning was still warm.

Because Genevieve must have known about her father's kiss. The time he'd kissed Claire when she was fourteen. In Genevieve's story, Joline had kissed Marc after asking him to close his eyes. And twice, in that story, he'd thought about the kiss, and seemed to savor it. Had Genevieve wanted Claire to recognize it? And she knew Genevieve couldn't have guessed it, knew that, because Genevieve had also known about Pakistan, it couldn't have been a coincidence, and her mind raced. Could this woman have met her father in Pakistan, in the month he was there before Claire was injured? But that was fifteen years ago, and Genevieve would have been barely fourteen herself then. And she'd picked her up hitchhiking on the highway, and she couldn't have known Claire was driving, couldn't have known she'd be out on that long stretch of hot, empty road.

She wanted Lucy. She wanted to talk to Jack. She wished she

had a cell phone. The corner of her mouth was quivering as Genevieve slept.

She thought to herself, *You are a mother. Of a beautiful blue-eyed girl. You own a motel in California. You're married to a good and decent man whom you look after, and who looks after you. You met him in Nebraska. This morning, you'll drive through Lincoln, where you lived for a while. And you're on your way to Michigan to visit your mother and father.*

She repeated these sentences, and tried to calm herself. She dug into her pocket for her keys, and held them up to the street-light so she could see a tiny photo of Lucy that dangled from the keychain, and she reached for it and let it rest in her fingertips. Lucy with a wand blowing a huge bubble. But because her hands were unsteady, the keys slipped from her fingers, and she tried to catch them with her free hand, and missed. Her sudden movement didn't rouse Genevieve, who continued to sleep.

Set into the starlight she could now see vast expanses of farmland, rows of corn now several feet high, but not yet tassel-ing, and farther away a farmhouse with one lit window. She thought she caught the faint scent of someone cooking an early breakfast. She ran her hand along the edge of the truck bed, where the man who'd said *buoyant* had rested his, and with her fingers she took up a few drops of dew that had settled there as she slept.

She glanced over at Genevieve again, and wanted to wake her. Amid another wave of fear, she looked back at the lit sign.

Last Day of Classes: June 13th. Have a smart summer! It was difficult for her to imagine, as Genevieve had, the children pouring out of the doors. In an hour or two, she told herself, it would be a beautiful June morning. It had never rained. Beyond the creek she'd seen before they slept, she could now see a ball field cut into the rows of corn.

"Your crickets are back," Genevieve said. Claire looked back at her, and she was up on an elbow. "And maybe before sunrise we'll hear an owl, too. Remember how quiet it was last night?"

She listened to them, and watched the occasional firefly glow near the water. Beyond the field, another light came on in the farmhouse.

"Doesn't this place seem familiar to you?" Genevieve asked. "Isn't it kind of like where you grew up?"

But Claire couldn't answer her.

"Something wrong, Claire?" Genevieve's head was framed by the light that still seemed to glow beyond the ball field.

"Lie down next to me, please," Claire said. They both lay back on the mattress so that they were shoulder to shoulder. Together, for several moments, they looked up at the sky.

"See anything heavenly up there?" Genevieve asked with a lilt, but when Claire didn't respond, she asked again, "What's wrong?"

"That kiss. The story you told about my father, when I was falling asleep. Joline kissing him with his eyes closed. The way he kissed me when I was fourteen. And Pakistan."

Claire continued to watch the sky. Genevieve didn't turn to look at her, but instead reached for her fingers, squeezed them, and then lay with her hand over Claire's.

"How did you know my father, Genevieve? How could you know him? You said you were in Pakistan, but you would have barely been fifteen when he was there. And he was there for only a few weeks in a city with millions of people. And then the highway where you were hitchhiking. That's worse. You couldn't have known I was driving down that road."

The trills of the crickets were muffling the trailing noise of one or two cars along the freeway. Now she faintly heard the water running in the creek, and Genevieve, for a few moments, seemed to be listening, too.

"I'll tell you about that after you finish the rest of your story. In fact, you won't even have to ask."

"I want to know how you knew my father."

"I'll tell you. I swear, I'll tell you. Afterward."

But Claire was still fighting a sense of panic. The story she'd told about the time with Seth, now almost half her life ago, had made that memory vivid, had further pushed out the familiar rhythms of her life at the motel in California, already unmoored by the phone call about her father, by the road, and by Genevieve. She was remembering clearly those nights with Seth, was sensing again how night fell into night, one tipping forward into the other, like an end-to-end collapse of houses set closely together, and she knew what would happen in the last of that row. Having recalled for Genevieve how much desire she had felt for Seth, she was troubled, now, by how little she remembered of him.

She'd met his mother once—a woman who couldn't have been more than fifty, but back then seemed too thin and stooped at the shoulders—who had said to her, "Well, aren't you a pretty young thing. You should hear how he raves about you." But what could he have told his mother about her, after all?

Claire imagined she was on another stretch of highway, back in Nevada, coming around a bend and seeing Seth with his thumb out. "What took you so long?" he said and smiled, after he jogged up to the truck; he was still twenty years old, but he slowly turned his face and showed her his knife wound, healed in the same rough way as her own.

"You won't need to ask," Genevieve said again. "I promise."

"Why do you want to hear it so bad?"

"I told you. Because it's the story you never tell."

"But you don't know all that much about me, and what stories I might tell."

"Do you really believe that at this point?"

Claire was expecting the sky to lighten, but instead more stars had emerged. She heard the cars and trucks in the distance, their rushing past offering that heard sense of the wind. The sounds of the insects were syncopated by the twang of a frog.

"I like this place," Claire said faintly.

"It's a good place for you to finish your story. Better than the highway, you know? I mean, think of all those kids in that school over there, gathered during the winter months to hear their teachers read books to them. It's a place where stories are told. And when you're done, if you want me to, I'll tell you the rest of the story about your father. And then we can head down the road, and before you drop me off in Chicago, we can talk about other things."

"Okay, Genevieve."

Claire closed her eyes, held a deep breath, and then released it.

"I wouldn't say, the night after we took the walk to the bakery, or the days that followed it, and there weren't that many, that things changed completely. But they were different. We still drank at night. We still ended the drinking with one of us pulling the other into the bedroom. And Seth still talked to me while we were making love, but he had pulled back some from the violence of the fantasy I told you about. When he'd come in from work, and I'd be standing in the kitchen, making some sort of simple meal for us, he'd come up behind me, breathe in the scent from my neck, and tell me he loved me. He'd keep his face buried in my hair until I said it back to him, as if he needed to hear it. Most times, I didn't mind telling him that I did love him, though I knew I didn't mean it anymore.

"For a while, I wondered if he could tell, and was looking for reassurance, but one afternoon, when I'd come back from the sandwich shop, and I was vacuuming the floor—I guess I liked our little domestic arrangement, the sense that I was taking care of a home—I didn't hear him come in, and when I didn't, he pulled the vacuum cord from the outlet, and he gave me sort of a half smile and sat down on the stool near the door where we usually threw our coats. But by then it was late March, and spring had come early, and I'd bundled up our coats in a plastic bag, and stored them in the back of our one closet. I remember thinking that was a hopeful thing, because it meant that come October or November, I'd be taking them out again.

"I was waiting for Seth to say something, but he just sat on the stool, with the end of the vacuum cord in his hand, rolling it over in his fingers so the plug looked like the moving head of a small animal. Finally, I said, 'What? You got something against a clean floor?' and tried a smile, but he shook his head. Then he said, 'I lost my job.' I knew that soon April rent would be due, and my check might cover it, but how we'd eat next month I didn't know, and those were the first thoughts that crossed my mind. I asked him what happened, and he told me, 'I'm really sorry, Claire. They laid me off three weeks ago. I should've told you. I didn't tell you because I was trying to find work. I figured if I had a new job, what would it matter if pay was minimum wage, anyway, but no one seems to be hiring.' He was still rolling the cord between his fingers, only now he was looking at the plug itself instead of me."

Claire thought she had never in her life lain looking at the sky as the stars faded into dawn, and she was still waiting. "Do the cars on the highway sound like wind to you?" she asked.

"Yeah. They always have, when there're a lot of them. But I like it best when I hear a lone car traveling late at night on the freeway. I think of the person in there as someone going on a long, long trip, like you've been, or someone who has just said good-bye, or someone going home after a long time away."

Claire wondered if Genevieve was thinking all three were true of her, but she didn't ask.

"It's funny, you know," Claire continued. "I know how things are always changing under the surface, and just because you don't observe them doesn't mean it isn't happening. But when I saw Seth turning that cord over and over, and the head of it bobbing like he had a mouse in his hand, I knew then that period of my life was over. I wondered if he was fired, but I didn't ask. Finally, he said to me, 'I've found a way to make some money. But it isn't, you know, exactly legal.' 'What do you mean by *exactly*?' I asked him. It turns out he was running drugs for a man he knew who had offered him several hundred dollars to take a bundle of marijuana to Florida. He would borrow the man's car and run it down there, and then bring back the cash. This didn't necessarily alarm me at the time. I remember thinking it wasn't cocaine, or heroin, only weed, and that he'd be back in three days. Seth told me he would be leaving the next morning.

"When he did, I went to work at the store and made

sandwiches, just like every other day, but I remember how that afternoon even the store and the Korean man who owned it seemed changed. I noticed for the first time how boxes of condiments in the storeroom were covered with dust, and that someone had drawn into the dust a word in Korean script. They'd been sitting there a long, long time. And toward three o'clock, when people stopped coming in for lunch, and I was only doing the next day's prep work, a man came in and spoke to my boss a single sentence in a whisper, and then the man handed him a playing card that was cut in the corner. I figured it had something to do with gambling, and I knew not to say anything. But it helped me recognize that after Seth had gone, whatever could have been described as the innocence of that period of my life had passed.

"Those nights I missed Seth. But I was also thinking how little I knew about him. I'm not saying he deliberately kept things from me, because I don't think he did. But I realized that our time was about learning what our bodies liked, and drinking enough that our memories of what brought us to each other receded. When he was gone, I could remember only one story he'd told me about his childhood, a time when he went fishing with his grandfather, and how he'd hooked a big bluegill and got so excited that he stood up in the boat and went over the side, and when his grandfather pulled him out of the water he was still gripping the pole in his free hand, and the fish was still on the line."

She stopped for a few moments, and Genevieve asked, "Why do you think he told you that story?"

"I don't know, Genevieve. I think it was one of those days for him that seemed perfect in some way."

Genevieve shifted onto her elbow, her face dim in the starlight.

"When I was a kid, I had a friend, and one spring day we hid in the woods and pretended we were both Snow White, and we held out our fingers for the birds to light on them like they did in the cartoon. And one actually flapped about a foot away from my finger before it realized I wasn't a tree. That was a great day. Do you have any favorites?"

Despite herself, Claire smiled. "You like birds, don't you, Genevieve?"

"Well, they can fly," she said.

She laughed at this. "Yes, I suppose they can. But I already told you about that time in northern Michigan, on that river, when I was sixteen. Those were perfect days."

"Any others?"

"I'm sure there are." She thought about it for a few seconds. "I had a friend, too. Her name was Chloe. And I remember one of our rituals most summer afternoons was a long walk around a nearby lake to a candy store. We couldn't have been more than ten years old. We'd get a dollar from our mothers and go out and buy some kind of treat; I think it gave our moms a break for the afternoon. One time when we were walking, we saw a dead squirrel on the street, and we felt sorry for it. We were both pretty squeamish about dead things, but I grabbed a long stick and pushed it into the high grass along the shoulder of that road. And when I was done, I started smelling my hand because I'd been pushing the squirrel's little corpse, and Chloe said, 'What's the matter, Claire? You afraid your hand's gonna smell like stick?' And something about that struck us so funny, that we collapsed laughing, right along the side of the street."

Genevieve laughed at this quietly, and then said, "That's a nice memory." Claire wasn't certain, but this may have been the first time she heard her laugh. Neither of them said anything for a while. Something fluttered by the hood of the truck, an insect, but then flew off again.

"Anyway, while Seth was gone, I was thinking about how he had begun waiting for me to tell him I loved him, and that I didn't know enough, anymore, to say that to him with any confidence. I never had a time like Joline, in your story, Gen, the way the father of her child saw her, when I felt like the way he looked at me was some kind of transformative moment. I loved learning his body, what a man's body could do, and how it would respond. But during those days he was driving to Florida, after I left work, I spent hours walking around the city. I remember seeking out the abandoned buildings, the ones with shattered windows, and floors covered with paper and trash. I was seeing empty buildings, broken buildings, no lives being lived in them, no businesses working out of them anymore.

"And I was thinking they had pasts that weren't difficult to imagine, people at desks or working on assembly lines, and I was thinking that wasn't true about the apartment I had with Seth, where so many lives had been lived that you couldn't imagine only one, and then I was thinking about the house I grew up in, where by this time my father and mother had separated, and how someone standing outside it would see a pretty home with a blossoming cherry tree, because it would have been blossoming by that time, and I wondered whether they could see, too, the tension of the lives being lived there, lives that were still going on. Whether they could see the house, and the beautiful tree, and see the beauty, but also feel the tension. Once a building was abandoned, like those I looked into on those long walks, I knew the imagined lives in them were over. And those two nights, coming home late to that empty apartment, I could tell that my life with Seth was over, too. Not because he was gone. Not because of what he was doing. It's just that those tiny rooms already looked like a place someone had once lived in, long ago."

She could hear Genevieve breathing in the foreground, the sounds of the insects behind her. She thought of the motel, and how far away it seemed, how Lucy and Jack were there, maybe Lucy lying on the couch next to Jack, who had fallen asleep while quietly turning the pages of a magazine in order not to wake her. But she was having trouble picturing them.

"He came back the evening of the third day. He'd called to tell me when he was arriving, and I'd made a good dinner for him. I wasn't going to break up with him right away. Particularly because when he came through the door, he was so happy. He almost bounded in. I asked him how Florida was, and he said everything went fine, and that it was fun to drive into summer, and to see palm trees, which he'd never done before.

"But he didn't say much of anything else. He kept telling me how delicious the meal was, which was just chicken and potatoes and green beans, and yet he was savoring each bite, looking into my eyes and smiling as he chewed. But I was already watching his jaw move, seeing the way he looked at his meal, then back up at me, and the way he pushed his food around on his plate—it was like a videotape that I was playing back, years from now, rewinding and playing back, in order to remember him, because I was already amazed at how faded this time of my life had become.

"We still drank together after that dinner. We still pulled each other to the bedroom afterward. He didn't talk while we made love, and, instead of rolling off of me afterward, he fell asleep on top of me while I stroked the hair around his neck. So when the man broke through the apartment door, he was still there, his chest on mine, his knee thrown over my thighs."

Claire wrapped her arms around herself. She closed her eyes in order to remember, to block out the simple, tame beauty of the early morning, the empty school, the dark ball field, and the starry sky, which was increasingly feeling like the only place in the world.

"What happened next wasn't all that dramatic. I mean, it was so quick, when I think about it now. The man broke through the door and bellowed Seth's last name. It wasn't hard to find us, even though the lights were out. The place was so small. Seth had gotten to his feet, and was standing on the mattress, trying to keep his balance, and just as the man came through the doorway to the bedroom, I had pulled myself up, half-blinded by fear, and was reaching for Seth, reaching for him, but then I was overcome by some unexpected fury, and I turned toward the man and tried to hit him, and then fell toward him, and I have no idea whether he intended to hurt anyone or only terrorize Seth to get the money Seth had stolen, or hadn't given to him, but I felt the knife enter at my shoulder, I felt it puncture my lung and go all the way through, and then the man pulled it out and I heard him say the first words of a sentence. 'Fuck! I didn't know—' but then it was like he was speaking a different language, even though he couldn't have been, and I heard Seth scream and dive forward, and he fell on top of me and I could hear the sound of someone running away. Seth was up on his arms, looking down, asking me a question, and I could feel droplets falling from his face, but it was still dark in the room, and I couldn't tell what they were. He turned me over and was pushing on my chest, where the blade had come through, and I couldn't understand what he was saying. He went away then, for what seemed a long time, and when he came back, I was cold, so cold, and shivering, and he covered me up and put his hand to my shoulder again. I could feel how wet the bed was around me, and he was pressing on my chest, but I could also hear him sobbing, his shoulders heaving, and he was repeating something over and over, but it was like I'd lost all capacity to understand language, and could only hear the words being made. I remember hearing sirens, though they were far off, and I was thinking of the Sirens of Greek mythology, and the way they would lure men toward their deaths. And I thought for a minute that I could be dying, and that Seth's voice was the voice of a Siren. But then all I felt was the cold again, and I felt myself shaking, and Seth was gone, and I was alone in that room, and it was incredibly large and growing larger, with its receding walls, and I was alone, alone and—"

She stopped there because she could remember nothing else. She wanted to open her eyes, but was afraid to. She wanted to open them to California and that other life. She felt Genevieve shift next to her, she felt her shadow over her, and when she felt her lips on hers she didn't flinch, didn't turn her head. Genevieve left them there for several seconds, and when she pulled away, Claire raised her head to keep them there a moment longer. She opened her eyes, and Genevieve was still close, blacking out most of the sky.

"I'm sorry, Claire," she said. Genevieve rested her hand on the side of Claire's face, her thumb lightly stroking her temple. "There's no Lucy. No Jack. No motel in California where you learned to love the summers."

"I know that," she said. "I know that now."

She felt the ache in her belly and arms where Lucy had never been, but she would not cry.

"And I promise you, I promise you, that he won't know that you know. That I would never tell him that you know."

Claire did not think to ask who he was.

"Do you still want to hear the rest of Marc's story?"

"Yes."

"Claire, it would make him so happy that you still want to hear it."

"I know that, too. I do know that, Genevieve."

She closed her eyes and waited.

~ 15

Marc could discern only the sounds of a city slowly waking—cars on a street several blocks away, the warning signal of a truck backing up, then a shout, a train in the distance braking on its rails. A man coughing as he walked past. He was still turned away from the window, but light now shone dully off the walls.

He realized he was barely breathing, waiting for Josephine to continue, waiting for her to rescue Claire from the moment of her . . . the moment of her . . .

But she goes on living, doesn't she? he thought. She'll climb out of the back of that truck bed, and when the sun rises, she'll drive down the toll road toward Chicago, and Genevieve will tell the story of Marc and Kathleen at the lake house, and in the quiet and the cold, they'll find a way to start talking again, and that night Marc will sleep curled next to Kathleen, and when Claire and Genevieve arrive outside of Chicago, Claire will drop her off at an L station, and they'll say good-bye, and Claire will think about Lucy as she drives the two hours that will take her to the hospital where Marc lies dying.

He waited. But Josephine sat so quietly she may as well not have been in the room. He made a quarter turn toward her and felt the pain in his shoulder where he'd fallen.

"You're not going to leave her there, are you?" he heard himself say. "Alone and dying in that room?"

"Marc, it's dawn. It's all we have time for."

"I don't hear anyone."

"They're coming."

"I don't hear anyone yet. How can you leave her alone like that, after everything?"

"It's her story to tell. And she's not alone. She's with Genevieve."

As she said the name, he heard the car quietly pull up outside the door. He felt himself break into a sudden sweat.

"Turn and look at me, Marc."

He heard a car door thump, then another.

"Turn and look at me."

He knew he had only the moment, and something like panic filled him, as if this opportunity to see her face were his last line to the world, and he ignored the sharp pain in his shoulder as he rolled over, and the two men came through the door where Saabir stood guard.

She sat with her large hands in her lap, looking down at him, her hair covered by a deep-blue hijab, her mouth drawn into the slightest smile, her lips full. The bones of her face were slightly masculine, her skin so pale in the light of early dawn that she looked luminous, though plain, her eyes decidedly gray. She held his gaze as the men pulled him up to his knees, her expression almost serene, and then one of the men yanked a black sack over his head.

"For whatever it may mean, Claire wants to hear the rest of your story, too."

This was the last thing she said as the men lifted him to his feet and led him through the door to the car. But her face seemed imprinted on the black cloth, if not onto his own face, and cloaked an image of Claire's that he couldn't reach. He thought it was the kind of face that someone could look at for a long time, not for minutes or days, but for weeks and years. And as the men pushed him into the backseat of the car for what he knew would be a short drive, it struck him that it was the last face he would ever see.

↝ Epilogue

For a long while I thought, *Now, the sunrise. Now, a woman at my bedside who says she's my mother. Now, a morning cup of coffee.* Don't misunderstand me. I knew the way to pull the sheet under my chin, knew to loop my finger around the handle of the coffee mug, knew what a mother was and believed the woman when she said she was mine. And in a few months, as I healed, I saw the emerging pattern of the days, and I remembered to expect the rising heat of a July morning, expect—as I made my way down to the porch, and spent long afternoons in a rocking chair, my strength slowly returning, my hair growing in—the slow turning of the heads of the flowers toward the summer sun, wildflowers that my mother had planted, plants that I could name—cosmos, daisies, black-eyed Susans—but could not tell you where I learned to name them, and couldn't tell you how I arrived at expectation at all. It was some kind of underweaving that had preserved language and the naming of things that weren't people, weren't the ones that I loved, or that I had once loved. I couldn't remember loving anyone.

Or, more accurately, I could remember the capacity to love, but could remember no one at all. For two weeks, my mother wouldn't even speak to me about the attack, and then she wouldn't tell me how it happened, and she never did tell me why it happened, since she said she didn't know, and I believe she is being honest about that. She told me, once I was released from the hospital to come to her house, that I was twenty years old, and, when I stood and could bear to see my reflection in the mirror, my hair covering the scar on my scalp, a T-shirt over the bandage over the wound where someone drove the knife through, I did look young, but for what it's worth, for whatever it may mean, I felt years and years older.

Someone had phoned 911 when I was hurt, but he'd reported a name that wasn't his, though the address where I lay was real, and by the time the paramedics reached me, apparently I'd lost a lot of blood, and banged my head badly on the floor or a corner table, and between the blood loss and the surgery on my skull, the doctors said, I had lost my memory, had lost any recognition of anyone I ever knew, including myself. They told me they thought some things would return to me when the trauma eased, but it's been months, and nothing has, or, if it has, it's impossible to discern what I remember from what others have told me, several others, but especially my mother, who I try to remember to address as Ma or Mom, rather than by her name, Lynne.

She is a lovely woman. Bright blue eyes that are youthful well into her late forties, a rope of hair that she keeps in a long, blond braid because, she said, when she was praying for my life, she'd had it woven into that braid, and worried if she changed anything, anything at all, from what she was eating for breakfast to what she wore to the hospital, it would tip the balance. She told me that before the attack, I'd been going through what she called a *wild period,* and she said from the time I was small I'd always been spirited, and that she'd hoped that spirit was revealing itself for a short time in wildness. But after I was hurt she was consumed by guilt, consumed with the realization that she'd let me move away from her, further away than she should have, though not in terms of miles, and if she hadn't, if she'd tried harder to stay close, none of this would have happened.

"People always say that," I told her as she sat across from me almost knee to knee on that porch.

"What people?" Lynne asked. "Are you remembering someone right now?"

I said, "No, I don't mean it that way. I'm just saying of course you would have done different things. But you should know I didn't end up here because you didn't do them. You should let yourself off the hook, Lynne. I mean Mom."

She nodded, and then her eyes filled up for the thousandth time since I'd regained consciousness.

"Why is it so hard for you to remember to call me Mom? I'm staying at home, taking care of you, like a mom, aren't I? I've told you everything I can remember to tell you about who you were. Who you are."

And she was doing that. She'd taken family leave from the marketing company she worked for, at least for the first three months, and then even afterward she'd check in throughout the day, afraid that I might have wandered off. But for a long while I was afraid to take so much as a few steps from that porch, even those days when the temperature hit ninety, and in my little enclosure I could see the heads of the flowers nod in a breeze that didn't reach me, one that I could remember would feel cool on my skin.

And I thought then that mothering is different from being a mother, and that I wished I could remember everyone that ever mothered me, even if I wouldn't call them *Mom.* But seeing the look of hurt on my mother's face, I regretted slipping up again. So I said, "I'm sorry, Mom. It's just so strange because I don't remember your face. But you're right, you've taken such good care of me. I can tell you've been doing it all of my life."

She nodded her head, glassy-eyed, and smiled thinly. "You're so different from how you used to be. The way you say things. Your tone of voice. Even sometimes the words you choose. It's like you've become brutally honest."

I didn't know about the brutal part, but if there is a blessing that goes with remembering no one, it's that there's nothing to conceal, and no one you reflexively feel that you have to or want to protect. But only for a while, and I knew that time was ending.

So I told her, "I love you. My body remembers loving you, anyway. It always feels good when you give me a hug. It's the closest thing I have to a specific memory."

I said this to make her feel good, but I also meant it, and she stood up and smiled and came over to me, and I squeezed her hard, to show her the strength that was building in my arms.

Strangely, I didn't ask about my father for weeks and weeks. You'd think I would, and, if not, that Lynne would have volunteered a story about him, or at least his whereabouts, but neither happened, and with my memory erased, it simply didn't occur to me to ask, and I didn't even have the curiosity that an adopted child might have about her biological father. When I did finally ask, it was almost impulsive. I was lying on the couch on a late August evening, my mother sitting in an armchair across from me, reading, while I watched the ceiling fan spin above my head as it circulated the air in the room. I was tracking the blades with my eyes in a way that seemed irresistible, and when I got tired of this, I closed my eyes, and saw the fan circling in the darkness under my eyelids. And I heard myself whisper, because she often fell asleep in the armchair while watching over me, "Mom, are you still awake?" I'd remembered not to call her *Lynne*.

"Yes, sweetheart. I'm right here."

My eyes were still closed, following the fan blades.

"What happened to my father?"

After I moved west, it was the sense of this, the way everything at my mother's house in those months seemed both sudden and familiar, even the apparition of my father, emerging in parts from my mother's description of him as I watched the ceiling fan, that I described to Jeremy as he lay next to me in my bed in the apartment above the little diner where I wait tables in this tiny Nevada town. I'd met him when he'd stopped to eat one evening on his way home from the mines. He was older than I was by maybe ten years, and his face was rough-cut out of that dry land, and permanently red from working on it, his eyes brilliantly blue. He was kind and quiet. When we started seeing each other, he didn't ask many questions about me, though this seemed to come from a well of respect for my privacy rather than disinterest. The first few times we went out, we would go for long drives in his truck, because no place you'd want to visit during a cold November in northern Nevada is close to anyplace else. During those drives, we were mostly silent, other than the country music on the radio. Once he turned to me as we headed down another empty stretch of road, and said, "You know, most women aren't content to sit quiet like this."

I smiled at him. "Maybe most women from around here."

"I always thought back-east women could talk a mile a minute."

"Michigan isn't what I'd call *back east,* Jeremy."

He gave me his strong smile, his teeth bright in his red face.

"East of here, Miss Claire."

I'd told him about my home, about my mother, who hadn't wanted me to leave, and how my father was killed in Pakistan, but for a while I didn't want to tell him how I lost my memory. He seemed content to wait for me, in the way that a good man who gets used to the desolation of that land—the rocks stacked on rocks, the outcroppings of wind-beaten pines, the mountains on the far horizon that always make me feel lonely when I take a few moments to look at them—knows that it yields its stories warily.

On an evening when he'd taken me to a movie in Elko, after holding my hand for the half-hour drive back to the diner, I was ready to have him come up to my room. That first night, he didn't ask about the heavy purple scars on my back and chest. I could tell, for him, it had been a long time since he'd slept with anyone, and he felt as much relief as desire at lying naked together, and when he was inside me, I felt how some of the isolation that my loss of memory caused was driven out of me for a while.

Next morning, when we woke up together, he watched from the bed as I made coffee in the kitchen, and when I walked over to hand him his mug, my robe fell open, and I saw him glance at the scars.

"That must've hurt," he said. It was a cold morning, with a winter storm moving in, and his skin was run over with goose bumps, but he was used to it and didn't cover his bare chest with the blanket.

"I don't really remember," I said, after setting my own cup of coffee on the nightstand and crawling back into bed beside him.

"Seems like it'd be a hard thing to forget."

He was looking at my face, and in his eyes I could see concern and perhaps the first glimmer of love. So I told him what I knew about what happened to me, the things my mother said, the details I'd sought from the brief articles on the Internet, how they'd not caught the man who'd stabbed me or found the man who'd lived with me. But mostly I described what it was like to wake each morning in my mother's house and recognize everything but remember none of it.

He listened very carefully, glancing occasionally out the window as the panes rattled in the wind, and a few flakes of snow were whipped about. Finally, he said, "So for all you can tell, last night might have been your first time with a man."

"No, no. I'm sure it wasn't," I told him.

"How do you know?" he said, smiling. "You're young."

I smiled back at him. "Did it feel to you like it was my first time?"

He looked away from me and lay back against the pillow.

"No, I got to admit, it didn't."

"My body can remember other men. My body does. It's only my brain that doesn't."

He thought about this for a while, running his hand over his whiskered face. I liked the way the winter light made the pale skin glow on his arms and chest, and his muscles underneath reminded me of fish just under the surface of the water.

"What are you thinking?" I asked him.

"Well, I'm trying to figure out if I envy you. I mean it's an awful thing to be attacked like that. But I'm talking about losing your memory. On one hand, it would be terrible to not be able to remember anybody. Your friends. Your family. Gotta be hard on your mom and . . . sorry."

He glanced at me, but when I said nothing, he looked out the window where the wind was howling.

"On the other hand, maybe it's better not to remember being hurt. And it's kind of like a fresh start. Not obliged to anybody. Nobody bothering about who missed you at Christmastime when you didn't show up." He looked back at me. "I didn't tell you I got a kid."

"No, you didn't. Were you married?"

"Yeah, for a year or so. But that was long enough. It's not like it was a bad scene. I was just never home. Couldn't blame her for divorcing me, really."

"Boy or girl?"

"A little girl. Miss her bad, and see her maybe six times a year. It's not like I don't want to miss her, but it hurts, you know? Some days I'd like not to have to remember all of that."

He thought about this and looked over at me again, and then closed his eyes. Something pulled at the corner of his mouth.

"I guess that's not true. I'm sorry. It's gotta be hard. Must be like waking up to a life someone else dreamed up for you."

My skin flushed warm after he said this. I pushed myself up on my forearms and kissed him lightly.

He opened his eyes and said, "What was that for?"

"It is that way sometimes."

He was looking at my face, and ran his hand through my hair, and then tucked a strand behind my ear.

"I've been meaning to ask, because you don't usually see a pretty girl behind the wheel of a beat-up Taurus with a *Drink Pepsi* bumper sticker. Is that your daddy's car you drive around in?"

I said that it was, but we left it at that, because I had to go downstairs to work. When she told me about my father, that summer afternoon in her living room while I watched the ceiling fan spin, my mother said he'd left me some money through an insurance policy, and I asked her to hold it for me for some time when I needed it. But I did take his car. It was ten years old, a Ford, and smelled of spilled coffee and rust and perhaps sweat, or some other distant smell that had come from the hours and hours he'd spent driving it, and the seat was slightly squashed from the weight of his body. I liked thinking that I was peering through the windshield as he had, heading toward an as yet never-seen destination. My mother told me he'd loved to travel, that once he'd driven all the way to New Jersey with me in the backseat of that car when it was still new because I'd wanted to see the ocean. While I couldn't remember that ten-year-old girl, it was still possible, glancing in the rearview mirror, to imagine her sitting there.

It had been well into August before I'd learned that my father had been killed. My mother's explanation for not telling me, she said, was to protect me while I healed, but she had left my father in the months before he went to Pakistan, and I think that complicated her reasons for keeping his death a secret. When I asked about him, she told me his mother, my grandmother, was still alive, still living in the place my father had grown up.

We drove out to her lake house the following Saturday, on one of those late August days when the humidity is high and not a leaf moves in the warm, heavy air. My grandmother cried when she saw me, her dog hunkered down next to her knees. I didn't recognize the white-haired woman in front of me, and she glanced for a moment at the place on my skull where hair was still growing in, and then pressed me close to her chest, and said, "If I'd lost both of you . . . If I'd lost both of you." She took me around the small house, and showed me the room my father had slept in when he was a boy, but she'd remodeled it long ago, and there were no signs of his time there except for a wooden candy dish she told me he'd made in shop class in eighth grade that she kept on an end table and filled with peppermints. She showed me photograph albums that we looked through while sitting next to each other on her floral-patterned couch that had the faint smell of mildew. I liked the pictures of my father as a boy, sitting next to his sisters, holding two fingers behind one of their heads in a gesture I recognized from my own childhood. And I could recognize myself in the photographs my grandmother had of me, and I could see myself in the child sitting on her father's lap with her hands raised in the air, and in the photograph of my unhappy face when I was older while I stood next to him in front of a Christmas tree. I thought I could see that he loved me.

When we had lunch, my grandmother served us peanut butter and jelly sandwiches with potato chips and sliced apples, and then apologized for the simple meal, but she said these were his favorite foods when he was a boy. We sat at the round wooden table, but really, there was nothing much to talk about. I watched the lake out the window while she and my mother talked, and when we finished eating, I asked my grandmother to take me outside while my mother cleaned up the dishes.

The lawn that led to the lake was small, and her dog, a springer spaniel named Penny, loped down to the water in front of us and started sniffing among the lily pads for small fish and minnows. The lake was mostly calm at midday, the cottages that circled the front half of it slightly hazy and quiet with the occasional exception of a slamming screen door. The children who would normally be outside playing had likely gone home for the start of the school year. The land on the opposite side was undeveloped, and there were trees along the bank, and some farmland on one end where, tucked away from the lake's edge, you could see a corner of a field of corn.

We stood silently for a while near a willow tree that grew just short of the bank. I finally asked my grandmother, "Did my dad like coming out here to visit?"

"He did, I think. As much as any grown man enjoys visiting his mother. I don't think he ever came out here without saying something about how small the place seemed compared to when he was little, when he could still swing out over the bank on these willow branches. Some afternoons, he'd pull a lawn chair out to the edge of the lake and sit there for an hour or so. Just looking out over the water. I wish I could tell you what he was thinking about, but he seemed to find it peaceful."

"It is peaceful."

"You used to come out here on the weekend to visit all by yourself. We bought you some ice skates one Christmas when you were only five or six, and I had to call you in those winter evenings or you'd have kept skating on into the dark."

I smiled. "Is it nice in the winter?"

"It's cold! But it's beautiful after the water freezes over. The only time I saw the whole lake ice up at once was on one of those weekends you stayed over. It was right after the New Year, and we had a fresh snowfall. We were lying on the couch together, and you were asleep. You might've been in third grade back then. The lake was choppy, with little whitecaps every-where, and they looked pretty because they matched the snow on the banks. I'd set aside the book I was reading to you, and kept glancing out the window, but fell asleep myself for a minute or two. Then I thought I heard someone walking in the front of the yard, and it woke me, and I sat up, and no one was there, but the wind had died, and I could see this perfectly clear skin of ice slowly spread itself over the water, from the banks to almost the middle of the lake."

She looked up at me then, and smiled shyly, as though she'd revealed something about herself that she hadn't intended.

"When you woke up, you asked to put your skates on first thing," she said.

I gave her a hug, and told her I'd like to sit out near the lake for a few minutes by myself, like my father used to do, and she squeezed my hand and brought back a lawn chair for me before she went inside.

Can you grieve for someone you don't remember? About whom you've only heard stories, even if those stories include a version of yourself you can't recall? Or is it like waking in a theater at the end of a movie where everyone around you is crying?

I sat for a long while trying to recall my father, trying to imagine him as a boy swinging on the boughs of a willow tree, splashing his sisters in the water out at the end of the dock where my grandmother's old boat was tied, and I imagined my father, too, pulling the oars that would lead the boat across the water, and I imagined I may have sat in the bow a time or two while he rowed across the lake.

I thought of him as a man visiting his mother, sitting where I was late on a summer evening, that time of night when the vacationers who filled the rented cottages would have doused their charcoal pits, and their kids would long since be out of the water and immersed in the deep slumber that comes from a day of play on the lake. There might be a few fireflies still lit along the banks, and the wind would have died down by then, and there would be only a faint lapping of invisible waves that he could hear against the black line of sand at the lake's edge. A late-night fisherman might be rowing in, or someone in a canoe, maybe a couple of teenagers, or a newlywed couple, who had paddled to the other side of the lake to whisper to each other or exchange kisses.

My mother had told me a woman was somehow involved in my father's kidnapping in Pakistan. I hadn't searched very deeply to find out more about her; there didn't seem to be much reason. They thought she may have been from upstate New York, but no one could find her mother or father. The photo they had online did what they always do, which was to make her look haunted, angry, and unattractive. As I looked out over the lake at a fisherman casting his line, I tried to imagine the woman in a room with my father, a room in a country he never had the chance to know, where at the end all he had was his memory to comfort him, the opposite of what I felt in those first mornings after I'd been attacked, waking in my bedroom where I grew up. I wondered if my father had said anything at all to the woman about me. I wondered what life he'd dreamed up for me when I was born, and what life, if any, he'd wanted for me before he died.

Sometimes, now, on the rare weekend when Jeremy's daughter is visiting, while she lies sleeping between us and I've wakened early to watch the first morning light brighten the bed where she and Jeremy are curled in toward each other, I think I know what he might be dreaming of, even in his waking hours. That the two of us could marry. That we could raise his daughter in that hard-scrubbed landscape, that her eyes would take on the blue of the sky, and we would build a little home near a stand of pine trees where I'd hang clothes outside in the clean wind that rolls over the mountains, his little girl's blue dress flapping in the breeze. I could go to college in Elko, learn a trade or have a career, and we could live a happy life carved out of the stark beauty of that land. Part of me wants that.

But during those nights his daughter visits, in the living still-ness made by the knowledge that she is asleep between us, my own dreaming returns. At first come shadows, forgotten rooms, and then familiar faces, half sentences someone is speaking to me that I remember, but then dissolve when I open my eyes. I don't know that these memories will continue to return, but I do know they are out there, along with all of the things I can't remember. Even though I can't name them, I think of them in the world, I think of them in the minds of other people, as if these others are the caretakers of my memories—for me, or for maybe everyone who has forgotten anything or has been forgotten—people living in different times, people in faraway lands.

It's like waking to a life someone dreamed for you. Maybe, at some point, that's partly true for everyone. I think of Jeremy opening his eyes in my bed, and, in the half second before he remembers me, seeing a woman in a strange kitchen making coffee. I think of my mother, waking to a morning when the man she'd loved, lived with, then left had been killed, his body never found; and, months later, on another morning, waking to a daughter who had disappeared.

And then, one early morning, when Jeremy has gone to work and left his little girl sleeping beside me, I dream of a man who says he is my father. He is sitting with me in a café in Karachi, where my mother told me my father was killed. We sit sipping from cups of tea in the bright late-afternoon sun, neither of us speaking, as women pass by in hijabs, men in suits, my father wearing a jacket and tie and set back in his chair, his legs crossed. I feel his eyes on my face, but when I turn toward him he is always looking elsewhere, at a boy waving to someone from a window, and then at a limping man pushing a cart down the street.

"How's your mother?" he asks me, and loops his finger into his teacup.

"You know I haven't seen her in months."

My father still won't look in my eyes, but he nods. He turns his hand up and studies his fingernails. A waiter comes by and puts the check on the table, and my father looks up at him and gives him his good smile.

After the waiter walks away, my father says, "I suppose you're in love with this Jeremy." Now he's looking out over the roofs of low buildings, their shadows advancing in the low sun.

"I don't know," I say. "I don't remember what that's like."

He nods again, looks down at his watch, and then reaches in his pocket and pulls out a coin and places it on the check. He stares at it as if he wonders if it will be enough, and then begins to glance through the crowd of people moving past. Finally, he finds a mother walking through the marketplace holding the hand of her daughter, and he says, "Back when you were that little girl's age—"

But I say, "Don't."

Then he finds a young woman without a head scarf, and says, "Of course, by then you were—"

And I say, "Stop."

At last, he looks at me. He lightly touches his fingers to his face as if he needs to make certain it's his. The sun has dipped behind the buildings, and we're in shade.

"Claire, don't you want to remember?"

I nod my head, because I do. I do want to remember. But I'm in that space between sleeping and waking where images of a dream collide with the coming demands of the day, and I want to go on dreaming.

So instead, I say to him, "Tell me a story."

✐ *Acknowledgments*

For their unflinching support and friendship, thanks to Claude Hurlbert, A. D. Feys, Tim Johnson, Dave Martin, Mark L. Shelton, Tom Sweterlitsch, and Jay Letto. With admiration, thank you to Stewart O'Nan, Laila Lalami, and Christopher Scotton. For their dedication to good books, thank you to my astute and extraordinary editors, Amy Einhorn and Caroline Bleeke, and to all the fine people at Flatiron. At the Gernert Company, thank you to Flora Hackett, Anna Worrall, and especially my agent, Andy Kifer, whose brilliance lit the lantern for my manuscript and guided it down every right path. And to depths I can't express, thank you to Erin Cawley, who through draft after draft of this book turned over each word with intelligence, acuity, and devotion.